ABSOLUTION

The Protectors #1

SLOANE KENNEDY

ISBN-13:
978-1530629343

ISBN-10:
1530629349

Absolution

Sloane Kennedy

Trademark Acknowledgements

Acknowledgments

Thanks to Jay, Missy and Chloe for beta reading for me.

A special thank you to Kylee for coming through for me when I needed you the most and more importantly, for reminding me to breathe.

Trigger Warning

Listed below are the trigger warnings for this book. Reading them may cause spoilers:

This book contains references to sexual assault against a child so please proceed with caution if this is a trigger for you.

absolution

noun ab·so·lu·tion \͵ab-sə-ˈlü-shən\

The act or an instance of forgiving

Prologue

JONAS

"Welcome home, Mr. Davenport."

"Thanks, James," I murmured as I gave the pilot a quick nod. Even after more than four years of flying back and forth from Paris to the States via the luxurious private jet, I still hadn't managed to get the pilot, co-pilot or flight attendant to call me by my first name. It was always Mr. Davenport...a name I still hadn't gotten used to using again after so many years of not needing it. In truth, I hadn't been a Davenport in a very long time – not since the day my father called me a faggot and gave me five minutes to pack my shit and get out. I'd only been fourteen at the time but luckily I'd been smart enough to leave things like my comic books and video games behind in favor of a few changes of clothes, my savings account passbook, the twenty-three dollars in quarters I'd been stuffing into my Spiderman piggy bank for the better part of a year and of course, my sketchbook. I'd hated leaving behind my carefully mixed paints and brushes but I'd had hopes that my parents would ultimately store them, along with the dozens of paintings littering the walls of my room, until I could come and get them. They didn't.

Being a Davenport had never been easy but I'd done it surprisingly well. Probably because I'd learned quickly that if my parents were pleased with how I came off to those in their social circle, I was more likely to get something out of the deal. I traded in my good grades, perfect manners and unfettered obedience for art supplies and classes and nearly weekly excursions to every art museum throughout New England. That is, until I turned thirteen and my parents decided my genius IQ should be nurtured at an elite boarding school in Switzerland. Which had nothing to do with the fact that they were planning a yearlong excursion traveling the world on their friends' yacht, they'd assured me repeatedly in the months and days before I left.

Exactly one year later I was back home in my parents' stately Beacon Hill penthouse trying to explain why I'd been expelled for kissing the son of a very wealthy British Ambassador. The obvious explanation that I'd kissed said boy because I'd wanted to hadn't netted me the lecture I'd thought it would…it had earned me a one-way ticket out the front door with my mother looking on, tears streaking down her perfectly made up face. I'd felt an obscene surge of hope at the sight and waited for her to step in to stop the whole thing, but that had only lasted as long as it had taken for me to hear her ask my father why *I'd* done this to *them*. It was then that I'd finally understood that the tears weren't *for* me, they were *because of* me.

After that, home stopped being a physical place for me and it wasn't until almost a year later that I found out that home didn't always mean a roof over your head.

"Jonas!"

I nearly tripped on the top step of the stairs leading down from the jet to the tarmac when I heard the high-pitched squeal and I couldn't help the broad smile that spread across my face at the sight of my family standing in front of the Suburban SUV, a huge paper banner that read *Welcome Home Jonas* strung out between their hands. My eyes fell on the two children who were bouncing up and down, skimmed briefly over the tall, dark-haired man desperately trying to hold on to the giant Mastiff tugging to escape his hold and then finally settled on the young woman in the middle. Even from where I stood in the doorway to the jet, I could see tears spilling down her

2

cheeks. She was my home. She had been from the moment she'd saved my life eight years earlier.

"Uncle Dev!" the little girl shouted to the man behind her and I could see he was holding her by the collar of her dress to keep her from charging me the way she clearly wanted. I guessed he didn't want her anywhere near the jet's engines as they wound down, so I quickly hurried down the stairs and toward the car. Once I crossed whatever invisible line the man had set in his mind, he let go of the dog and the little girl at the same time. Amazingly, the little girl got to me first but the dog wasn't far behind.

"Hi baby girl," I said as I gathered the child's body in my arms and lifted her just as the Mastiff slammed into me. I was used to Sampson's tactics though, so I managed to stay upright as I gave him a quick pat.

"Mama says you're not leaving again," the little girl said as she grabbed my cheeks and held me still as if needing to look me in the eye to determine if I was telling the truth when I answered.

"Your mama is right, Izzy," I said. Her ear-splitting shriek had me biting back another smile as the eight-year-old threw her spindly arms around my neck. Hearing Isabel Prescott refer to my best friend as her mother was still an oddity for me. Not because I doubted the relationship Casey had with the little girl who was actually her niece, but because Izzy ironically still called Devlin Prescott, Casey's husband, her uncle even though he wasn't related to her by blood, but had been in her life longer than even the mother who had died shortly before Isabel's fourth birthday. But I'd seen enough to know that Devlin and Izzy's relationship was that of a father and daughter and the lack of using a certain title or shared DNA wouldn't ever change that.

As I crossed the tarmac with Izzy rattling off questions in my ear, I hugged twelve-year-old Ryan Prescott who looked more and more like his father with each passing year. "You staying out of trouble?" I asked, as I ruffled Ryan's hair.

"No!" Izzy answered for him and Ryan actually blushed. "He likes a girl," Izzy announced and poor Ryan looked mortified.

I chuckled and bumped his fist with mine. "Nice," I said.

"We're just friends," Ryan said sheepishly.

"Nuh-uh," Izzy said, to which Ryan's blush grew considerably.

"That's my cue," Devlin Prescott said as he reached out and took Izzy in his arms. Then his big arm was wrapping around me and even though we were nearly the same height, I couldn't help but feel the warmth spread through me at the contact. Not only had this man changed Casey's life for the better, he'd done the same for me and he'd gone a step further and become a surrogate father. "Welcome home, Jonas," Devlin said softly in my ear.

I found myself overcome with emotion, so instead of answering, I just hugged him tighter. But as soon as I turned my attention to Casey, I lost it and began crying as I tugged her into my embrace. The fact that her slim arms wrapped around my neck like a vise had me closing my eyes, because it was something I would never get used to. In the three years that Casey and I had spent on the run together, she'd rarely hugged me and on the few occasions I'd touched her in an effort to provide comfort, she'd always flinched and pulled away. But Devlin had somehow fixed that too.

By the time Casey finally released me, we were both a mess and she laughed and reached up to wipe at my face with the edge of her sleeve before doing the same to her own. I, in the meantime, let my eyes drop to her very prominent baby bump. I lifted them back up to meet hers as I let one of my hands rest on her belly, but neither of us spoke. We didn't have to. We both knew that we'd been incredibly lucky to end up here in this place. The scar that I could feel through the thin fabric of her shirt was a reminder of how close I'd come to losing her and the slight flutter of motion against my palm was proof that she'd found the life she was meant to have.

Now if I could only figure out how to do the same.

Chapter 1

MACE

FOR WHAT WAS PROBABLY THE THOUSANDTH TIME, I LOOKED through the scope of my rifle and rested my finger on the trigger as I drew in a breath and held it. The dank smell of mold permeated my nostrils as I focused on the scene before me, and I cursed the fact that the only window that had a good view of the building across the street was in the cramped bathroom. I supposed I could have gotten used to the mold if that had been the only issue with the confined space but it was the stench of rotting eggs wafting out of the broken toilet that really did me in. I'd made the mistake of lifting the plastic lid on the very first day as I'd scoped out the place to figure out the different views the two-bedroom apartment offered, and now every time I jammed my body into the narrow space between the toilet and the leaky shower, I had to bite back the revulsion of knowing the nastiness that was just inches from me.

The prudent thing to do would have been to call the maintenance guy to come fix the shitter but since I'd already made an impression with paying three months of rent up front in cash, I wasn't exactly looking to become memorable in any other way. And since there was a second bathroom in the place that didn't actually rival the portable toilets you only used when you absolutely had to,

I'd figured I could live with the noxious smell and God-awful image that was burned into my brain long enough to do my job and get out. That had been my thought three weeks ago when I'd first spied my target through the scope on my M23 semi-automatic sniper rifle. Yet here I was, twenty-one long days later, my burning muscles protesting the same unnatural position I had forced them into and my tortured nose sending a reminder to my tired brain to get some fucking nose plugs or grow a pair and finally pull the goddamn trigger.

I'd like to say that my phone ringing at that exact moment was the reason I let up on the trigger and flipped the cover down over the scope, effectively obliterating my target from view. But I knew that was complete shit because I'd already made the decision long before the *Blue Oyster Cult* ringtone started playing on my phone. I lowered the rifle and leaned back against the wall as the sounds of *Don't Fear the Reaper* chimed through the small room. Reaching into my pocket, I pulled out the phone and swiped to answer it without looking at the caller ID because I already knew who it was.

"You fucking changed my ringtone?" I snapped as I dropped my head back against the wall and turned so I could keep an eye on my mark.

"It's a classic," the voice on the other end said. "And it beats the hell out of that classical shit you listen to."

I didn't bother arguing because I'd likely end up with a boy band song next if I made too much of an issue out of it. I also didn't ask what the caller wanted because I already knew that he wouldn't bother wasting my time or his if he didn't have something of value to share. It was one of the many things I respected about Mav. It was also the reason I chose Mav as my second whenever he wasn't out on his own assignment.

"Since your mark posted an online ad a few minutes ago, I'm guessing you still haven't done it," Mav said.

"What kind of ad?" I asked, ignoring his not so subtle dig.

"He's looking for help. Handyman type shit. Painting, electrical work, plumbing."

"Pull it."

"Already did," Mav drawled and I heard my phone ding a moment later and saw the ad flash on my screen.

"Can you intercept any calls he makes to the site to check on the ad?"

"Yeah. I've already hacked his computer too, so if he tries to reach customer service that way, it's covered."

"Anything interesting pop up on his PC?" I asked, hoping against hope that Mav would be able to give me the proof I needed that would let me pull the fucking trigger so I could get my ass out of this shithole.

"No, it's clean. Only pictures and sites he's interested in are for artsy shit."

Fuck. I bit the bullet and said, "That make sense to you, Mav? A pedophile with not even one pic on his computer?"

Silence on the other end, then, "Could be he's got another PC stashed somewhere. Or he's old school and doesn't like digital."

I glanced back across the street at my mark and cringed when I felt my cock stirring in my pants. The young man had stripped off his shirt and while I couldn't see as much as I wanted, I still felt my mouth water at the sight. In a perverse move, I put the phone on speaker and set it on the window sill and then raised my rifle back up and flipped up the cover on the scope. I was greeted with the sight of pale, firm flesh that had smatterings of color all over it from the spray of paint that would occasionally fly off the end of the paintbrush as the young man's arm and wrist stroked lovingly over the canvas in front of him. I lifted the gun enough to take in the dark brown hair that was threaded with streaks of gold. I sent a telepathic message to the guy hoping he'd turn enough so I could get a good look at the crystal clear blue eyes I'd so far only seen in pictures but no such luck, so I settled for imagining what it would feel like to trail my fingers over the hard line of his jaw before tracing them over his full, pink lips.

"You about done visually molesting the guy?"

I bit back a curse and lowered the rifle as I reached for the phone. Mav knew me way too fucking well. I should probably take that as a sign that it was time to get the hell out of this business.

"Anything else?" I asked as I willed my cock to settle the fuck down. No way in hell was I going to be fooled by the veil of innocence this guy had managed to cloak himself in. My conscience might need a little more convincing before I could let myself pull the trigger but I wasn't about to let something as inane and useless as lust be the deciding factor as to whether this guy deserved to keep breathing or not.

"No. But Grisham's getting impatient. Says you haven't been sending in your reports."

I wanted to say Grisham could go fuck himself but figured Mav would take just a little too much pleasure in delivering that message to our team leader so I merely said, "Anything else?" again.

"Pull the trigger and be done with it, Mace," Mav said quietly. They were words I'd repeated to myself over and over these past three weeks. But I said the same thing to Mav that my gut had been telling me for just as long.

"Not yet."

❋

JUST MY LUCK THAT MY FIRST CLOSE UP VIEW OF THE GUY I WAS supposed to put a bullet through was his perfectly shaped ass cradled in a tight pair of khaki pants. At least he was wearing a shirt. I cleared my throat to make him aware of my presence but instead of responding, he crawled farther under the table and began fiddling with a screwdriver. The sight of him on his hands and knees did nothing to cool my raging libido and a surge of anger went through me that I was thinking more about how my dick would feel sliding into all that tight heat rather than acknowledging that now would be the perfect time to pull the gun from my ankle holster and finish the job I'd been entrusted with.

"Hey," I called out again, slightly louder but then nearly swallowed my tongue when the guy stretched his long body in a way that had his white T-shirt riding up to reveal a line of smooth, supple skin at his back. My dick went from semi-hard to hard just like that and I cursed my lack of control. Then I cursed the faceless young man before me and reached out to prod one of his bare feet with my steel toed boot. He let out a ragged shout and then a moan, a second after his head connected with the underside of the table.

I suppose I should have offered him an apology as he crawled out from underneath the table and pulled out the earbuds that were blasting some kind of rock music into his ears, but I was too busy trying to school my reaction when I caught the sight of his profile. The scope on my rifle was good, but by no means had it done the guy justice. Even the pictures had failed to capture his naked beauty. His lips were much fuller than I'd thought and I could see them stained with just a little bit of color like he'd been worrying the sensitive flesh with his teeth. His eyes weren't the simple blue I'd been expecting – they were so pale that they had an almost eerie, silver look. His spiky brown hair looked like he'd been running his fingers through it and I actually found myself wanting to reach out and smooth a few of the strands to see how they would feel.

"Sorry," he murmured, breaking me out of my trance. His hand was rubbing a spot on the top of his head and as he climbed to his feet, I actually reached out to help him before I realized what I was doing. It was a monumental mistake because the electricity fired through my blood the second my rough fingertips brushed over the soft skin just above his elbow. And if that wasn't bad enough, his sharply indrawn breath said he'd felt exactly the same thing.

A mix of rage and disgust went through me at my body's reaction to the monster standing before me. His charming, lop-sided smile and innocent eyes were exactly what would have drawn a kid like Evan to him. Fuck, this guy probably didn't even need to use the standard lure of, 'Hey kid, will you help me find my puppy?' to entice any little boy his sick mind wanted.

"I'm Mace," I bit out, my hard-on dying an instant death at the reminder of Evan. "We have an appointment."

I could tell the guy was put off by my rough manner and I reminded myself that I was here for a reason – to figure out why I couldn't just pull the fucking trigger and end this scumbag's life.

"Right," he said quickly, his smile fading as he took several steps away from me. I didn't miss the fact that he didn't extend his hand

and I had no doubt it wasn't just my tone of voice that I couldn't get a hold of. My entire body felt poised to strike and I actually didn't realize my hands were fisted, the knuckles white, until I reached out to shake his hand.

He swallowed hard at the sight of my extended hand but then took a deep breath and shook it quickly without moving any closer. "I'm Jonas Davenport. Thanks for coming," he added as he wiped his hand on his pants.

I glanced at the screwdriver he had clutched in his other hand and when I did, he let out a harsh chuckle and released his death grip on the tool and put it on the table. "Someone bolted it to the floor," he said a little too loudly.

"What?" I asked.

Another swallow and then he put a shaky hand on the table. "They bolted it to the floor. I thought that was something you only did on cruise ships," he said with another unnatural laugh. "I was wondering why they left it behind but I guess they must have stripped the screws…"

His voice trailed off as his eyes settled on a spot on my neck and I knew he was likely focused on the tattoo there. Under any other circumstances, I would have used his fascination to my advantage but since I wasn't interested in fucking a kiddie rapist, I focused on the task at hand and said, "You're looking for help."

My cold tone did the trick because his eyes lifted to meet mine and I saw the hesitation in them. I'd already decided that I needed to get close to the guy to get a better read on him and my attitude so far was clearly not going to get me the job. Which was why I was glad Mav had had the foresight to pull the ad the guy had posted. But even with his options limited to just me, he could just as easily tell me to take a hike and do the work himself or go the route of hiring a professional contractor. So I reached past him and grabbed the screwdriver off the table. I didn't miss the way he tensed as our bodies nearly touched. Yep, I'd definitely freaked him out. Time to pull a Hail Mary.

Chapter 2

JONAS

THE SECOND MACE DISAPPEARED UNDER THE TABLE, I STARTED planning my escape because I knew what the look in his eyes meant. No, I had no clue what had put it there but hatred was hatred and I'd learned long ago that ignoring that look was tantamount to signing your own death sentence. Only this time, I wasn't some desperate kid whose sole focus was earning enough money to ease the ache of starvation that had taken up permanent residence in his belly. I was going to tell this guy to get the hell out, but the only place I was going to do it was up at the front of the building, preferably out on the sidewalk where there was plenty of foot traffic.

"I'm going to need some other tools to work this loose," the man said from beneath the table and as he started working his way out from underneath it, a rush of panic went through me and I started backing away from the scarred, stained table and towards the doorway that led to the main room. My eyes never left Mace as I watched his huge frame pull itself upright, the screwdriver in his hand. And in that moment I was exactly what I'd said I wasn't – I was the same desperate, stupid kid because just like that, I was back in a darkened alley, backing away from the gleam of the knife fisted in the man's beefy hand…

I saw Mace's mouth move as he pointed at me but I couldn't hear anything he said above the voices in my head – mine telling me to run and the man's telling me not to move. By the time I made the decision to listen to my fourteen-year-old self, I was too late because the man was reaching for me and even as my back bumped into the alley wall at my back, I knew I'd waited just a moment too long to run.

Pain radiated through my shoulder as I hit the wall but when the wall gave way behind me, I instantly returned to the present and realized I'd run into the pile of old lumber that had been leaning upright in the corner of the room. I started to fall but a strong hand wrapped around my wrist and yanked me forward and even as the pile of wood crashed around me, I knew that none of it would hit me because somehow Mace had managed to put his body between the danger and me and while his body blocked mine from each impact, I heard every little grunt as piece after piece of wood struck him.

While I knew the whole thing had lasted only a couple of seconds, it took me much longer to recover and when I did, I could feel Mace's warm breath fanning across my cheek as he asked, "You okay?"

I nodded even as I struggled to catch my breath, because not only had I not managed to escape the man, he had somehow succeeded in pinning me against the wall, his big arms caging me in. I forced my eyes up and saw his nearly black ones watching me intently. Not with hatred this time but with something else. Something I couldn't put my finger on but that had the fear in my gut twisting into something that was no longer about the danger this man represented. A fierce surge of energy fired throughout my entire body. It was the same thing I'd felt when my eyes had spied the curl of black ink peeking from underneath the collar of his shirt and I'd wondered what it would feel like to trace the outline of the tattooed arc with my fingers.

Mace was a good deal taller than me – at least three inches, if not four. Which put him at nearly six and a half feet. And I didn't even want to guess how much he outweighed me by. He wasn't huge

like some of the guys from the wrestling shows I'd watched in fascination when I was younger and just starting to realize I was more
drawn to muscles than curves. No, Mace was built but not bulging.
His hair was a muddy combination of blond and brown and on the
long side. His dark eyes and darker skin tone had me thinking he
had some Latino blood running through his system. Everything
about his face was hard and rough – sharp jaw line, coarse stubble
that I suspected would feel good against my suddenly itchy skin, and
a slightly crooked nose that suggested he'd seen his fair share of fist
fights where he hadn't walked away unscathed.

The heat wafting off of Mace was intense but I didn't get to
enjoy it for long because he pulled his eyes from mine and straightened, and then let out a curse as he reached to shove away a piece
of wood that had been leaning against his body. But the second I
saw the blood coating his fingers as he tried to look over his shoulder
where the wood had hit him, I knew it hadn't just been leaning on
him – it had impaled him. A glance down at the wood showed three
rusty, blood soaked nails jutting out from the end of the offending
object.

The sight of the blood actually helped bring my fading panic,
and the other emotions I didn't want to examine too closely, under
control and I pushed away from the wall and stepped around Mace
to examine the back of his shoulder. There wasn't a ton of blood
but enough that I couldn't actually make out the three holes I knew
would be in his shirt and in him. Guilt went through me at the sight
and before I could think too much of it, I wrapped my hand around
his lower arm and said, "Come on."

❋

IT ONLY TOOK A MINUTE TO CLIMB THE STAIRS LEADING TO MY
studio but I spent all of it intensely aware of the man behind me. I'd
had enough sense to release his arm once I was sure he would follow
me but since he was only a half a foot behind me, I could still feel
the strength and heat that radiated from his big body. But it was the
unexpected scent of citrus and mint that was driving me crazy,

because I wanted to know if he just happened to be chewing some kind of fruity gum that had given off the aroma or if he smelled that good all over.

"In here," I said as I opened the door at the top of the stairs. I stepped back to let him pass and then shut the door and tried to swallow back the nerves that were threatening to overtake me. Although the guy had put himself between me and potentially serious injury, I couldn't shake the way he'd looked at me earlier. But one glance at the smeared blood on his shirt reminded me that his motives didn't matter. I'd patch him up and then get him out of here and then I'd figure out how to find the help I needed to get the repairs done to the first floor in time. I'd purposefully posted the ad on a general *Help Wanted* site in the hopes of finding some cheaper labor but since no one else had answered the ad except for this giant of a man, I'd have to find a way to come up with more cash to pay a professional to do the work...preferably someone who didn't look like he wanted to rip me limb from limb.

"Sit here," I said to Mace as I pulled out one of the only two chairs I owned. I'd found them at the thrift shop and was glad I'd splurged on the sturdy wood ones instead of the spindly metal pair I'd been eyeing, because I doubted they would have been able to hold Mace's weight. I hurried to the bathroom at the other end of the open space and searched out the few first aid supplies I had. When I came back out, I saw Mace hadn't heeded my instruction to sit and was exploring my combined studio/apartment. Although calling it an apartment was a generous use of the term. The building I'd chosen for my studio and gallery wasn't designed for residential living but it hadn't made sense to waste money on an apartment when I wouldn't be spending much time there. I had all the things I needed including space for my bed, a bathroom that included a small but working shower and a kitchen area that had probably been more of a break area in its former life. I didn't have a stove, but my microwave and mini fridge met most, if not all of my needs. Takeout food took care of the rest.

But none of that was what Mace was looking at. No, he was standing near the wall of windows that faced the street below and his eyes were glued to the large canvas that was leaning up against one of the foundation columns. I made my way back to the kitchen and tried not to keep sneaking looks at him as he studied my painting. Over the years, I'd gotten used to even the most critical eye studying my work but, for some reason, my gut knotted at the sight of Mace absorbed by whatever it was he saw in the swath of colors that I'd spent the better part of a week trying to get just right.

"We should get that taken care of," I finally said when Mace made no move to return to the kitchen. His stony eyes lifted to hold mine and I tried to figure out what he was thinking. And to my dismay, I really wanted to hear what he thought of my painting. Which was ridiculous because my art was the one area in my life that I'd never let anyone else touch. No amount of praise or criticism had ever affected why I put my brush to canvas or changed the colors I saw in my head. So why did I want Mace to tell me he saw what I did? Why did I care if he saw the things I'd felt when I'd picked up my brush and made my first stroke?

But he said nothing. His expression remained blank as he started walking towards me and I was just about to drop my gaze when I saw his fingers reach for the first button on his shirt. And then time slowed as I watched the man close the distance between us, his swagger confident as he finished working the buttons free, each one exposing another small piece of tanned flesh. My mouth suddenly felt dry as he peeled the shirt back and I couldn't say if it was the sight of his bronzed, muscled chest or the intricate tattoos that covered his body that had me unable to catch my breath.

An array of colors and shapes covered Mace's arms from his shoulders to his wrists and the artist in me wanted to examine every line and explore every color but my eyes caught on the large letters scrawled across his chest just above his nipples and spreading across his pectoral muscles to meet up with the ink on his arms. Somehow I managed to make out the words *Fiat Justitia*.

"Let justice be done," I automatically murmured as I translated the Latin.

Mace came to a stop before me but I couldn't rip my eyes from the tattoo – I had so many questions I wanted to ask about why those words, and what they meant to him, but even more, I wanted to reach out and trace the edges of each letter to test the texture. I wasn't a stranger to tattoos, but somehow seeing them on this man was like I'd never understood their true beauty. His body was so much more than just the canvas to display some tattoo artist's work. *He* was the art, the masterpiece.

I was about to throw caution to the wind and ask him about his ink when my eyes dropped just a little bit and I nearly swallowed my tongue. A glint of metal shone on either side of his right nipple and it actually took me several long seconds to realize it was a piercing. The lust that had been simmering in my belly exploded as I imagined what it would feel like between my teeth and I actually had to lick my lips to try and get some moisture on them because my entire mouth had turned into the fucking Sahara.

A small exhale of breath caught my attention and I finally looked up and saw that Mace was staring at me...no, not me, my mouth. He looked like he wanted...

Fuck.

I nearly stumbled backwards as it hit me that the gorgeous man standing just inches from me was likely gay and if the hunger in his eyes was anything to go by, he wanted me. It was another look I was all too familiar with but instead of feeling the need to escape like I usually did, I felt my body drawing up tight with anticipation. And then I made the mistake of looking down and any doubts I had fled when I saw the clear outline of Mace's erection against his pants. This time I did step back and nearly tripped over the chair I'd forgotten about. Mace's hand came up to steady me.

God, I needed to get a fucking grip. "Um, you should sit," I stammered as I put a hand down on the chair to turn it towards him. I tried to not let on that I was also using it to support much of my weight.

Mace stood there for a long, pregnant moment and I wondered what he would do next because his eyes had flared to life with heat and need as soon as he'd touched me. I was also wondering what I would do if he dragged me to him. I was terrified to realize that I already knew the answer to that question.

Luckily, Mace finally released me and sat, his back to me. As beautiful as his front was, his back was a not so distant second. Another tattoo graced the span of his upper back and it was more intricate than any of the others. And its meaning didn't need any explanation. This time I did run my fingers over the tattoo before I could stop myself. I let my eyes take in the detail of the angel's wings while my finger followed her body down the middle of Mace's back. He trembled beneath my touch but didn't move otherwise. My eyes fixed on some letters beneath one of the angel's wings but I managed to not speak the word this time around.

Evan.

A lover perhaps? A family member?

"You can read Latin?"

Mace's voice wasn't particularly loud when he spoke but it may as well have been a cannon going off because I yanked my hand away from his back.

"What?" I asked.

"You know how to read Latin?"

I nodded and then realized he couldn't see me. "Yeah," I said as I reached for the gauze and antiseptic. "I learned in grade school."

I focused my attention on the wound on Mace's left shoulder and started cleaning it. I wasn't particularly surprised when Mace didn't even flinch when the antiseptic came into contact with his injury. I was very glad to see that the nails hadn't damaged the tattoo.

"Grade school? Isn't that a little young?"

"I guess. I sort of liked the challenge of it, though. Made all the other languages seem like a cakewalk," I admitted with a laugh.

"Languages? With an 's'?"

"My parents were real big on impressions and nothing scores more points than having your kid be able to say, 'It's a pleasure to make your acquaintance' in five different languages. I felt like those Von Trapp kids singing that goodbye song."

This time it was Mace who actually chuckled and I let the sound settle over me like a comforting blanket.

"I bet they're really proud of what you've got going here," Mace said so softly that I almost didn't hear him. And I wished I hadn't because the pain that spiraled through me was unexpected.

"You okay, Mr. Davenport?"

The use of my surname snapped me out of my thoughts and I automatically said, "It's Jonas." I knew my tone had been too curt so I added, "Please."

I wasn't so sure why it mattered so much that Mace refer to me that way since it wasn't unusual for someone seeking a job to speak to a potential employer with such formality but it still rubbed me the wrong way – even more so than when Devlin's help called me that out of respect.

I glanced down at Mace as he looked over his shoulder at me and I was sure my heart stopped when he murmured, "Okay... Jonas." He may as well have stroked his fingers down my spine because a shiver took over my whole body. And for whatever reason, he refused to release me from his gaze and my traitorous body was telling me to bend down and taste his wide, firm lips. I managed to pry my eyes from his and focused all my attention on placing a bandage over his injury.

I was both sorry and glad when I pulled my fingers away from his hot, smooth skin. "Your tattoo's okay," I said in a rush. "But you should probably get a tetanus shot."

Mace flexed his shoulder as if to test the bandage's staying power. "I've had one." He stood and thankfully began tugging on his shirt. He didn't turn to face me as he began buttoning it and I once again took in his whole appearance. The nice clothes looked really good on him but somehow didn't fit...maybe because of the tattoos, maybe because of his line of work. And then it hit me... hard. He was probably dressed nicely to impress me in hopes of increasing his chances of getting the job.

"I'd like to buy you a new shirt," I stammered as I dealt with the conflicting emotions that went through me. The man in front of me both terrified and intrigued me and that in itself was a dangerous combination. I couldn't get past the open hatred he'd shown me downstairs but I couldn't forget that he'd used his body to shield mine either. Maybe I'd misread what I'd seen in his eyes when we first met…maybe I was letting the past bleed into my current reality.

"That's not necessary," Mace said as he finally turned around. "I should get going," he added and then he was brushing past me.

I needed to keep my mouth shut and let him go. I could afford to go with a professional contractor – yes, it would cost more, but I wouldn't have to wonder about the things this man could do me… or what I would let him.

"Mace."

He turned and sent me a questioning look.

"Are you still interested in the job?" I asked, knowing that I would likely come to regret my decision but finding it hard to care as Mace's penetrating eyes swept over my entire body before coming to rest on my eyes.

"Yeah…yeah, I am."

Chapter 3

MACE

As Jonas asked me questions about my experience with construction work, I only half listened because my body was still humming from the feel of his fingers caressing my back. And that was exactly what he'd been doing when I first sat down. It hadn't surprised me that he was intrigued by the tattoo on my back but I was caught off guard by how good his touch had felt. Plenty of men and women had commented on it both in and out of bed but I'd never let any of them explore it the way they wanted...the way Jonas had. The angel had always been something I protected because she represented a part of my life that was gone forever... that had been stolen from me one cold Spring day almost eight years ago. But I'd let Jonas in. Another mistake – one on a list that was growing longer and longer.

The turn of events downstairs had caught me off guard. First, when Jonas looked at me but didn't really see me after I'd crawled out from underneath that table. And then again when I'd seen the disaster waiting to happen and instead of letting the young man taste even a small amount of the same pain he'd inflicted on others, I'd been more concerned with reaching him in time to keep him from getting hurt.

While the nails in my shoulder hadn't felt great, I'd lucked out that Jonas had dragged me upstairs to his personal space because it saved me from having to break in later to plant one of the listening devices I had with me. The second he'd stepped into the bathroom, I'd made quick work of placing the bug underneath the edge of the counter in the kitchenette and then covered the move by pretending to explore his apartment. And then I saw the painting…the one I'd seen him working on for hours the day before. I knew shit about art but I'd known the second I saw it why he'd spent so much time on it. Because he wasn't just painting some abstract image that made only sense to him. No, he was putting himself into every stroke of the brush, into every carefully selected color. Pain, hope, grief…I saw it all. And as he'd returned to the room, all I'd wanted to do was enfold him in my arms and ask him who he was and why he needed to use a paintbrush to tell the world what he was feeling.

And then I'd gotten pissed…royally pissed. Because no sob story gave him the right to hurt those who needed to be protected the most. He'd had a choice – even if the worst had happened to him, he could have ended the cycle instead of continuing it.

"Mace?"

I jerked myself from my thoughts and saw that Jonas had actually stepped closer to me and his hand was resting on my arm. I casually pulled free of him as I tried to remember what he'd asked me. The fog of confusion finally cleared and I remembered him mentioning the hourly rate he was offering.

"That's fine," I said quickly.

"Great," he said with a smile. "How about I show you what I have in mind?"

I nodded and followed him from the apartment back to the first floor. I'd already gotten a pretty good look when I first entered through the unlocked front door. The main part of the space had been constructed of mostly brick walls and there were several interior walls that broke up the openness of the space. Since I'd already known Jonas was an artist, I'd assumed he was likely planning to use that part of the space as his gallery to showcase his work. I wasn't as sure what his plans were for the room we'd been in when the near miss had happened. The wood that had fallen was only a fraction of the debris that cluttered the area and I knew most of the work would need to happen in that room. A couple of the walls were exposed and many of the ceiling tiles were loose or gone all together and the linoleum floor was torn and dirty.

"So this is where the classes will be, so I want to get this cleaned up, close off the walls and put down some new flooring. The table would actually be a great place for me to put the paints so the kids can pick what they need…"

My ears caught on the word 'kids' and my whole body stiffened and a sour taste flooded my mouth.

"Kids?" I asked as casually as I could.

Jonas chuckled and shook his head. "Sorry, I'm getting ahead of myself. Yeah, I'm starting up an after school art program for some of the needier kids in the city whose schools had to get rid of their art programs because of budget cuts."

Jonas motioned around the room. "This will be the studio where they can work on different projects and up front will be the gallery where I can hang their stuff so they can show off their work to the community."

My ears were ringing so loudly that I barely heard the rest of what he said because after weeks of indecision, the young man in front of me had just sealed his own fate.

BY THE TIME I GOT BACK TO THE SHITTY APARTMENT ACROSS THE street, my trigger finger was itching and I felt a calm settle in my bones that I hadn't felt even once in the past three weeks as I'd watched Jonas through my scope. The sensation was familiar and comforting and washed away the temporary warmth that the young artist's touch had caused.

I snatched my rifle from the closet in the dark bedroom that had only a twin mattress in the middle of it and then strode towards the bathroom. The weight of the gun sent me to a whole other level as I pushed open the bathroom door. By the time I crouched on the floor and balanced the rifle on the window sill, my breathing had already slowed dramatically and my body had readied itself for the escape it would need to make before Jonas's body even hit the floor. It was unlikely the sound of the rifle would even be heard over the din of the traffic below but I wasn't going to take any chances.

I flipped open the scope and felt a rush of pleasure go through me at the sight of Jonas standing with his back to the window. He was near his painting but not looking at it. His phone was to his ear and I debated whether or not to take the shot while he was talking. If he stepped even a little to the left or right, he'd be out of my line of sight and I'd have to bide my time until I had another chance. I wanted this done now, damn it. I'd have to risk it.

As I rested my finger on the trigger and began the process of settling myself, my phone rang and I bit back a curse. Sweat began to form on my brow as the delay caused a shard of doubt to permeate my brain. I needed to get a grip and stop waffling back and forth on Jonas's innocence. I'd had the proof in my hands for three weeks – the arrest record, the medical records and statements of the three victims, the picture of the fourth victim whose body had yet to be found. And now the fucker had admitted that he was going to bring his prey directly to him under the guise of doing a good thing for those in need. Fuck, he'd even picked his targets perfectly – the most vulnerable kids who wouldn't have anyone watching out for them. A guy with Jonas's background would be able to spot the neediest, weakest kid in the bunch and do whatever he wanted to him.

My phone stopped ringing but then started up again within seconds.

"Fuck!" I shouted and snatched it up. "What?" I snarled at Mav, even though my anger had nothing to do with him and everything to do with me because my hesitation had let my gut take over again and the calmness that had settled over me earlier was gone.

"Listen," was all Mav said and then there was a click and I heard Jonas's voice come on the phone and I realized Mav had tapped into the bug I'd planted and was picking up the conversation Jonas was having with the other person on the phone.

"I don't know, Case. He seems nice but there was something about the way he looked at me...it reminded me of..."

Jonas's voice dropped off as he listened to whoever was speaking. I cursed the fact that I couldn't hear the other person talking.

"I know that in my mind, but I still feel like he's out there." Another pause and then Jonas said, *"No, I need to do this and I need to do it myself. You get that, right?"*

The combination of fear and determination in Jonas's voice had me looking through the scope. At some point, he'd turned around and was watching the traffic on the street below. A smile graced his lips as he said, *"His name is Mace."* His voice dropped as he coyly said, *"Yes, he is."*

Fuck, why the hell hadn't I thought to have Mav clone his phone so I could hear the whole conversation?

Jonas laughed. *"I am so not going to take creeper shots of him with my phone just to satisfy your curiosity."*

I couldn't help but smile at that.

Jonas listened for a few minutes and then said, *"Yeah, I will. Tell Devlin and the kids I say hi...I love you too."*

After hanging up the phone, Jonas stood at the window for a moment before finally turning his attention to the painting, putting his back to me once more. But I knew it didn't matter either way because I wasn't taking the shot.

The phone clicked and then Mav was saying, "I traced the call - he was talking to..."

I heard clicking of keys and then an indrawn breath which caught my attention. Mav was as cool as they came, so whatever he was seeing wasn't good.

"What is it?" I asked.

"Fuck, he was talking to Casey Prescott."

"Who?"

"Shit, Mace, don't you remember that story a few years back about Devlin Prescott?"

I stiffened. Devlin Prescott was one of the richest men in New York but he'd made headlines four years earlier when he'd gotten caught up in a custody battle for a little girl who'd been left in his care after her mother died.

"He's the guy who was trying to get custody of that kid."

"His nanny's four-year-old daughter," Mav said.

I snatched up my phone and brought up the browser and plugged in the man's name. As soon as I saw the first story, it all came flooding back to me. Devlin Prescott had ended up marrying the little girl's aunt but not before her sordid past was exposed.

Casey Prescott had once been Casey Wilkerson, the runaway stepdaughter of a wealthy pediatric surgeon who'd started abusing the young girl after he married her mother. The details of the abuse had played out in court when Casey admitted that she'd run away to escape the sexual abuse the man had been inflicting on her in addition to the torture she and her older sister had endured at both his and her mother's hands. Sadly, the young girl had only managed to exchange one tormenter for another.

"What the hell is going on?" I muttered more to myself than to Mav as I skimmed the article. My eyes caught on the tail end of the story that referenced Casey's escape from a pimp who'd forced her into prostitution. She'd fled to a remote town in northern Wisconsin and had run an animal shelter for several years before Devlin had tracked her down. After her crushing testimony about what her stepfather had done to her, she'd returned to Wisconsin but had been confronted by the pimp who ultimately tried to kill her and was serving a twenty-year sentence for the attempted murder.

Where the hell did Jonas fit into all this?

"Mav, see if you can find the connection between Jonas and the Prescotts."

There was moment of silence and then Mav said, "So it's Jonas now?"

I cringed at the slip. It was one thing to call the young man by his name in my mind, but to refer to him as anything other than a mark on the job was a massive fuck-up. "Just do it," I snapped as I hung up the phone and lowered the gun. Adrenaline surged through me and rattled my insides as I realized how close I'd come to pulling the trigger. In all the years I'd been doing this, my gut had never steered me wrong but my brief encounter with the young artist had managed to steal even that away from me.

There was nothing I hated more than feeling off balance. But that was all I'd felt from the moment I'd spied Jonas through the scope and I was starting to fear that even if I put all the pieces together and figured out who Jonas really was, it wouldn't matter because I'd already started to feel some of the things that I thought had died along with Evan eight years ago.

Chapter 4

JONAS

THIS WAS STUPID, I THOUGHT TO MYSELF AS I PUSHED THE FRONT door open and made my way past the empty walls of my new gallery. Even though I'd signed the lease almost six weeks ago, I still got a thrill every time I walked past the blank, brick walls. My agent, Candace, had been adamant that I should paint the walls white since I wouldn't agree to tear them down all together, but when she'd found out I had no plans to display my own art on them, she'd been apoplectic. I'd listened to her rant and rave all the way up to my studio and never said a word, and then enjoyed the sound of silence as she looked over the six paintings I'd finished since my arrival in New York. And just like that, her tirade about the walls ended and I practically saw the dollar signs in her eyes as she studied each canvas. All the paintings had sold within a matter of days and she'd found me spots in two upcoming shows in other galleries, and after that she never once voiced an opinion on what I was doing with my gallery.

Which brought me back to the present because what I wanted to do with it meant I'd had no choice but to endure the company of a man I couldn't figure out. In the week since Mace had accepted the job, he'd shown up every day at the exact same time, given me a polite greeting, explained what his plans for the day were and then had gotten to work. No venom in his voice, no lust in his eyes. Meaning I couldn't tell if he hated me, wanted me, both or neither. In fact, the only thing I'd managed to figure out was the guy had a thing for coffee. Since I didn't have a coffee pot in the gallery, he brought his own thermos with him and it seemed like he was endlessly filling his travel mug with it.

Buying Mace a cup of coffee from the café down the street where I got my daily latte had dumb written all over it, but the truth was, I wanted to extend an olive branch. Not that I necessarily needed to mend any kind of rift – I just really wanted to interact with him. Why? I had no fucking clue. I also wasn't expecting it to have any impact because my other efforts so far had failed. I'd offered to help work in the studio space on more than one occasion but the second I nearly tripped over a pile of old paint cans against one of the walls, Mace kindly suggested to leave the work to him since that was what I was paying him for. I'd extended an invitation to lunch, my treat, the very next day, but that had been politely rebuffed as well.

The progress with the renovation was slow but only because Mace had found a whole host of problems with things that he said weren't up to code. He'd patiently explained his findings to me but I'd been too distracted by his rumbly, strangely soothing voice to actually hear what he was saying and when he called me on it, I sputtered out an excuse about needing to call someone and told him to do whatever he needed to do to get everything up to code.

It was an odd thing to walk into my own space and feel like a stranger but that was exactly what happened every time I walked into the studio. Today was no exception and when I saw Mace, his back to me, on his knees near one of the electrical outlets, I actually leaned against the doorframe just to watch him work. I had no clue what he was doing but watching his large but nimble fingers work with the array of colorful wires had me wondering what those hands would feel like against my skin. My attraction to Mace wasn't a surprise since he was a truly stunning man and any man, gay or straight, would be hard pressed to say otherwise. My lust was what I

28

was having trouble dealing with. Just being in the same room with the man was as detrimental to my body as when I'd seen him in all his glory without his shirt. It was a reaction I wouldn't have expected considering my past.

"You need something?"

I started at Mace's voice and barely managed to hang on to both cups in my hands. I glanced up and saw that he wasn't even looking at me and I cursed myself for the sliver of disappointment that went through me. While I was very aware of Mace and my reaction to him, he clearly didn't have the same issue with my presence. I was beginning to suspect more and more that I was more like a gnat to him – always hovering around, a bit annoying but ultimately not worth the trouble of trying to get rid of.

"I brought you some coffee," I murmured as I straightened and walked across the room. His eyes finally lifted to study me and then he was climbing to his feet and by the time I reached him, he was towering over me. "I wasn't sure how long yours stayed hot in your thermos for," I stammered.

I stood there awkwardly as Mace watched me, his ever present unreadable expression filling his eyes.

"Thanks," he finally said as he took the cup from me. Electricity flooded my nerve endings when his fingers brushed mine but I covered the tremor in my hand by shoving it into my pocket and pulling out the cream and sugar packets I'd grabbed from the coffee shop. "I wasn't sure how you took it," I said as I opened my palm.

"Just black with a pinch of…" he began to say but stopped when I reached into my back pocket and pulled out a small container.

"Cinnamon?" I finished for him.

"Yeah," he said. "How'd you know?"

"Smelled it," I said as evenly as I could. I hadn't given much thought to how my attention to such a small detail would look. Desperate and maybe even a little stalkerish.

"What'd you do, steal this from the coffee shop?" he asked as he walked over to the table that he'd somehow managed to pry free from the floor at some point and had placed in the center of the room. He put down the coffee and carefully pried the lid off.

"Uh, yeah," I said with as much indifference as I could.

Mace removed the cap and turned the cinnamon over to sprinkle some into the coffee but when nothing came out, he flipped it back and then glanced at me before removing the entire lid. I felt heat crawl into my cheeks as he looked at the safety seal still in place and then at me.

"Guess they forgot to take that off before putting it out for their customers," I said sheepishly.

I was surprised to see a small smile tug at the edges of Mace's mouth. "So unprofessional," he said, though his tone held no doubt that he didn't buy my story about me stealing the cinnamon. Since the last thing I wanted to admit to was that I'd bought the cinnamon specifically for this moment from a small market down the street, I tore my eyes from him and glanced around the space.

"How are things going?"

"I've almost got everything re-wired so I should be able to start working on the ceiling in the morning."

I nodded like I knew what that meant. I hadn't even realized the extensive water damage that had occurred to the ceiling tiles until Mace had pulled one down to show me the mold that had started to form.

"I was thinking you might want to consider some different lighting options. I know you guys probably prefer natural lighting but since you're pretty limited in terms of windows in this room, I can install a few fixtures in the ceiling and then you can put in full spectrum fluorescent bulbs to mimic the natural light as much as possible."

"Yeah, that would be great," I managed to get out. I'd known the lighting would be an issue in the windowless space but hadn't thought it was something Mace would have even considered. "How did you know about the lighting?"

Mace shrugged and sipped at his coffee. "Did some research."

"Really?"

When there was no response, I glanced over my shoulder and saw Mace studying me over the top of his coffee as he sipped it. Whatever easiness I had spied in his gaze a few minutes earlier was gone and while he wasn't looking at me with contempt, I still couldn't shake the feeling that there was something off between us. It made me both nervous and frustrated. Nervous because there was a dangerous quality to Mace's silence and frustrated because I wasn't sure what I'd done to deserve such scrutiny. If I were smart, I'd head up to my apartment and get to work so I could ensure I had enough cash to fund my pet project but I hated the idea of hiding. I'd promised myself that after the events of four years ago, I'd never do it again.

"Is there anything I can do to help?" I asked as I turned my attention back to the damaged walls, already knowing the answer. Mace's silence annoyed me since I knew without a doubt that he was still watching me but I didn't turn around. I should have been more aggressive. This was my place after all. If I wanted to help, I should have just told him I was going to.

"You know how to patch holes in drywall?"

"No," I admitted before forcing myself to turn around. "But I'm a quick study."

❈

"Looks good."

A ridiculous surge of pleasure went through me at Mace's words. I'd like to think it was just the nuance of receiving praise for something I didn't have a natural talent for, but I knew better. I wanted Mace's praise and would have taken it in any form.

"Thanks," I said as I studied my handiwork. Patching holes in drywall wasn't something that took a lot of skill but I still felt absurdly proud of what I'd accomplished. "It's really real," I whispered.

"What is?"

Shit, I hadn't even realized I'd said the words aloud.

"Nothing," I said quickly and then turned to put the patching supplies on the table, but promptly slammed into Mace who'd somehow managed to sneak up behind me while I was lost in my reverie. His hands closed over both my upper arms and I instinctively froze. We both hung there like that for several long seconds and I found myself overwhelmed by the strength in his fingers as they pressed into me. I wondered if hands like his could deliver aching pleasure as easily as they could deliver punishing pain. And while my body wanted one of those things, my brain could only process the other. Because it was what I knew.

"Jonas, look at me."

My heart seized at the sound of my name on his lips. He hadn't called me Mr. Davenport anymore but he hadn't used my first name either – not since the day I'd tended his injury in my apartment. I wasn't even aware I'd dropped my eyes until he gave me the gentle command. I swallowed hard and did as he asked. The look was back...the one where it seemed like he was trying to figure me out.

I waited for him to say whatever it was that he was going to say but his eyes just stayed on mine until I finally felt him release my arm. His free hand came up to stroke over my cheek and I couldn't hide the tremor that shot through my whole body at the contact. It wasn't until I saw the chalky white substance on his thumb that I realized he'd only been wiping away some plaster from my face. I stepped back and wasn't surprised when he instantly released me.

"Hello?"

The voice coming from the gallery broke whatever trance had taken hold of us.

"Yeah," I called, my eyes still on Mace as I tried to figure out why I was so reluctant to walk away from him. There was no answer to be found in his eyes because while I was having trouble taking mine off of him, he wasn't suffering from the same condition. "Coming," I said loudly and then handed the supplies in my hands to Mace before hurrying up front.

I didn't recognize the man standing in the middle of the gallery. I guessed him to be around 6'3 or so and in his late twenties or early thirties. His black hair was closely cropped and even from where I stood, his stunning blue eyes stood out. But it wasn't just the unique, almost sapphire shade that had caught my attention – it was that they were shrouded with something so deep and so harsh that I felt an immediate kinship with him. He had the stance of someone in

32

uniform - my guess was military or law enforcement – but he wore civilian clothes, jeans and a white button down shirt.

"Hi, can I help you?" I asked as I closed the distance between myself and him. His eyes shifted past me for a moment and I knew that Mace must have followed me.

"Are you Jonas Davenport?"

The stranger's eyes weren't on me when he asked, but I knew he was talking to me. I glanced over my shoulder and noticed that Mace was only a few feet behind me, his jaw drawn tight, his lips pulled into a frown and his eyes narrowed.

"I am," I said as I turned my attention back on the stranger. I automatically extended my hand.

He shook it as he said, "I'm Cole Bridgerton."

The name didn't mean anything to me but I felt his hand tighten on mine just before he added, "I'm Carrie's brother."

Chapter 5

COLE

THE INSTANT I SAID CARRIE'S NAME, ALL THE BLOOD FROM THE young man's face drained and his mouth opened in surprise. He let out a small whoosh of air that had the man behind him taking a few steps forward and I wondered at their relationship. But I didn't have time to dwell on it because Jonas's free hand came up to cover his mouth. He had yet to release my hand.

"I...I..."

The combination of Jonas's starts and stops as well as the pain that flooded his eyes had me second guessing my decision to come here, but his discomfort was a casualty of me needing answers more than needing to spare him any painful memories my presence would stir up.

"I was hoping we could talk. In private," I added as my eyes shifted to the man behind Jonas. There was something about his hard eyes that had me instantly on alert. Jonas's throat was working overtime as he tried to swallow and another rush of guilt went through me.

"Of course," he said. I didn't miss the tremor in his hand as he finally let go of mine and then turned to the man shadowing him. "Um, I'll be back in a little bit, okay?"

The man gave him a barely-there nod but his eyes stayed on me. I didn't miss the warning look in his gaze as his eyes raked over me. A strange sensation passed through me at the perusal but I didn't have time to dwell on it because Jonas said, "There's a coffee shop down the street if that's okay."

I nodded and followed him towards the door. The hair on the back of my neck stood up as I felt the gaze burning into me from behind. It was the kind of feeling that would have had me reaching for my rifle if we'd been anywhere else.

Jonas led me down the block towards the coffee shop but didn't speak. I remained silent as I tried to adjust to the noise and chaos of the city. I'd only been discharged a little over a week earlier and I'd been warned on more than one occasion that returning to civilian life would be a challenge. The Navy shrink I'd been forced to meet with before I walked out of Naval Base Coronado in San Diego had gone over all the signs and symptoms of PTSD with me, and encouraged me to seek help if I felt I needed it. Who would have guessed that I would have happily chosen the debilitating disorder over the devastation I would have to face a mere seven days later?

Jonas kept his hands tucked in his pockets as we walked and he never once looked at me. In fact, his eyes never even left the ground and on more than one occasion, people coming towards us were forced to walk around him because he didn't notice them. I was tempted to reach out and draw him closer to me so that we wouldn't be taking up so much of the sidewalk but my gut was telling me he'd freak out even more if I touched him so I just kept pace with him. When we got to the coffee shop, he seemed to be on autopilot as he ordered a latte and when I went to pay for it, he didn't even seem to notice. I'd already figured that my appearance in his life would be a shock, but his behavior was making me wonder if I was really prepared to hear whatever it was that he was going to tell me about my sister.

We found a quiet booth in the corner of the small shop. The awkward silence between us stretched as I tried to get a read on him. He was younger than I thought he'd be. My contact in the Chicago Police Department hadn't had much information to go on other than a name but it had been enough of a starting point to lead me to his studio in a quiet area of Brooklyn. I'd expected someone closer to Carrie's age...or rather, the age she would have been had her life not been cut short.

"How'd you find me?" Jonas suddenly asked and I looked up from my own drink to see that he was watching me.

"A guy I served with works for CPD. He was able to look up Carrie's case for me and that's when your name came up."

"You're in the military?"

"I was. Navy. I finished my last tour ten days ago."

Jonas began chewing on his lower lip. "I'm sorry, she never told me her last name. I wasn't even sure if Carrie was her real first name...it wasn't unusual for kids like her – us - to use different names."

With that one sentence, Jonas had confirmed what I already knew, but hearing it from his lips suddenly made it all the more real and I found myself struggling to find words.

"We didn't know she was dead until a few days ago," I blurted out.

Jonas's eyes snapped up from where they'd been studying the lid on his cup. "What?"

Shit, this was not going the way I'd planned. I could feel my stomach rolling and I pushed my cup away from me and reached up to run my hands through my hair. It was already starting to grow longer than I normally wore it, and I wanted to laugh at the absurdity of one more little thing to get used to in a life that had changed overnight.

"They never told you?" Jonas whispered.

"There was some kind of mix up in their ME's office and her DNA was never entered into CODIS. They finally figured it out and loaded it a couple weeks ago and matched her to a missing person's report my parents filed after she disappeared eight years ago."

"Oh God," Jonas croaked as tears flooded his eyes. "Cole, I'm so sorry...If I would have known..."

I couldn't stop myself from reaching out to cover one of his hands with mine. The warmth I'd felt earlier was gone and his skin

36

felt cold and clammy against mine. I suspected mine didn't feel much different.

"Jonas, I didn't come here to blame you in any way," I began. He nodded and I reached for a couple of the napkins the barista had given us and waited until he'd pulled himself together. When he seemed as composed as he was going to get considering the shit I'd just dumped in his lap, I said, "I was hoping you could tell me some stuff about her…the stuff that's not in the police reports."

Jonas managed a nod but when he didn't say anything, I asked, "How did you two meet?"

"Bus station," Jonas answered, still somewhat in a daze. He was undoubtedly still trying to process what was happening. While the circumstances of my sister's death were limited, I knew enough to guess that Jonas had likely been caught up in the same life she'd found herself in after she'd fled our house in the dead of night, following a particularly heated exchange with our parents.

"I was…it was a good place to find guys looking for…" Jonas stuttered. His cheeks flooded with color and shame replaced the guilt in his eyes. He took a deep breath. "I'd just finished up in this alley behind the bus station when I saw her talking to this pimp. I could tell she was scared but I wasn't sure if it was because of being in the city or if she was scared of the pimp…Anyway, I knew what he'd do to her, turn her into, so when I saw him walk away from her to take a phone call, I went to warn her."

"How old were you?"

"Fourteen."

It took every skill I had not to react to that. I'd struggled with the knowledge that at seventeen, Carrie was too young to understand the harsh cruelties of the world and would have been easy prey but Jonas had been even younger. I wanted to ask him how he'd ended up in the same situation as my sister but I knew it wasn't my place. Jonas was already doing me a favor by linking me to the memory of Carrie and her final days.

"She listened to you," I said.

Jonas nodded. "I think she knew what the guy was but she was so overwhelmed that I don't think she really understood how much danger she was in. I took her back to my place. The first thing I told her was that she should go back home."

A shadow of sadness flashed in Jonas's eyes and I wondered if he wasn't thinking back to whatever circumstances had forced him into such an ugly life.

"She said she didn't have a home to go back to but she wouldn't tell me what she meant. I figured maybe her folks" – Jonas's eyes caught on mine – "your folks kicked her out or something." His eyes dropped again and I noticed him rubbing a fingernail into the logo on the coffee cup.

"I told her she could stay with me while she looked for a job. She was really sweet and we hit it off right away and I was actually glad to have the company. We liked a lot of the same things – cheesy horror movies, Chinese food." Jonas laughed and then said, "We couldn't actually afford takeout so we'd save the oriental flavored ramen noodles for Friday nights and eat them while we were watching a late night horror flick...we called it date night except it was always early in the morning because I was working..."

Jonas's voice dropped off and then his eyes went wide and he looked at me and said, "It wasn't really a date night! She and I were never together like that...I'm gay."

If I hadn't been hung up on Jonas's reference to selling himself for money, I would have laughed at his horror-stricken gaze as he tried to convince me, the big brother, that nothing untoward had happened between him and my baby sister.

Jonas must have realized I wasn't concerned about the nature of their relationship because he continued on his own. "She tried finding work but the few places that would hire her always fired her when she couldn't produce a social security card. I didn't want her working in the type of places that didn't care but I guess she felt guilty..." Again, Jonas's voice dropped off.

"She felt guilty that you had to work more to pay for her," I supplied.

Jonas didn't answer and I didn't need him to. It was the logical conclusion.

Jonas's gaze momentarily darted around the quiet coffee shop and when his gaze finally reconnected with mine he said, "Are you sure you want to hear the rest?"

I only managed a nod because deep down, I hadn't wanted to hear any of it. I'd wanted to believe that my sister was off living some fairy tale life and that all this was some fucked up nightmare.

"She'd been living with me for a couple of months when I came home one day and found her packing. I thought maybe she'd decided to go home but when she wouldn't look at me, I knew what she'd done. I tried to talk her out of it but she kept saying it was for the best."

Jonas dropped his eyes again. "Mateo was the worst of them."

As soon as the name of the man who'd murdered my sister fell from Jonas's lips, I had to clench my jaw to keep from telling Jonas to stop. I already knew the violent details of Carrie's death, but hearing the other brutalities her killer inflicted upon her before he finally took her life was something I had no way of preparing myself for.

"Did you work for him?" I asked, hoping the question didn't offend Jonas considering he hadn't actually come out and admitted he'd sold his body to survive.

Jonas shook his head but didn't say anything and I knew there was more there.

"I told her how dangerous he was but she was convinced that he cared about her and that she could handle what it meant to be one of his girls. I'd see her on the streets sometimes after she left, but she wouldn't talk to me."

I realized as Jonas spoke that he hadn't just been scared for Carrie; he'd missed whatever relationship they'd managed to forge in the time since they'd met. I desperately wanted to ask him more about what had driven him to that life but even more so, I wanted to comfort him, to take away the haunted look in his gaze. The observation confused me, so I kept silent.

"About a month after she moved out, she showed up at my door. She was pretty messed up and I could tell she was on something. It took me a while to get it out of her but she finally admitted that

Mateo had made her make a video with a few guys and another girl."

Bile crept up the back of my throat and I couldn't stop myself from covering my eyes with my hand. Not only had my sister been brutalized in every conceivable manner, her torment had been captured on tape and even now was likely being watched by all manner of men who were getting off on what had been done to her. Tears stung my eyes and my skin felt too tight for my body. Even breathing suddenly seemed to take too much effort.

"Do you want me to stop?" Jonas asked softly, his voice uneven.

Yes.

"No," I said as I took another moment to get myself under control. "Finish it," I ordered more harshly than I intended. "Please," I added, softening my tone as I dropped my hand. Jonas was watching me with concern and I didn't miss the sheen of moisture in his eyes.

"Once whatever Mateo had given her wore off, she started talking about wanting to go home. I told her she should call her parents but she was scared about what Mateo would do to her for leaving him, so she said she needed to leave that night." Jonas's voice dropped as tears began to slip down his cheeks. "She wanted me to go with her. She said your parents…she said they'd accept me."

"They would have," I said automatically. Although my parents and Carrie had butted heads on more than one occasion, they would have welcomed Jonas with open arms. They were just those kind of people.

The spark of hope I saw in Jonas's eyes was devastating. It was almost as if he was back in that moment – a scared, traumatized fourteen-year-old kid who was being given a second chance to be what he was supposed to be…a kid. The light in his eyes quickly died out as he snapped out of his reverie and remembered where he was and why he was there.

"We stopped at her place on the way to the bus station so she could pack. I was in the bathroom getting some of her stuff together when I heard someone knocking at the front door. She answered it before I could stop her." A harsh sob suddenly tore from Jonas's throat. "I'm sorry Cole, I couldn't stop him. I swear I tried…"

Despite Jonas's distress, I needed him to finish it so I said, "What happened?"

Jonas used his sleeves to wipe at his face. "He hit her. When I went after him, he punched me and then started kicking me when I fell. I saw the knife but I was so dizzy that I couldn't get up fast enough." Jonas's voice grew higher and higher in pitch as he spoke. "I could see him stabbing her over and over but by the time I got to him, she'd gone quiet."

"How did you get away?" I asked. I knew the question sounded accusatory but I was so raw inside that I couldn't temper my tone.

Jonas's voice quieted. "Another girl who worked for Mateo saved my life. She'd been waiting in Mateo's car. She followed him up to the apartment and saw him knock me down. As he was coming after me with the knife, she hit him over the head with a lamp and she got me out of there. We…we checked Carrie before we left but she was already gone…"

There was a moment of silence before Jonas whispered, "I'm so sorry, Cole," as one of his hands closed over mine. His touch nearly sent me over the edge so I yanked my hand away. My vision was already blurring with tears and I climbed to my feet, ignoring Jonas's stricken features. My only thought was that I'd gotten exactly what I asked for and I suddenly wished I'd never heard Jonas's name. I let my gaze briefly roam over the young man who'd just made my sister's death very real and then I did something I'd never done in my entire life.

I ran.

Chapter 6

MACE

"Jonas, I'm heading out," I said to the closed door after my knock went unanswered. I waited for several moments but then turned and hurried back down the stairs since I knew that I wouldn't be able to hear much through the heavy door leading to Jonas's apartment. There was no doubt in my mind that Jonas was still in there, since I'd seen him rush past me an hour earlier. He'd done his best to hide his face from me but it would have been nearly impossible to miss the tears streaking down his flushed cheeks. My gut instinct had been to grab him and demand he tell me what the fucker he'd walked out of the studio twenty minutes earlier with had done to him, but I'd managed to pretend that I hadn't noticed how upset he was as I murmured a bland greeting. That same instinct was compelling me to turn around and order Jonas to open the door and tell me what had happened, but I managed to quell it.

It took just minutes to lock up the studio with the key Jonas had given me the day before – a sure sign that I'd managed to earn his trust – and load up the van I'd bought for cheap and loaded with ladders and other supplies to help me sell my persona as a construction worker. I drove the van around the block and parked it in an underground garage where I knew Jonas would never see it, and then hurried back to the apartment building across the street from Jonas's studio. My computer was still sitting in the bathroom so I only had to grab the rifle from the closet. As I waited for the laptop to wake up, I lifted the gun and looked through the scope. My gut sank at the empty apartment and I realized that at some point as I'd been parking the van, Jonas had left the apartment.

"Fuck," I muttered. But a second later, my computer lit up and I saw that I'd left the program open that linked to the listening device I'd left in Jonas's apartment on the day we'd first met. The sound on the computer was muted since I'd been on the phone the last time I had it running but I could see the audio wave line moving up and down which meant the device was picking up some kind of sound. I hit the unmute button and froze as I heard the wracking sobs filter through the small bathroom. My stomach clenched at the strangled, agonized cries and I actually leaned back against the wall for support. I waited for the cries to end but they only let up long enough for Jonas to draw in a ragged breath and then they started all over. How many times had I heard wails like that? How many times had they come from my own lips?

I watched the waves on the program jerk up and down as my hands automatically began the process of removing the scope from my rifle. Once it was free, I stood up and began scanning Jonas's apartment again. Using the scope without the gun gave me a little bit more freedom in finding an angle that worked without risking someone seeing the rifle and I finally spied Jonas's mop of brown hair near the window in the far corner of his apartment. I couldn't see more than that but I didn't need to because I saw Jonas's arms come up to cover his head as he let out another few wails before finally quieting to an uneven combination of hiccupping sobs. Then his arms and head disappeared completely but he didn't get up so I figured he'd lowered himself to the ground because his crying sounded more muffled. It took another twenty minutes before the sounds stopped all together but he still didn't get up. I kept the scope in place as I searched out my phone and dialed.

"Yeah?" Mav said.

"Did you find any connection between the mark and the Prescotts?" I asked, pleased that I'd managed to not use Jonas's name this time around but not liking the sour taste that filled my mouth as I said it.

"No, I've got Benny working on it."

Fuck.

Benny was our tech guy who could dig up even the best kept secrets of any mark. And while that part was great, he also had our team leader's ear so anything Benny found would be filtered through Ronan first. Which wouldn't have been an issue if I was still in the early stages of studying my target, but since I'd been hedging on pulling the trigger for almost a month now, there was no doubt that Ronan Grisham would be watching my every move at this point. It was the main reason I'd been relying so heavily on Mav to handle the operational side of things when it came to this particular case.

As much as I wanted to light into Mav, it wouldn't change anything. "I need you to run a name for me," I told him. "Cole Bridgerton."

"Got it," he said.

"And Mav…"

"Yeah?"

"You run it, not Benny," I said firmly.

Mav was silent for a moment before he finally said, "Yeah, okay."

I hung up and checked the scope again. Although I couldn't see Jonas or hear him on the bug anymore, I was certain he hadn't moved. There was no reason for me to keep standing there watching for any sign of movement because I doubted Jonas would be leaving the apartment tonight. But I didn't lower the scope and I didn't move from where I was.

And I had no idea why.

❀

"JONAS, CAN YOU OPEN THE DOOR? I'VE HAD A BIT OF AN accident."

There wasn't even an ounce of guilt as I heard the lock disengaging less than a minute later. But even though I knew Jonas had had a rough night, I was still shocked at his condition when he opened the door.

I'd already known he'd spent much of the previous day crying and had been plagued by nightmares last night, because I'd heard every single one. The first one had happened shortly after midnight, about twenty minutes after Jonas had dragged himself off the floor and crawled into his bed. I'd set up the laptop next to my bed and had just managed to nod off when I heard the screams come through the computer's speakers. I'd jolted awake and had already reached for my gun that I kept next to the mattress before I realized what was happening. By the time I'd reached the bathroom and looked through the scope which luckily had night vision on it, Jonas had stopped screaming but his sobs were so loud that I could hear them in the bathroom even though I'd left the laptop in the bedroom. And with every sob, I'd watched his body curl tighter and tighter into a fetal position.

It had taken more than an hour before he'd fallen asleep again but I hadn't bothered trying to go back to sleep at that point. Less than fifteen minutes later, I listened as Jonas began quietly repeating the word "no" over and over until his screams once again ripped through the apartment. I'd returned to my perch in the bathroom and watched him for a while until he drifted off but didn't move back to my own bed because I knew there was no point. In the weeks I'd been watching Jonas, I'd watched him sleep on more than one occasion when my own nightmares kept me from enjoying the short-lived peace that I only found when the darkness of sleep claimed me, and I hadn't once seen any indication that Jonas was plagued with the same affliction. The reason for the sudden change was clear because only one thing had changed in Jonas's normal routine.

Cole Bridgerton.

"What happened?" Jonas asked as he opened the door wider and automatically reached for my left hand which I was holding lax in my right hand.

"Hammer got away from me," I said, injecting as much self-deprecation into my tone as I could. "If I could just get some ice, I'll get out of your hair."

Jonas's next move didn't surprise me at all. It was exactly why I'd deliberately smashed the hammer against the back of my hand in the first place.

"Come in," he said quickly as he carefully grabbed my arm. His red, puffy eyes skimmed over the injury as he held my hand in his and used his foot to kick the door closed. "Sit," he said softly as he led me to the same chair he'd had me sit in the first time his need to nurture had kicked in. I wasn't particularly proud to exploit his instinct, but I'd gotten what I wanted – the chance to see for myself that he was okay, and hopefully, draw him out. It wasn't something that made sense to me since my job was only to make him pay for the atrocities he'd committed but I'd given up on having that same argument with myself all morning long as I waited for him to come down to the main studio. Even then, just watching him through my scope should have been enough to satisfy me as to his condition, but it wasn't. Yet another revelation I didn't want to explore too much.

As Jonas went to his refrigerator to get the ice, I scanned his apartment. It looked exactly like it had the day before when I'd watched him after he'd returned from his meeting with Cole. The same exact dishes that had been piled on the counter next to the sink were still there, which had me wondering if he'd even eaten and a glance over my shoulder at his bed showed the bedding was still messed up. None of his paint supplies looked like they'd been touched, which was unusual in itself because in the entire time I'd been watching Jonas, he always spent at least part of his day painting.

Jonas returned to my side with a plastic baggie full of ice cubes and a towel.

"Thanks," I said as I started to stand but when I reached for the baggie, he dropped a hand on my arm and gently urged me back down. Just like every other touch he'd bestowed on me, whether intentional or by accident, it burned my skin in a delicious way.

"Can you move your fingers?" Jonas asked as he pulled up the other chair and sat across from me. I had to spread my legs a bit so he could move close enough to examine my hand and I had to fight the urge not to move in such a way that our legs were touching.

I wiggled my fingers slowly and didn't need to fake my wince. Apparently I'd been a little overenthusiastic with the hammer.

Jonas seemed satisfied and gently lowered the towel-covered baggie down to my hand. "Sorry, this might hurt," he murmured. His eyes remained fixed on my hand and I used the opportunity to take in the rest of his appearance. He was still wearing the same clothes he'd had on yesterday, and his skin looked pale except for the areas around his nose and eyelids, which looked red and chafed – further proof that his crying jags had continued during the times I hadn't been watching him through the scope.

I hadn't had a chance to connect with Mav this morning to see what, if anything, he'd found out about Cole Bridgerton, so I wasn't used to feeling so unprepared for a conversation. I usually had all the answers well before I asked the questions, but just like everything else with the young man in front of me, I was off my game.

"Do you want to talk about it?"

Jonas didn't lift his eyes but I felt the tremor in his fingers where he was using his palm to support my hand as his other hand held the ice in place. I was surprised when he didn't try to pretend he didn't know what I was talking about. Instead, there was an almost imperceptible shake of his head.

"Did he hurt you, Jonas?"

Fuck, I hadn't meant to ask that question. It was way too personal. His surprise mirrored mine because he lifted his eyes to look at me. I held my breath in anticipation of his answer because it shouldn't have mattered, but it did. It absolutely mattered.

"No," Jonas finally responded, his voice sounding hoarse. "He just...meeting him brought back a lot of memories for me."

"You'd never met him before yesterday?" I asked carefully.

"Um, no. I…I knew his sister." His voice dropped off on the word sister and I knew if I pressed any harder, I'd lose him. Besides, I was supposed to be keeping my distance so I could finally reach an unbiased conclusion about the young man's innocence or guilt. And I'd been doing a pretty decent job up until yesterday.

Until Jonas had brought me a cup of coffee. A simple cup of coffee and a fucking container of cinnamon and he'd done what he'd been doing from the first moment I saw him through my scope. He'd made me want to find some way to prove he wasn't like the others. I wanted the veil of innocence he wore like a mantle to be real. I wanted one reason, any reason, that meant I wouldn't have to put a bullet through his brain.

Jonas dropped his gaze again and I watched a single tear escape his eye. One fucking tear and I did exactly what I told myself I wouldn't. I touched him.

When I cupped the side of his face with my hand, he didn't move, barely breathed. I slid my thumb over the fallen tear and marveled at the way his skin glistened from the tiny bit of moisture. I was telling myself to pull my hand back when he suddenly closed his eyes and leaned into my touch. I knew I was treading on dangerous ground with what I was doing, but I couldn't pull my hand away, because I'd finally been able to give him what I'd spent the entire night wanting to give him as I listened to every heart-breaking, soul-wrenching sob that had worked its way out of his throat. And it wasn't enough. The need to take away his pain had me leaning forward, and even though Jonas didn't open his eyes, he tensed in my hold and I knew that he knew what I was planning.

I ignored every warning bell going off in my head as I slowly tipped Jonas's head up at the same time that I pulled him forward. And then it was over because the second my phone rang, Jonas jerked his whole body back so fast that the chair he was sitting in nearly tipped over. The bag of ice hit the floor and he quickly jumped up and scooped it up as I searched out my phone and silenced it.

"I'll just add a little more ice to this and then you can take it with you," Jonas stuttered as he hurried back to the refrigerator. I glanced at the phone, saw that it was Mav and sent the call to voice-mail. My muscles felt tight as I fought the need to finish what I'd started, but then I remembered the broken sobs that had tormented the young man in front of me for the last twenty-four hours.

"I think it's okay now," I forced myself to say as I stood up.

Jonas turned to face me, the small plastic tray of ice clenched to his chest like some kind of barrier.

"I'm going to be heading out in a bit," I said as I moved towards the door. I gave him another quick look and saw that he hadn't moved at all. "If you're up for it, I was thinking we could go check out some lighting options tomorrow."

"Um, yeah, that would be great."

I nodded and reached for the door.

"Mace?"

"Yeah?"

"Thanks," Jonas whispered and I knew he wasn't talking about the trip to the lighting store.

I was too confused by my own reaction to do anything but give him a brief nod. I no longer felt the pain in my hand as I walked down the stairs to the main floor. I didn't feel anything except an uneasy rolling in my belly as I started to understand what I'd almost done. Kissing Jonas would have been the epitome of stupid. I knew that but I still wanted to turn around and go back upstairs and wrap myself around him until my obsessive need for him was satisfied.

It took me only a few minutes to clean up for the day and I used the bathroom at the back of the studio to try and get as much of the drywall plaster off my hands as I could. By the time I reached the studio again, I knew I was no longer alone. And I could tell the instant the visitor sensed my presence because his whole being drew up tight.

Cole turned from where he'd been examining the one remaining open wall that I still needed to finish. His gaze settled on me and I saw the same guarded look in his eyes that I'd seen yesterday.

"Is he here?" Cole asked, his voice sounding somewhat hoarse.

"No." The lie fell easily from my lips because I still had the sound of Jonas's mournful cries in my head and felt the dampness of his tears against my fingers.

Cole's jaw hardened and I knew he didn't believe me. It made me wonder if he was just really good at reading people, or if my growing attachment to Jonas was allowing my confused emotions to bleed into my voice or facial expressions. I had no doubt that he was military – I'd known that the instant I'd seen him yesterday because it was written into the manner in which he held himself, alert, at the ready, always aware. I also hadn't missed the way he'd kept his attention on me even as he'd spoken to Jonas – like he'd known I was the greater threat. He'd been right.

"Any idea when he'll be back?" Cole asked.

"Not a clue," I answered, my body tightening in anticipation as Cole's tone made it clear he wasn't going anywhere. I was between him and the doorway that led up to Jonas's apartment and a strange thrill went through me at the thought of this man trying to get past me. I chalked it up to wanting to pick a fight with someone who matched me both in size and skill. Maybe if I pounded on Cole for a while, I'd be able to work out every single one of my frustrations that had been building from the moment I'd spied Jonas through that small bathroom window.

But as Cole's eyes stroked over my body, I nearly cursed out loud at my dick's untimely response. It wasn't that the good looking, clean cut soldier was looking at me with open desire like Jonas had that first day in his apartment – it was the flash of confusion I saw in his eyes that had me swallowing hard. Apparently I wasn't the only one wanting to work out my frustrations in a physical way. Unfortunately, I wasn't so sure a fight was what I was looking for anymore.

"Mace, are you still here?" I heard just a second before footsteps sounded on the stairs behind me and Jonas appeared, an envelope in his hand. "I have your check-"

Jonas's words dropped off suddenly as his eyes fell on Cole. "Hi," he finally said, his voice quiet and unsure. He cast me a quick glance as he handed me the envelope and then he was folding his arms around himself as he took a few steps towards Cole. He clearly hadn't sensed the tension he'd walked in on.

Cole's eyes shifted from me to Jonas and I felt an unreasonable surge of jealousy. Only problem was, I wasn't sure which man I was actually jealous of.

"I'm sorry," Cole said, his cool demeanor shifting into something more vulnerable. "I shouldn't have left like that yesterday," he said to Jonas. Cole hadn't moved at all but Jonas had, because now only a couple of feet separated the men.

Jonas shook his head. "You don't owe me any explanations and you certainly don't owe me an apology."

Cole's eyes dropped to the floor. "I thought I'd prepared myself for the stuff you were going to tell me since I'd already read the details in the police report but…"

"I made it real," Jonas supplied.

Cole nodded and sucked in a deep breath. To my surprise, I actually felt like I was intruding on the moment between the two men though neither had asked me to leave. And worse, I really didn't like the sudden vulnerability in Cole's stance. The cool, collected soldier was gone and what was left was…a man.

"I was hoping you might come to the funeral," Cole said after several long moments of heavy silence. "It's on Tuesday." He finally raised his head to look at Jonas and I was stunned to see tears swimming in his eyes. "Most of her friends have moved on-"

Before he could even finish getting the words out, Jonas closed what little distance there was between them and wrapped his arms around Cole's neck. Cole seemed caught off guard by the move but then his hands came up to return the embrace. While it was an "all in" hug for Jonas, Cole seemed uncomfortable at first but then something shifted and I glimpsed a shroud of pain come over his face that was so intense that I actually took a step forward before I realized what I was doing. Thankfully, Cole didn't seem to notice, because he'd tightened his hold on Jonas and buried his face against Jonas's neck.

The sight of the two of them together clinging to each other did something strange to me and I actually had to retreat to the bathroom to collect myself. Because in that moment I'd felt like an inter-loper. Not just because I was intruding on such an intimate moment but because I wanted to be a part of it. I wanted to share in what they were feeling and draw it from them. I wanted them to know that I understood loss. I understood it in my bones.

"Mace?"

At the knock on the door, I turned off the water that I'd been splashing on my face in an effort to settle my turbulent thoughts. Jonas was waiting for me on the other side of the door when I opened it.

"Is nine 'o clock tomorrow okay?" Jonas asked.

I stepped out of the bathroom and glanced around the now empty studio. Jonas looked shaky, but he was dry-eyed so that was something. I wondered how Cole was doing and then cursed myself for the ridiculous thought.

"What?" I asked.

"Is nine a good time for us to go check out the lights?"

"Uh, yeah," I said distractedly and then stepped past Jonas to grab my coffee thermos. "See you tomorrow," I said over my shoulder as I hurried out of there.

"Mace!"

I cringed at the sound of Jonas's voice behind me but forced myself to stop and turn.

"You forgot your check," he said, the envelope clenched between his fingers. "You okay?" he asked as he handed it to me.

"All good," I answered as I took the envelope, careful not to touch him since I didn't trust myself at the moment not to drag him into my arms. It had been years since I'd been this off-balance and I could feel the crushing need to lose myself come over me. In the past I'd had the luxury of finding a warm body or a bottomless bottle of scotch or both to forget who I was, but since neither of those things were an option, I needed to get the hell out of there.

"Night," I said without making eye contact with Jonas. I went through the motions of parking the van, but as I began walking towards my temporary apartment, I found myself stopping at a small, shabby liquor store. The feel of the paper wrapped bottle felt comforting in my hand as I climbed the stairs to the rat trap I was staying in but I knew that I wouldn't be drinking even a drop of it. The first thing I'd do after unlocking the door was dump every drop of the pretty amber colored liquid down the kitchen drain. I couldn't explain why the ritual worked for me, it just did.

That was the plan anyway. But as soon as the door swung open, I knew I wasn't alone. It took just seconds to pull my gun from my ankle holster since my other one was tucked away in my toolbox. I began methodically clearing each room as I moved towards the back of the small apartment but once I reached the bathroom, I already suspected who my unwanted guest was. But when I stepped into the small room, I froze at the sight of the man holding my rifle, the barrel pointed in the same direction I'd been pointing it for the better part of a month. The scope that I had removed the day before was once again affixed to the gun. I glanced out the window and saw that Jonas was in his spot by the window, his paintbrush in hand, a blank canvas in front of him. At any other time, I would have been pleased to see him back to doing what he normally did, but in that moment all I felt was fear since I knew what an easy target he was. And Ronan Grisham wouldn't hesitate to pull the trigger...nor would he miss.

I actually felt my hand tightening on my gun as my options fired through my brain. Would I really be willing to take the life of the man who'd saved mine?

"He is beautiful," I heard Ronan murmur as he kept his eye on the scope. Tension rolled through me as I locked my eyes on his finger which was resting lightly on the trigger. He held there for several long seconds before he finally lifted his head and glanced over his shoulder at me. His eyes settled on my gun which I still had resting by my leg and I had no doubt that he knew exactly what I'd been contemplating. I didn't relax even a little bit as he unfolded his big body and stood. Ronan was one of the most lethal men I knew and also one of the most unreadable so I didn't move or even breathe as he closed the distance between us. It wasn't until he handed the rifle to me that I finally took a breath.

"You should have kissed him when you had the chance," Ronan said as he moved past me.

I flinched at the realization that he'd been watching me and Jonas when I'd gone to get ice for my hand. It took me several long seconds to get myself under control and follow him. I found him in the kitchen studying the bottle of liquor I'd left on the counter as I'd made my sweep of the apartment. It was foolish considering what had just transpired between us but him seeing the bottle of liquor actually made me feel ashamed.

Everything about Ronan was dark and dangerous. At 6'5', he matched me in height and build but I knew from experience that he could take me in any fight. He was the only man I'd ever truly feared and not just because he could best me physically. He knew all of my weaknesses, and he knew that the things he'd done for me had bought and paid for my absolute, unquestioning loyalty…until now.

Ronan's gray eyes finally shifted to me but he didn't say anything. Instead, he pulled a business-sized envelope from his pocket and handed it to me. I leaned the rifle against the counter, making sure it was out of Ronan's reach, and then tucked the revolver in the waistband of my pants.

"You wanted to know his connection to the Prescotts."

I didn't miss the fact that Ronan didn't use Jonas's name. There were several pages in the envelope but I knew within seconds of reading the first few lines what I was looking at. It was an email transcript between Jonas and Devlin Prescott.

I need you, Jonas. Our place. Tomorrow.

I can't wait to feel you inside me again Devlin-

Disgust rolled through me as I flipped to the next email which was more of the same. The last page was a list of dates and the name of an expensive hotel in Manhattan. The dates lined up with the dates on the emails.

"How long has it been going on?" I asked.

"Benny found emails going back almost eight years…long before Prescott met his wife."

Which would have made Jonas a teenager when the affair

54

started. I was right when I'd guessed he'd been a victim who'd turned into an abuser himself.

"If you're too close to this-"

"No," I said sharply. "It's done." Even as I said the words, I wanted to call them back. But I couldn't.

Because I'd finally run out of reasons not to finish what I'd started.

Chapter 7

JONAS

I could feel Mace's eyes on me as I examined the different lights as we walked through the small store. Mace had already been waiting in his van when I'd left the gallery a few minutes before nine, but when I'd climbed into the passenger seat, I'd known instantly that we were back to where we'd been when we first met because Mace had only grunted a greeting and I'd seen a flash of something dark go through his gaze. It wasn't the same outright hatred I still wasn't a hundred percent sure I'd seen on that first day when he'd come to interview for the job, but it was still unnerving. Especially after what had almost happened in my apartment yesterday.

Since Cole's appearance in my gallery two days ago, I'd been on a roller coaster of emotions. It wasn't that I hadn't thought of Carrie in the years since she'd died, because I had...all the time. But the loss was something I'd had to experience by myself since Casey hadn't known Carrie personally. And although I'd given some thought to Carrie's family over the years, I'd automatically assumed that her relationship with them was similar to the one I'd had with my parents or, at worst, it was similar to the abusive one Casey had had with her mother and stepfather. So to have Cole show up like he had had thrown me for a loop because I'd seen in his eyes how much he'd loved her.

From the moment I'd started talking about Carrie, every detail of that terrible night had come back to me. I could still hear Carrie's soft gasps as she struggled to breathe, Mateo's knife plunging into her body over and over. The stench of blood had flooded my senses and I could still feel the hot stickiness of it as it coated my skin and dripped down the back of my throat. But I'd left all those details out as I told Cole what he wanted to hear. When I'd gotten to the part about Casey saving my life but that we'd been too late to help Carrie, I'd heard the words Cole hadn't said out loud.

Why you and not her?

It was a question I had asked myself in the years that followed, especially as the stain of my former life began to recede. It was that question that had tormented me as I'd watched Cole walk out of that coffee shop. I'd listened to its echoing taunts as I'd hurried back to the studio and ducked past Mace so I could hide out in my apartment. I'd barely managed to get the door locked before I'd let go. And then it all came back to me with a vengeance. Time ceased to exist, there was no need for food or water, and every time I'd managed to take a painful breath between the sobs that had ripped me open, I'd remembered the words Carrie said to me just before I'd walked into the bathroom to get her things.

We're going home, Jonas.

We.

In all the years that I'd mourned Carrie, I'd been mourning my loss as well because she'd given me something I hadn't had since I myself had stepped off the bus at the busy Chicago bus station. Only there'd been no one there to warn me about the danger that was waiting for me.

"How about these?" I said as I tried to shake myself from the past.

Mace's fingers reached past mine to check the label on the lighting fixture. "I can make that work," he said.

My gaze caught on his fingers and when I glanced up at him, I knew he was thinking the same thing as me. Even now the idea of

Mace's lips finding mine both thrilled and terrified me. And that only confused me even more because sex wasn't something that I'd wanted or needed in my life again. I couldn't deny my attraction to Mace but I couldn't understand my need to act on it, considering how fucked up things had gotten with the only man I'd dated after my life on the streets. And my attraction to Victor hadn't been anything like what it was with Mace.

My eyes got stuck on Mace's fingers as he began working the fixture loose from the display it was hanging on.

"I think six of these should do it," he said. His words finally knocked me loose from my trance and I nodded.

We didn't speak again until we reached the gallery and unlike the other days, I had no desire to linger and see if Mace needed any help. The studio was coming along nicely and I expected it would be done in a week at the most. Seven days. I just needed to get through seven more days of wanting Mace but not wanting to want him.

I helped Mace dump everything on the wooden table in the middle of the room and then headed for the stairs leading to my apartment.

"Jonas."

I flinched at the sound of my name on his lips. I'd like to say I tensed up but I couldn't because that was the way my body always was around this man. I forced myself to turn and watched as Mace strode towards me.

"Your receipt," he said once he reached me.

I stared at the piece of paper in his hand and then looked up at him. "I…"

I what? What the hell did I want to say?

I wish your phone hadn't rung yesterday.

I wish I hadn't pulled away.

I wish you'd try again.

"I hope your hand's better," I murmured before I grabbed the receipt. But as I turned to go, he gently grabbed my wrist to hold me in place.

"It would complicate things, Jonas," he said softly.

Even as Mace spoke, he was pulling me closer and I was happy to go because the heat coming off his body was drawing me in. I didn't bother to ask what he meant because in that moment, I wasn't interested in playing games with him. "For you or for me?"

But Mace didn't answer me. Our bodies were just inches apart and he was still holding onto my wrist. I felt his thumb brush over the skin there and I felt the exact moment he realized what he was feeling because his thumb stilled. I dropped my eyes to my hand as he turned it over and then his finger started moving again as it explored the raised scar on my wrist. We could have been standing there like that for minutes or hours before he finally spoke.

"For us both," he finally said.

I nodded as I tugged my hand free. I didn't bother saying anything as I turned to go upstairs because it wasn't the first time the scars of my past had ended something before it had begun. I doubted it would be the last time either.

✺

TUESDAY CAME MUCH FASTER THAN I WANTED IT TO. I HADN'T HEARD from Cole in the days since he'd shown up at my studio to ask me to come to the funeral, except for a text giving me the address for the cemetery. I hadn't expected to see Cole after the coffee shop, but when I'd walked downstairs to give Mace his check for the week and saw Cole standing there, his big body stiff and unyielding but his eyes filled with agony, I'd needed to tell him he wasn't alone. But the words had gotten stuck in my throat because they didn't seem like enough. So I'd hugged him. And then I'd regretted it because as soon as I'd touched him, his entire body seemed to lock up and I'd been sure he was going to shove me away. But he hadn't. Not even a little bit.

The feel of Cole's arms around me had been both a blessing and a curse. A blessing because I'd felt like maybe, just maybe, it was Cole's way of saying he forgave me. I'd known it was a stretch to read so much into one touch, but I'd needed something to ease the torment of knowing the pain I'd inflicted upon him. The curse came when I'd started to want more. I'd wanted the mouth that was resting against the spot where my shoulder met my neck to skim over the skin there. I'd wanted the fingers that were pressed against my back to draw me closer. I'd wanted to know that there was a place for me in his arms.

Complete and utter stupidity.

I wasn't sure when I'd become so needy. Maybe it was something about finally being home. Maybe it was seeing the peace on Casey's face in those quiet moments when we'd be having dinner and she'd rest her hands on her swollen belly and stare at the man and the two children who'd given her life meaning...who'd helped her find the peace in her life she'd so desperately craved. I'd accepted those were things I probably wouldn't have, but accepting didn't mean the wanting went away.

I shook off my maudlin thoughts as I hurried out of the gallery. Mace was just getting out of his van when I stepped out onto the sidewalk so I left the gallery unlocked. The air was awkward between us so I merely nodded to him and said, "I'm not sure what time I'll be back." I didn't wait to see what his response would be because I was simply too embarrassed to spend any extended amount of time in his company. I'd had all weekend to try to get past the humiliation of knowing Mace was likely aware what had caused the scar on my wrist...that and the naked neediness he probably could see in my eyes every time I looked at him. By the time Monday rolled around, I hadn't even bothered leaving my apartment. In fact, I hadn't even left my bed.

I'd been lucky to find a parking spot in front of the gallery a few days earlier when I'd gotten back from having dinner with Casey and Devlin at their house in the Hamptons, but that was as far as my luck held out, because as soon as I turned the key in the ignition, the car sputtered for a moment but didn't turn over. A few more turns just produced the same results.

"No, no, no," I muttered as I tried the key once more, jamming it forward as much as I could as if that would somehow magically fix the car.

A tap on my window had me turning to see Mace standing there and I barely resisted the urge to drop my head on the steering wheel.

"Pop the hood, I'll take a look," Mace said through the window.

Several minutes of him telling me to try the engine again passed and then he was slamming the hood shut. I bit back a curse and climbed out of the car.

"Could be a couple things...the starter, a bad fuse..." Mace said.

I nodded. "Thanks for trying," I mumbled as I glanced at my watch. If I didn't get on the road now, I'd be late but a cab to New Haven was going to cost a fortune.

"You need a lift somewhere?" I heard Mace ask.

"Um, no, I'll call a cab," I said idly as I began scanning the street.

"The funeral's today, isn't it?"

I looked at Mace in surprise.

"Your friend..."

"Cole," I supplied.

"I heard Cole mention it when he stopped by last week." Mace tossed the towel he'd been using to wipe the grease from his hands into the back of his van. "Come on, I'll give you a lift."

"No," I quickly said. "It's in New Haven," I added thinking that the idea of driving me to Connecticut would put a quick end to the discussion. The bottom line was that I was just too raw to deal with the confusing emotions this man stirred in me and spending a couple of hours cooped up in his van seemed like a supremely bad idea.

"It's no problem," Mace added as he closed the back doors on the van.

I must have hesitated because Mace came up to me and softly said, "Your friend needs you, Jonas."

Everything about the statement was wrong. Cole wasn't my friend and he didn't need me. But it wasn't just the words that were messing with me. It was the intimate way Mace said it to me and the way his fingers gently brushed over my bicep as if trying to urge me forward. Maybe if he hadn't said my name the way he did...like we were more to each other than employer and employee, I would have been able to resist.

We didn't speak until we'd left the city limits. And even then, Mace's voice caught me off guard when he asked, "Did you guys go to school together or something?"

"What?" I asked, my body feeling numb as we drew closer and closer to our destination.

"Cole's sister. She's the one who passed, right?"

"Um, yeah," I said. "No, we didn't go to school together. We met a long time ago," I hedged, not wanting to have to try to explain how Carrie and I had met. The idea of having Mace know the things I'd done to survive made me sick. It was bad enough that Cole knew the truth about me.

"He mentioned a police report..." Mace probed

"Mace," I whispered, my throat feeling tight.

"Yeah."

"Can we talk about something else?" I asked, my eyes glued to the traffic flying past us on the Interstate.

"Sure," he said. "Why the kids?"

"What?"

"The art studio you're building. Wouldn't most artists be interested in displaying their own work?"

"I've been pretty lucky," I said on a sigh, grateful that this was a topic I could handle.

"How so?" Mace interjected before I could even continue on my own.

"While I was in school, I met someone who took a liking to my work. She bought several of my pieces and started spreading the word about me to her friends. She even helped set me up with an agent when I got back to the States."

"States? You went to school somewhere else?"

"I got a scholarship to an art school in Paris. I studied there for a couple of years and then stayed for a couple of more so I could immerse myself in the culture. But I missed home so I came back a couple months ago. I had enough saved up from the sale of my paintings to lease the studio and fix it up."

"Why do it for kids though?"

"Because I think about what art gave me when I was younger and I want other kids to have that."

"What did it give you?"

"A voice," I said without hesitation. "Even when there wasn't someone around to hear." I risked a glance at Mace and was surprised to see him watching me. It was just for a moment of course, since he had to stay focused on the road but I liked what I saw. Like he got what I was trying to say. Probably just more fanciful wishing on my part. I turned my attention back to the passing scenery. "Even if all they get out of it is seeing their art on display, think how they'll feel for that minute or hour or day."

Mace didn't say anything after that and I was kind of glad. Once we got closer to the city, I used my phone's app to get us to the cemetery and I was glad to see the service hadn't started, even though we were a couple of minutes late.

"Thanks," I said to Mace as I climbed out of the van.

"I'll be right here," he said with a simple nod. I knew he meant that he'd be there to drive me to Cole's house for the gathering afterwards and then ultimately to take me home, but I pretended he meant something else. Something that gave me enough strength to stiffen my back and walk up the small incline to where a handful of mourners stood, unaware that the reason Carrie was dead stood among them.

Chapter 8

COLE

THE ATTENDANCE AT CARRIE'S FUNERAL WAS EVEN SMALLER THAN I'd expected and I felt another piece of my heart shear off as I realized how little of my sister's memory still remained in this world. As I scanned the few faces gathered on one side of the flower-draped, silver coffin, I had the insane urge to tell everyone to leave because none of them really understood what we'd lost. None of them got that losing Carrie had set off a chain reaction of events that had destroyed the family we'd been.

As the priest took his position and opened his Bible, I saw Jonas hurrying up the side of the hill. I felt a strange sensation in my chest as his eyes caught on mine – like some kind of knot inside me was starting to unwind itself. I expected him to hover on the edge of the small group but instead, he came up right next to me and took my hand in his and gave it a gentle squeeze. He didn't have to say anything because I got the message in the way he touched me, in the way his gaze held mine.

I'm here.

It was the same thing he'd given me when he'd hugged me in his studio last week. It was like he'd known I was broken and he was trying to help me hold together the pieces.

Jonas's hand went lax in mine as he made a move to step away and while I released his hand, I couldn't stop myself from grabbing his arm and holding him there next to me. It made no sense to me since I'd known him the least amount of time but I couldn't let him go. And even though I had to physically release my hold on him so it wouldn't look strange to everyone else, Jonas didn't move after that.

Although I had asked the priest to keep the service quick, since I wasn't sure how long I'd be able to keep my father in check for, it still seemed to drag on. I didn't really hear the actual words that were said but hadn't really realized I'd tuned out completely until I felt Jonas's hand at my back. I glanced at him and he motioned to the nearly empty container of red roses near the casket. The casket was draped in a handful of roses and most of the funeral goers were already picking their way down the hill towards their cars. I reached for my father's arm and felt him sway as he stepped forward with me. To any other onlooker, he would have appeared overcome with grief. But I knew better.

I handed one of the roses to my father but he struggled to figure out what he was supposed to do with it so I took it from him and placed it on Carrie's casket. Mine followed and then I was turning my father away from the site that would be his daughter's final resting place. I saw Jonas look at me with concern, but I forced my eyes from his so I could focus on getting my father to the waiting car. Yet I couldn't stop myself from looking over my shoulder to watch Jonas place his rose. His hand lingered on the casket and then I saw him place a folded piece of paper on it. I couldn't dwell on it though because my father chose that moment to come out of his stupor.

"Need a drink," he grumbled as more of his weight pressed against me.

"We'll be home soon," I managed to say as we neared the car.

"I want a fucking drink!" he shouted as he wrenched away from me and then stumbled to his knees. My father was not a small man by any means so it took me a moment to get him righted and as I was in the process of pulling him to his feet, I saw Mace watching me from where he stood near what I presumed was his van.

"My little girl," my dad suddenly whispered brokenly and I felt a rush of pain go through me. I hated my father's drunken jags, but I hated his lucid moments even more because they teased me with glimpses of the man I'd lost. It was a painful reminder that the man who'd raised me, who'd made me into the man I was, was buried under the stench of alcohol...close enough to see but not enough to reach.

I wrestled my father into the back of the Town Car I'd rented for the occasion and just as I was getting into the car, I glimpsed Jonas reaching Mace's side. I felt a pang of envy go through me when I saw Mace's hand reach out to settle on Jonas's upper arm. I felt my own skin tingle in the same place Jonas and Mace were connected, and it took everything I had left to force myself to tear my eyes from them and climb into the car next to my father.

By the time I got home, our neighbor, Mrs. Pellano, had already started greeting the mourners who'd arrived ahead of us. I'd been reluctant to give her the key to the house so she could start preparing all the food she'd spent most of the morning dropping off in various crockery dishes, but I hadn't really had much of a choice since she'd insisted on handling the entire affair. In truth, I hadn't wanted any of it – period - but I'd learned from an early age not to question my elders, and as my mother's best friend, Mrs. Pellano was high on that list.

"Cole, your mother would have loved that service," Mrs. Pellano announced as soon as I got my father through the kitchen door so the guests wouldn't see him. Bringing up my mother in every conversation was something else Mrs. Pellano did a lot...and something I fucking hated.

At the mention of my mother, I felt my father flinch. "My Scotch," my father grumbled.

"Thank you, Mrs. Pellano," I murmured as I hurried past her, my father in tow. I didn't miss her look of disapproval when I snagged a half empty bottle of Scotch from a cabinet on the way to the den.

As soon as my father was settled in his worn out leather recliner, I handed him the bottle and sat back on the coffee table and watched as he took a long drag on it. It may as well have been water for all the concern he showed about the quantity he was taking in. Under normal circumstances, I would have tried to limit his intake but today I needed him to be out so I wouldn't have to try run interference with him and our guests. I didn't have much left to give my father, but I could give him the dignity of keeping his need to drown himself in alcohol private.

It took just a couple of minutes for my father to start to nod off and I reached out and took the bottle from him before it slipped from his lax fingers. I took my time going back to the kitchen and managed to stow the bottle before anyone else saw it. I could only hope that Mrs. Pellano would have enough respect for my father, as well as the memory of my mother, to not share my father's condition with everyone. It would likely make it around the neighborhood at some point but today maybe I could still pretend that that one part of my life was still normal.

I hadn't even made it to the living room where the half dozen guests lingered when Mrs. Pellano appeared in front of me in the hallway and said, "He insisted," and then motioned towards the doorway. Up until that point I figured I'd been holding it together pretty well but the sight of the man standing by the front door had something breaking apart inside of me, and I was on him before he could even get a word out. I slammed him hard into the door at his back and then yanked him forward, pulled the door open and pushed him backwards so that his ass hit the concrete walkway leading up to the front door.

"What the hell, Cole?" the man muttered, his hand coming up to push the strands of hair that had fallen in his face.

Jimmy Cortez was someone I'd considered a friend once, but just the sight of him had me wanting to go back into the house to get the gun I kept locked in a safe in my closet.

Jimmy climbed to his feet and brushed his hands over his slacks. "I have a right to be here," he shouted. "I cared about her too!"

"Get the fuck off my property," I snarled at him and then turned to go back into the house.

"She knew the score, Cole!"

"The score?" I asked. "The score?" I repeated in disbelief. "She went to Chicago looking for you, you fuck!"

"I told her to go home! When she called to say she was in town, I told her it wasn't going to happen because I'd met someone else."

My entire body went cold as Jimmy's words filtered through me and then I was moving down the porch steps. "You broke up with a seventeen-year-old girl over the phone while she was alone and waiting for you in a bus station in downtown Chicago? You fucking left her there?"

I had the pleasure of watching Jimmy pale at my approach. "I-"

That was all Jimmy got out before I slammed my fist into his jaw. It felt so fucking good that I did it again. The warm spray of blood across my knuckles was like a balm to my soul, but before I could close my hands around Jimmy's throat like I wanted to, big hands were wrapping around both my arms, dragging me back.

"Enough," I heard a deep voice say and then Mace planted his big body between me and Jimmy. When I tried to shove past him, he grabbed me again, his fingers biting painfully into my upper arms. But I welcomed the pain and a feeling of elation went through me at the prospect of being able to do battle with a man who would fight back.

Mace must have sensed something in my gaze because he suddenly dragged me forward and whispered against my ear, "Not the time or place, Frogman." The SEAL nickname shook me free of my rage and I stilled enough to notice how his warm breath fanned across my skin as he said, "Something tells me we'll have our chance soon enough."

With that, Mace pulled back a little and I felt something shimmer in my belly when his eyes fell to my mouth for the briefest of moments. And then he released me and stepped back. Jonas instantly took his place and grabbed my bruised hand. I let Jonas lead me back towards the house but when I gave Mace one final look, I saw him lean down, grab Jimmy by the collar and drag him to his feet. And just before I went into the house, I saw Mace murmur something to Jimmy that had him going even whiter than he already was, and then Mace escorted him from the property.

❋

"Do you have anything to wrap this with?" Jonas asked me as he finished wiping the blood from my hand.

The first thing Jonas had done when he pulled me into the house was ask me where the kitchen was. After I'd told him, he snagged an ice pack out of the freezer and led me towards the kitchen sink. But one look at a few guests who were hovering near the entryway to the kitchen had him asking where my bathroom was. I'd followed him passively, my nerves still rattled from the fight with Jimmy and the strange encounter with Mace afterwards. Once he locked us away from prying eyes, he'd sat me down on the closed toilet and had placed the ice on my hand while he'd gotten a washcloth ready. Then he'd sat down on the rim of the tub and began the task of cleaning up the spattered blood.

"It'll be fine," I murmured. "Sorry you had to see that."

Jonas withdrew the washcloth and gently placed the ice on my knuckles again as he supported my hand with his. I barely felt the cold from the ice but I sure as hell felt the heat from his skin touching mine. What the hell was going on with me?

"Did she tell you about him?" I asked. "About Jimmy?"

"Not specifically," Jonas answered. "She mentioned she'd been in love with someone but it hadn't ended well."

"Love," I huffed.

"Was he a friend of yours?" Jonas asked.

"Jimmy?"

Jonas nodded.

"Sort of. We hung out for a little while when we were freshmen but grew apart over time. His thing was drinking, drugs."

"What was your thing?" Jonas suddenly asked, his eyes studying me. "Sorry," he quickly said as if realizing the question was off topic.

"Athletics, mostly," I answered just as quickly.

"You were a jock," Jonas said with a smile.

I laughed and the feeling was so foreign that I was caught off guard by it. "I guess," I said. "But I was focused on my grades too."

"A jock and a nerd?" Jonas said softly. "You would have been my dream come true in school," he said with a chuckle and then his eyes widened as color flooded his cheeks. Another apology fell from his mouth but I barely heard it because I was focused on the way his eyes kept shifting back to mine.

"Did you know Carrie went to Chicago for that guy?"

The reminder of Jimmy ripped me back to reality. "We figured she'd runaway to be with him but we didn't know where to. After graduation, Jimmy left the state to go to college but got kicked out after a couple months. I don't know how he and Carrie met but my parents were unhappy about their age difference. The guy was pretty bad news but the more my parents tried to stop her from seeing him, the more rebellious she became. Carrie had always been stubborn but I don't think my parents ever thought she'd just take off like she did. Fucker showed up here last week when he heard her body had been identified – I guess he moved back to the area a couple of years ago, but was too much of a fucking coward to tell any of us Carrie had ended up in Chicago."

"Was that your dad at the service?"

I nodded but couldn't find the strength to say anything else. I knew Mace and Jonas had both seen my father's condition and heard his words so they had probably already figured out what he was, but to have to say it out loud was a different story.

"Your mom?" Jonas asked gently.

"Died a couple years ago," I managed to get out. "She had a heart condition and the doctors said the stress was just too much for her…"

I felt one of Jonas's hands close gently around my wrist and I closed my eyes. How did this man know just when I needed his touch most? And why did I all of a sudden crave it more than I craved my next breath?

"How does this feel?" Jonas asked, as he shifted the ice pack to study my knuckles.

In truth, I hadn't felt much since Jonas had first touched me so it was easy to say, "Feels okay."

I couldn't make sense of what I was feeling around the younger man. Jonas's touch wasn't exactly sexual but if a woman had been touching me in the same way, I wouldn't have hesitated to act on the curiosity that was flooding through me now. Was what I was feeling about attraction or was it about just needing to connect with another person in a way I hadn't in a really long time? I'd never once in my life even looked at another man in the same way that I had women.

It had to be the stress. There was no other explanation. And my body was reacting to Jonas because we had a connection that was born of terrible circumstances. If I'd met Jonas on the street, I wouldn't have given him a second thought.

What about Mace?

"I should probably get back to the guests," I muttered as I pushed back the memory of the sensation that had rushed through me when Mace had had me in his grip.

It's fucking stress.

Jonas nodded and removed the ice pack.

"Jonas, can I ask what you put on Carrie's casket?"

The younger man was in the process of reaching for a towel when I asked the question and I didn't miss the way he stiffened.

"It's okay, you don't have to tell me," I said.

"It was a picture," he said as he began drying off my hand from where the condensation from the ice pack had dampened it.

"A picture?" I prodded.

"A drawing," he clarified. "Of you," he admitted, lifting his eyes to meet mine. "I would have done your entire family if I had known what your parents looked like," he added. "I'm pretty good at remembering faces," he said quickly. "I didn't sneak a picture of you or anything."

I smiled at that. "Thank you for doing that for her."

"I, um…I did one for you," Jonas said softly and then he reached for a sketchbook that I hadn't noticed sitting on the edge of the sink. I could see his fingers trembling just a little bit as he pulled a loose piece of paper from between the pages of the pad.

It seemed to take Jonas a moment to work up the courage to hand it to me. I'd prepared myself for a simple sketch of Carrie's features which would have been undoubtedly distorted considering how much time had passed since Jonas had last seen her. But the girl I saw looking back at me was exactly the Carrie I remembered. Jonas hadn't just gotten her features right; he'd gotten everything right. The way her eyes lit up from the inside, the slight lift in her smile that made you wonder what she was thinking and the coy way she tilted her head as if she knew exactly what *you* were thinking.

"She looks exactly like the last time I saw her. We played cards for hours and hours on Thanksgiving night during my last leave before she disappeared...It's perfect," I whispered and then I did what I'd wanted to do since the day I'd gone to Jonas's studio to apologize. I enfolded Jonas in my arms and I felt a big breath escape me as his arms wrapped around my waist. We were still both sitting so the angle didn't let me pull him up against me the way I wanted to but I still reveled in how at ease I finally felt. I tried not to think on it too much that I liked the soft fragrances of aftershave and man teasing my senses, or the way Jonas's hard body flexed beneath my palms. Or that the feel of his jaw brushing my neck felt insanely good. And I definitely did my best not to dwell on the fact that it would be so easy to turn my head just a little so my lips could taste his skin, flutter over his pulse, skim over his full lips.

I was lucky that Jonas finally pulled back on his own because I was struggling to be the first one to end the contact. But then Jonas sent me a tremulous smile and I knew I was fucked. Completely and royally.

Chapter 9

MACE

THE FIRST THING I NOTICED AS I PULLED THE VAN INTO AN OPEN spot in front of Jonas's gallery was a gorgeous ass in a tight pair of jeans sticking out from beneath the hood of Jonas's car. I had no doubt who the ass belonged to, since I'd caught myself looking at it more than once. The last time had been the day before when I pulled Cole off the unlucky bastard he'd decided to let his rage loose on. Jonas and I had arrived at Cole's house just in time to see Cole shove the skinny, stringy haired guy down the porch stairs. I hadn't actually heard anything the two men said to each other so I had no idea what had caused the fight, but a part of me had enjoyed seeing someone as cool and collected as Cole lose it. But I hadn't liked the crowd that'd gathered around to watch Cole's meltdown.

It actually hadn't been easy to drag Cole off the guy and I hadn't missed the hungry look in Cole's eyes as he fought me, albeit briefly. His unspent fury felt familiar to me and I'd actually felt a perverse need to let him do whatever he needed to do to lance the wounds that drove him. I'd also felt something else that I was trying very hard not to dwell on.

I hadn't seen Cole after that because I'd stayed in the van during the service. I'd spent much of the time trying to figure out my next steps, because the call from Mav that I'd finally managed to return after Ronan left had only left me with more questions than answers. I knew Cole was a decorated Navy SEAL who'd been honorably discharged in recent weeks and I'd wondered why a man in the prime of his career would walk away from it. At twenty-nine, Cole still had plenty of years left to serve his country and from his stellar record, he'd done more than his fair share of it. I hadn't seen any signs of PTSD and from the information I'd gleaned about his sister, the discovery of her death occurred after his discharge.

Which led me to the problems I was having with figuring out Jonas's connection to Cole and his sister. While Cole had mentioned a police report that described Carrie's death, he'd also hinted at Jonas knowing something about what had happened to her. The problem was that Mav hadn't been able to find any details about Carrie Bridgerton's death. All he'd found was a missing person's report her parents had filed years earlier.

I'd had Benny send me all the emails between Devlin Prescott and Jonas from the time their relationship started, and while there weren't a lot of them, they were regular enough to prove that they'd been seeing each other from the time Jonas was fourteen up through the time he'd spent in Paris. Which meant Jonas would have likely met Carrie while he'd been living in Boston or possibly during one of his trips to Manhattan to meet up with Devlin.

The idea of Jonas and Devlin Prescott made me physically ill, and I'd been tempted on more than one occasion in the last couple of days to grab my rifle and head up to the Hamptons to take out the monster who'd started this whole thing…the man who'd turned Jonas into what he was. But first and foremost, I needed to figure out what the hell was going on with Jonas because Ronan's patience would only last for so long. I knew in my gut that something about this whole thing was really fucked up but I just couldn't figure out the piece I was missing.

As I got out of the van, I heard Jonas's car start up. My plan had been to fix the car I'd intentionally disabled before Jonas got up. I hadn't planned on Cole showing up though.

"Morning," I said to Jonas as he climbed out of the car, a smile on his face.

"Morning. Cole fixed it," he said, motioning to his car where Cole was in the process of releasing the hood so he could close it.

Cole's cobalt eyes shifted to me when he said, "Loose wire on the distributor cap. Surprised you missed it."

"Huh," I said non-committedly. "Glad you figured it out."

"He's a lifesaver," Jonas said as he started loading some boxes that were stacked up on the curb next to the car. "It would have sucked trying to get these into a cab."

"Didn't expect to see you again so soon," I said to Cole.

"Jonas left his sketchpad at my house," Cole responded as he began helping Jonas with the boxes. "I knew it was important to him..."

"Cole's going to help me deliver some of these art supplies today," Jonas added. "If you need anything, you can call me on my cell."

Right. Because I was the fucking help.

"Sure," I murmured as I went through the motions of getting my shit out of the van. I did my best not to watch Jonas and Cole laugh as they struggled to fit the boxes into Jonas's little hatchback sedan. I hated the jealousy that ate away at me but I hated knowing that my irritation stemmed more from being an outsider rather than Jonas and Cole being together. Because there was something about the two of them...

"Bye, Mace," Jonas called as he and Cole got into his car. I returned his wave as I got the last of my things out of the van but I didn't bother taking them into the studio. Instead, I put the tools back into the van, slammed the doors shut and locked up the gallery. It took just minutes to walk to my regular car which was parked in an alley one block over. Following Jonas and Cole wasn't really necessary but I convinced myself otherwise and brought up the app on my phone that linked to the GPS tracker I'd placed in the wheel well of Jonas's car the day before.

It took just minutes to catch up to them but I made sure to maintain my distance. They ended up making three stops at various schools and I was surprised how much time they spent at each one. I would have liked to see how Jonas interacted with the kids but figured with Cole's presence, he would probably hide any interest he might have had in any one kid. Even as the thought crossed my mind, I wanted to spit out the bitter taste that flooded my mouth. And it wasn't because I believed that Jonas was guilty of the things he stood accused of...the things I had proof he'd done. It was because I needed him not to be. Because I knew, had known for a while now, that I wouldn't be pulling the trigger, no matter what happened. I'd thought after seeing the emails between Jonas and Devlin that I could do what I needed to do but as I'd lain in bed that night listening to Jonas's cries as he struggled with his relentless nightmares, I'd known then that I couldn't punish him for something that had been done to him.

Only problem was, if I didn't pull the trigger, Ronan would send someone who would. Someone who wouldn't see Jonas's kindness or gentle nature or his need to comfort...or the pain that consumed him. They wouldn't care that he'd suffered at the hands of another. They would deliver justice, not mercy.

I knew I wouldn't be able to stop the men that Ronan would send so I was left with only one choice. Take Jonas and run. Find a place for him to start a new life and make sure he got some help so he wouldn't hurt any more kids.

He'd hate me of course. There was just no way around that. But I wanted him alive more than I wanted him to keep looking at me like he always did – with equal parts of want and need and just a hint of fear.

As I followed Jonas and Cole to a deli, I parked across the street and far enough down the block that I wouldn't be visible, but had enough of a view to watch them as they ate in the outdoor seating area. Jonas looked so at ease with Cole that I felt envious. What would it be like to have Jonas smile like that at me? What would his laugh sound like?

What did it fucking matter? I was about to destroy his entire life.

A rush of anger and frustration surged through me and I started up my car and headed back to the gallery. I'd seen that there were still boxes in Jonas's car so he likely had more stops to make before he got back to the gallery, but I didn't want to risk not being there if he came back early.

I'd made a lot of progress on Jonas's studio and had only a couple more days' worth of work. It didn't leave me much time to make plans for figuring out how to get Jonas out of the mess he was in.

It was close to three o'clock when I heard the gallery door open. I expected to hear heavy footsteps but when there was nothing, I left the studio and walked up front. I was surprised to see a pregnant woman wandering around the space, her hand resting on her protruding belly. I knew instantly who she was because I'd seen her picture in the many articles I'd read in the hopes of understanding her connection to Jonas.

"Can I help you?" I asked.

The woman startled and I felt bad when I saw a rush of fear go through her briefly before she gathered herself.

"Sorry," I said.

She laughed and shook her head. "No, it's my fault. I was thinking about something else. Um, is Jonas here?"

"No, he's not, but he should be back soon."

"Are you Mace?" she asked as she gave me a quick once over. I liked that she closed the distance between us. With my size and my tats, I wasn't exactly the most approachable guy.

"I am," I said as I automatically held out my hand when she introduced herself.

"I'm Casey Prescott. I'm a friend of Jonas's."

"Nice to meet you," I said. An uneasy rush of emotion went through me as she spoke because the lilt of her voice and her warm smile reminded me of someone I'd lost long ago…someone I'd driven away. Someone who'd once been my entire world.

"This place looks amazing," she said as she looked around. "May I?" she asked, motioning to the doorway that led to the studio.

"Please," I said.

"Wow," she said as she took in the now clean room. I'd managed to get the last wall up the day before and had started on hanging the lights.

"Case, you here?" I heard Jonas call.

"Back here!" Casey called. She met him in the doorway and there was no hesitation between them as Jonas dragged her into his arms. A twinge of anger went through me at what Jonas was doing with this woman's husband behind her back, but I reminded myself he was a victim.

"I thought that was your car out front," Jonas said as he pulled back. I could see Cole standing just behind the pair.

"Devlin had a Board meeting to attend, so I thought I'd tag along and see how things were coming along. It's perfect, Jonas," she said as she looked around the room. "The kids are going to love it."

The wide smile that spread across Jonas's lips had me shifting uncomfortably. He looked so genuinely happy that I had to wonder if he'd somehow compartmentalized his actions, because I couldn't explain his complete and utter lack of guilt.

Unless he didn't have anything to feel guilty about.

The thought was so unexpected that I actually took a step back. Was that even a possibility?

"Case, this is Cole," I heard Jonas say despite the roaring in my ears. "Cole, this is Casey Prescott."

I picked up on the sudden tension in Jonas's voice and that helped settle the disturbing thoughts that had started to rattle around my head.

"Hi," Cole said as he extended his hand. But like Jonas, Casey wasn't having any of it and she stepped forward and wrapped her arms around Cole. And just like with Jonas, he seemed caught off guard by the hug but he recovered quickly.

"I'm so sorry about Carrie, Cole. I wish I'd gotten there sooner..."

At Casey's words, I froze. Had she known Carrie? How was that possible?

I thought back to what little I knew about Casey's life before she'd married her husband. The possible connection between her and Cole's sister hit me hard and fast and I was actually reaching for my phone to call Mav before I remembered where I was.

"Mace?"

I had no idea how Jonas's voice pierced the fog that clouded my brain but when I looked up, I saw all three of them looking at me with concern.

"What?" I asked.

"You okay?"

I nodded. "Yeah, sorry," I stammered. "Was someone talking to me?"

"I was asking if you might be able to come to Jonas's birthday party tomorrow night at our house in the Hamptons. We're celebrating a week early because we're leaving for Ireland on Friday," Casey said, her voice thick with concern.

"Yeah, sure – I'd love to," I rattled off.

I tuned out again after that and automatically began gathering my tools. I needed to get the hell out of there and call Mav. I needed some fucking answers. I needed to know that I hadn't nearly done the unthinkable.

"You sure you're okay?" Jonas asked when he reappeared by himself in the studio.

"Yeah, just a little tired," I said. "I'm going to head out if that's okay."

"Sure," Jonas quickly said. "About the party, you don't have to come if you don't want to. And it's not really a party, more of a dinner. She wrangled Cole into coming too so…"

I wasn't sure if he was telling me that because he could sense the tension between me and Cole, or if he just didn't want me there. In truth, I was too shaken to even worry about it so I didn't answer him.

"So, I'll see you tomorrow?" Jonas asked awkwardly.

I nodded but as Jonas passed me on his way towards the stairs that led to his apartment, I said, "Casey's really nice. Have you guys been friends for a while?"

Jonas smiled. "Almost eight years. She saved my life," he said softly. "Night, Mace."

"Good night."

I was already dialing Mav's number by the time I reached the van and he picked up just as I slammed the door shut.

"Hey-"

"I need you to look up the name of the man who tried to kill Casey Prescott," I barked before Mav could even get another word in. Mav must have sensed my mood because he didn't ask any questions and I could hear him typing.

"Mateo Santero."

"What was the name of the girl he killed in Chicago?"

More typing, then, "She was a Jane Doe."

"That's not good enough, Mav," I snapped. "I need a name!"

Mav didn't answer me but since I could hear him typing, I tried to rein in my frustration.

"Fuck," I heard Mav breathe. "Carrie Bridgerton."

I closed my eyes as a wave of heat flooded through me. What the hell had I done?

"Mace-"

"No!" I snapped. "Not over the phone. Meet me at our place. One hour!" I hung up the phone without giving Mav a chance to respond and then I slammed my hands down on the steering wheel over and over again until I felt some of the initial rage ease from my system. I knew I needed to get a grip since Jonas could easily see me either from his apartment window or if he came down to the gallery for any reason, so I started the van and went through the motions of parking it in the garage. It took me another ten minutes to get to my car and then I was heading out of the city.

I beat Mav to the nearest motel in the cheap hotel chain we typically used for debriefs, and got a room. I didn't bother texting him which room it was because he knew which one I'd go for. The one farthest from the street and on the corner. I left the door slightly ajar and paced back and forth as I waited. My mind was racing as I tried to finish piecing together what I knew and what I didn't. By the time the door swung open, I was in a complete fury and I didn't even slow down as I strode up to Mav, grabbed him by the shirt collar and slammed him against the back of the door, effectively closing it.

"Tell me what you know right fucking now!" I snarled.

"I swear, Mace, I don't have a clue what's going on," he said as he held his hands up in supplication.

Of all the men in the group that I'd worked with, Mav had been the easiest to read. And the fact that he wasn't fighting back told me he knew we'd fucked up.

I shoved away from him and began pacing again. "How the hell did we miss this?" I asked.

"The mark's-"

"Jonas!" I yelled. "His fucking name is Jonas!"

Mav nodded. "Jonas's name never showed up in either investigation but there was a reference to a witness to Carrie's murder. But because they were underage, there wasn't any specific information about them…name, age, gender."

"And Casey Prescott's case?"

"Jonas isn't mentioned at all. Nothing to indicate they even knew each other."

"They've known each other for eight years!" I snapped. "The only way he could have known both girls was if he was in Chicago. And if he went with Casey to Wisconsin after Carrie's death, he wouldn't have been in Boston when those sexual assaults were committed."

"Maybe he wasn't with her in Wisconsin."

I shook my head. "He said she saved his life. He had to have meant from Santero. They were just kids – I can't imagine they would have split up and gone their separate ways."

"What if he went home?" Mav offered. "His parents live in Boston. He could have reconnected with Casey after she got to New York."

I shook my head but didn't say anything because it was a slim possibility.

"I saw the emails Benny found. Jonas's parents would have run in the same social circles as Devlin Prescott. They could have met that way after Jonas got back from Chicago," Mav said softly.

"So Jonas runs away to Chicago as a kid, meets and befriends Casey after Carrie is killed, then goes back home to Boston and starts fucking the same guy who goes looking for Casey three years later to help him get custody of her niece? Jesus, Mav, you can't even call that a fucking coincidence! It's such a fucking stretch…"

"Then tell me how he ended up a suspect in not one but four sexual assaults in Boston? I checked, Mace – he wasn't in Paris when that nine-year-old boy disappeared! Customs has him arriving at Logan airport in Boston three days before the kid was snatched."

Fuck! An hour ago I'd been so sure this was all some monumental mistake but I didn't have the answers to Mav's questions. Tomorrow night - Jonas's party at the Prescotts. I'd get my fucking answers then, even if I had to drag them from Jonas himself. Because I was done with this.

"This conversation doesn't leave this room," I snapped at Mav as I stormed past him and out of the motel room.

Chapter 10

COLE

I QUESTIONED WHAT THE HELL I WAS THINKING FOR THE HUNDREDTH time as I rolled through the large iron security gate that opened after I announced my name in the small speaker box, and began the long drive up the perfectly manicured driveway that wound through a grove of trees before giving way to acres and acres of freshly cut lawn. I'd told myself to call Jonas and tell him I couldn't make it to his party but every time I picked up my phone, I couldn't bring myself to do it. Not because I thought Jonas would be overly disappointed if I wasn't there but because I wanted to see him again. Even though I'd spent the better part of the day with him only twenty-four hours ago, I needed to hear his voice again, see his infectious smile.

When I'd seen his sketchpad lying on the bathroom floor next to the tub the night of Carrie's funeral, I'd been strangely glad to have the excuse to see Jonas again, even though I'd spent the rest of the day after he'd patched me up trying to sort through the strange feelings both he and Mace brought out in me. An unexpected mix of excitement and peace went through me whenever I was around them and I couldn't make sense of either of those things. I'd spent all night lying in bed repeating my mantra that it was just the stress, but as random images of Mace and Jonas filtered through my head, I'd found myself reaching for my cock before I even realized what I was doing. Even as I'd stroked myself, I'd tried to call up some of the faces of the women I'd been with in recent years, but I always came back to Mace's fingers gripping my arms, his eyes on my mouth and the feel of Jonas's body flush with mine. And just as Jonas's mouth had closed over mine while Mace's hands traveled down the length of my body, I'd come in a rush of pleasure so intense that I was whispering both their names as they murmured praise in my ear, before turning their attentions to each other.

While I couldn't understand my sudden attraction to these men – and I knew after that mind blowing orgasm that that's what it was – it didn't freak me out as much as it probably should have. Maybe because it was coming at a time in my life when everything was already so fucked up that in the scheme of things, my sudden expansion in sexual preferences didn't seem consequential. So much in my life no longer seemed as important as it had once been.

My childhood had been decidedly uneventful and entirely stereotypical. I was the typical Army brat though, in my case, it had been the Navy that controlled nearly every aspect of my family's lives since my father had been a Naval Intelligence Officer. While my sister had struggled under my father's disciplined, orderly rule, I'd thrived on it. I couldn't even remember a time when I hadn't wanted to be exactly like my father and I'd breathed in his praise like oxygen. It hadn't hurt that I naturally excelled at everything I did, but having the highest GPA in my graduating class and being scouted for college football teams had never once deterred me from my goal to follow in my father's footsteps. Carrie had often ribbed me for being a kiss ass but it hadn't only been about pleasing my father. I'd loved the challenge of pushing myself both physically and mentally so trying out for the SEALs had been a foregone conclusion because I never did anything in half measure. Failure wasn't an option for me and defeat wasn't even in my vocabulary. But while I was an unstoppable force in the field, I wasn't capable of dealing with the chain of events that unfolded after the night my sister took off.

One event that left me powerless and helpless for the first time in my life.

The only thing that had kept me functioning was my team and our missions, because when I had those things, I turned off the endless loop that ran through my head of the terrible things that might have happened to my sister. My men often called me the Ice Man because I never reacted to even the evilest of atrocities we bore witness to. None of them knew that I was dying inside as I watched my family fracture and slowly implode. Every time I went home, I lost more of my mother as she sought the quiet of her darkened room. My father spent his days and nights trolling websites that described unidentified bodies found all over the country. On more than one occasion, he would show me pictures of cast models that artists created to try and show what a deceased victim might have looked like at the time of their death.

As the years passed, holidays ceased to exist, birthdays were barely remembered and Carrie's room was turned into a shrine. And then my mother gave up. That wasn't what the autopsy said, of course. But that's what it was. There'd been no solace that she'd gone in her sleep, because even what some coined a "peaceful" death didn't make up for the years of torment she'd suffered at not knowing what had happened to her youngest child. After that, my father stopped looking for Carrie. Maybe because he'd failed to bring her home to her mother, maybe because he'd done what I'd done and started envisioning Carrie living a happy, successful life somewhere else. Whatever the case was, he found his solace at the bottom of a bottle. And I did what I did best – I became the man my father had always wanted me to be. Because I was certain there'd be a day when he'd come out of his drunken fog and he'd need to know that he hadn't lost everything.

But that day hadn't come. What had come was a call from my father's doctor, who also happened to be an old family friend, telling me my father would be dead in less than a year if he couldn't get his drinking under control. I'd spent the first few days after my discharge trying to get my father sober enough to talk to me about getting some help, but the man who'd told me to leave him the fuck alone wasn't my father. The news of Carrie's death had come the very next day.

As the Prescott house came into view, I tried to push thoughts of my father to the back of my mind. I'd asked Mrs. Pellano to check in on him and I had plans to meet with his doctor tomorrow to see what my options were for forcing my father to seek help. My guess was they'd be limited and nothing that would be a long term solution. And from the words my father had spat at me when I'd first broached the subject, he wasn't interested in anything long term.

I pulled my car to a stop in the turnabout part of the driveway as I took in the sight of the massive Tudor style house that was just yards from the water. I didn't know much about Jonas's friends other than the little bit he'd shared with me about his and Casey's life after they'd escaped Mateo. I suspected he'd glossed over the hardships they'd faced as two teenagers trying to carve out a life for themselves, but I hadn't pressed him for anymore because I hadn't wanted the smile that had been glued to his face all day to disappear. I'd had more fun than I'd had in a really long time and most of that had come from watching Jonas interact with the kids at the various schools we'd stopped at. Although his intent had just been to drop off art supplies, he'd gotten roped into an impromptu art class on more than one occasion after the kids got done unpacking their new supplies. He'd been in his element and I'd been envious.

As I got out of my car, I scanned the grounds and saw Jonas's car parked near the multi-car garage. A man I didn't recognize was checking something on Jonas's car.

"Hi," I said as I approached him. He was a good looking guy in his late thirties and was dressed in a pair of jeans and a white button down shirt.

"Hi," he said back as he stood and reached out his hand but then withdrew it when he noticed how greasy it was. "You're either Cole or Mace."

"Cole," I said.

"Devlin Prescott. Good to meet you."

"Is Jonas still having car trouble?" I asked as I motioned to the car.

"No. He picked up a nail in his tire so I decided I'd change it for him just to be on the safe side."

I nodded and watched as he began tightening the lug nuts.

"Daddy?"

"Over here, Ryan," Devlin called.

A young boy in his early teens at best appeared and gave me a quick wave as he circled around me. "Mom says the pilot needs to talk to you about tomorrow."

"Uh, yeah," Devlin murmured as he glanced at the tire and then his son.

"Go, I'll finish up," I offered.

Devlin hesitated and then said, "You sure?"

"Yeah, absolutely."

"Thanks," Devlin said as he handed me the tire iron. I watched him follow his son into the house and then turned my attention to the car. I began tightening one of the lug nuts but as I moved to the next one, I lost my grip on the tire iron and it shifted upwards and hit the inside of the top of the wheel well. Before I could even check for damage, I heard a clicking sound and looked down to see a round, black object fall to the ground beside the tire. I picked it up and turned it over in my hand and then froze when I realized what it was.

I'd seen more than my share of tracking devices but I couldn't even begin to fathom what the hell it was doing on Jonas's car. His car was an older model that didn't come with GPS but it wouldn't make sense for a civilian to use this type of device as a stand in for a LoJack system.

"Cole?"

Jonas's voice had me tucking the tracker into my jacket pocket. It was clear that someone was keeping tabs on Jonas but I didn't want to freak him out until I knew more. I was already making a plan in my head when he appeared.

"Hey, what are you doing?" Jonas asked.

"I offered to finish putting on your tire so Devlin could take a call," I responded as I tightened the last lug nut.

"I told Devlin not to worry about it," Jonas said as he glanced at the tire. Then his eyes met mine and he said, "Thank you." His smile did something to my insides and I had the insane urge to touch him.

"It's no problem," I said as I brushed past him, ignoring the way my body responded when my chest came into contact with his arm. I put the tire iron in the back of the car and closed it.

"Thanks for coming," Jonas said as we began walking towards the house. "I know Casey didn't really give you a choice."

I was saved from having to answer by the sound of an engine coming up the driveway and I automatically stiffened as Mace's van pulled up and parked next to my car. The man had been uncharacteristically quiet yesterday during Casey's visit to the gallery, but today he looked stiff and unyielding. He reminded me of a soldier going into battle. His grim features barely shifted at Jonas's greeting and I felt the urge to kick his ass when I saw Jonas shrink back.

The house was surprisingly chaotic considering there were only a few people in attendance. Jonas made the introductions and besides Casey, Devlin and their two kids, there were several dogs and cats running around including a huge Mastiff that nearly knocked me to my knees when it came to check me out. The atmosphere was friendly and relaxed and not at all what I would have expected for such a well-off family. And watching the way they treated Jonas, I could tell he was definitely a part of the family. While most of Jonas's time was monopolized by twelve-year-old Ryan and eight-year-old Isabel, Devlin and Casey spent much of their time interacting with me and Mace. Mace managed to hold up his end of the conversation but I didn't miss how his eyes kept shifting back to Jonas. I knew Mace had an interest in Jonas beyond their professional relationship, but I couldn't tell if he'd acted on it.

As much as I enjoyed watching the happy-go-lucky Jonas who blossomed in the presence of his family, I started feeling the pang of my own loss as the evening went on, and I ended up excusing myself shortly after dinner on the pretense of checking my messages. I found my way to the back of the house and went to stand out on the massive deck that stretched the length of most of the back of the house. The salty ocean air felt good against my skin and I started walking towards the beach to explore a bit when I heard a horse whinny. I glanced to my right and saw a small barn with several large paddocks around it. A gray horse stood in the paddock closest to the barn. I could tell there were two other animals in the enclosure but I wasn't sure what they were so I began walking that direction. It wasn't until I reached the fence that I realized they were donkeys. Both came up to greet me at the fence but the horse stayed where it was, its dark eyes fixed on me.

"That's Jack."

I turned to see Jonas walking towards me and I felt a ripple of desire go through me. Jonas's lean body nearly touched mine as he stood next to me and draped his arms over the fence. "And this is Judy and Dot," he added as he began petting the donkeys. "You guys hungry?" he asked the docile animals as they began sniffing his hands expectantly. "What do you say, big guy?" he said to Jack. "Dinnertime?"

I followed Jonas into the barn and watched as he went to a bin at the end of the aisle and began scooping grain from it. "You mind opening the doors?" Jonas asked as he motioned to the doors at the back of each stall that presumably led out into the paddock that the horse and donkeys were in. I did as he asked and then watched as he finished feeding the donkeys which had each entered a stall. Jack was the only one that remained in the paddock even though I'd opened his door. I leaned against the outer stall door and watched Jonas as he stood by the inner door and began talking softly to Jack. It took a couple of minutes but the horse finally entered the stall. But instead of eating, it stood tentatively before Jonas for several long seconds before it finally stepped forward and pressed its head against his chest. I didn't say anything as I watched Jonas's fingers ghost over the horse's face. He soothed the animal for several minutes before leading it to the bucket where the grain was waiting. I was surprised to see him wiping at his eyes when he exited the stall and closed the door.

"Sorry," he said with a little laugh. "I still haven't gotten used to it."

"What?" I asked gently. I hadn't even realized I'd moved closer to him until I felt his body bump mine as he turned to latch the door.

"He never used to let me touch him," Jonas said, motioning to the horse. "Casey was the only one who could handle him and even that took months of her gaining his trust after he arrived at the shelter."

"Shelter?"

"Um, yeah. After we left Chicago, Casey and I ended up working at this animal shelter in a small town in northern Wisconsin. The old lady who ran it let us live there for free in exchange for helping her out with the stuff she couldn't do anymore. She left it to us when she died...well, Casey technically, since I was underage."

Jonas studied the horse for a moment. "She never used to let me touch her either," he suddenly whispered.

"Casey?" I guessed.

Jonas nodded and then looked at me, his eyes glistening. "After everything that happened, I never really believed I'd get here, you know? You stop hoping after a while because it's easier that way."

"What is?"

But Jonas just shook his head. "I'm sorry she didn't get this, Cole."

The words hurt, but it hurt more to see Jonas in so much pain. I wanted...no, needed to take that from him, once and for all, but I didn't know how. I lifted my hand to palm his cheek and said, "You knew her, Jonas. Would she have wanted you to keep blaming yourself?"

Jonas shook his head but when silent tears began slipping down his face, I shifted my hand to the back of his neck and drew him forward until his face was pressed against my neck. I felt the moisture seep into my shirt collar, and before I could stop myself, I shifted my head enough so that I could skim my lips over the sensitive skin just behind his ear. "She's at peace, Jonas. You deserve to be too."

I felt Jonas nod against me and he stayed there for several seconds as I let my fingers massage the back of his neck where I still held him. My other hand had gone to his waist and automatically tightened when Jonas tried to pull away from me. I felt the instant he became aware of the intimate way I was holding him, because his body stiffened and his breathing ticked up just the slightest bit. He lifted his head so that he could look me in the eye and I saw the confusion there as he tried to get his bearings. I wasn't sure if I was afraid he'd pull away before I got my chance to finally taste him or if I would be the one who would end up chickening out, so I added just enough pressure to the hold I had on the back of his neck to urge him forward the few inches it would take for our lips to meet.

"Jonas!"

The sound of Ryan's voice from somewhere outside shattered the stillness between us and Jonas pulled back enough that I was forced to release him. But then I heard him gasp and saw his eyes widen as he spied something over my shoulder and I knew without a doubt that we weren't alone. And I knew without looking that it wasn't Ryan who'd put that look of horror on Jonas's face.

I turned just as I heard footsteps come running into the barn but my eyes bypassed Ryan and settled on Mace who was leaning against the barn doorway.

"Jonas, Izzy's trying to open your presents!"

"Coming," I heard Jonas say, his voice uneven as he shoved past me. He hung his head as he hurried past Mace. I followed more slowly and stopped once I was on the opposite side of the barn door.

"Cock-blocked by a twelve-year-old," Mace drawled.

His voice was disinterested and amused but his expression said something else. I studied him for a long time before I said, "I can't figure out if you're such a callous asshole that you actually like fucking with his head, or if you don't even realize that you're doing it."

The smug smile faded and then he was moving towards me. I was already leaning back against the side of the entryway to the barn so there was nowhere for me to go, but it wouldn't have mattered because I had no desire to move. Maybe I'd get the fight I'd been craving. Maybe I'd get something else I'd been craving even more.

Mace stopped when his body was only inches from mine and I could feel the heat wafting off of him. I'd always thought his eyes were black, but I could see now that they were a very dark shade of brown. His lips were wide and full and slightly parted but my eyes drifted to his neck and I wondered if it would feel the same as Jonas's…if his heat would burn my skin if I touched him there.

"He's your first, right, Frogman?" Mace said softly but his voice was laced with steel.

"First what?"

"Your first time wondering if dick might taste just as sweet as pussy."

I didn't bother responding to the crude words because I knew he was saying them just to goad me into something…anything.

"Do you even know what he was, Mace? What he was forced to do to survive?"

Mace stilled at that and I saw a flicker of indecision go through him.

"That's what I thought," I muttered as I moved away from Mace and made my way back up to the house. I glanced over my shoulder and saw that Mace hadn't moved from the position I'd left him in.

Chapter 11

JONAS

As far as birthday celebrations went, it hadn't been one of the better ones. I'd known that having Mace and Cole in the same room for extended periods of time wouldn't go over well, since they seemed to naturally rub each other the wrong way, but in the end it hadn't been either of them that ruined the evening for me. Nope, that was all on me. Because I'd read into something that wasn't there. I'd twisted Cole's offer of comfort into something it wasn't and not only had I humiliated myself in front of him, I'd given Mace quite a show too. My only consolation was that I wouldn't have to be around either man for much longer…in fact, I doubted I'd see Cole again anytime soon. As for Mace, I could tell just by looking at my nearly done studio that he'd be out of my life for good within a day, maybe two.

As I let my gaze take in the clean walls and newly installed floor, I let my back slide down the wall behind me and marveled that a week from now, I'd be able to start welcoming kids into the studio.

I'd gotten home from the party a few hours ago, but as darkness had started to fall, I'd found myself too restless and agitated to paint, so I'd spent the last couple of hours unpacking and organizing the supplies that had arrived earlier in the day. I was excited at the prospect of watching kids who'd never held a paintbrush before get to experience the freedom that came with it. And I was looking forward to finally have some normalcy back in my life. Being around Mace and Cole had brought back a mess of feelings I'd thought I'd buried long ago.

As I studied the plain white walls in the studio, I began to contemplate the idea of painting murals on them but my thoughts were interrupted when I heard the gallery door unlock. I couldn't see who it was from my position but I could guess, because the only other people who had keys were Mace and Casey, and I knew Casey would be knee deep in preparations for their flight in the morning. So knots of tension started to form as I got to my feet and walked into the gallery.

Mace paused when he saw me, but he didn't speak and I noticed the same agitation he'd had when he'd muttered his goodbyes just before leaving Casey and Devlin's house. I'd long ago lost my fear of Mace but there was something in the way that he was looking at me that was off, and I couldn't make my feet move forward towards him. But I didn't have to because he came to me. I didn't even realize I'd backed away from him until my back hit the brick wall behind me. I held my breath as Mace reached out to cup my face with his hand. I thought maybe he was going to kiss me, but he just held me that way, his dark eyes latched to mine.

"I fucked up, Jonas," he whispered. "I need you to believe that I didn't know."

"Know what?" I managed to ask in spite of the ball of anxiety that was bouncing around in my gut.

"Tell me about Cole's sister."

"What?" I asked, surprised by the change in topic.

"How did you know her?"

"I met her in Chicago…"

"How old were you?"

"Fourteen," I answered, still not sure what he wanted from me. His body was brushing mine and his hand was still wrapped around my cheek, but his thumb had started brushing back and forth over my skin.

94

"Why were you in Chicago?"

"I…I didn't know where to go after my parents kicked me out. I ended up at the bus station and I saw this poster for Chicago and I had just enough money for a bus ticket there. I kept thinking they'd have a lot of art galleries in Chicago…" I said numbly as I was transported back to that moment that I'd stood surrounded by people going about their daily lives, as I was trying to figure out what had just happened to mine.

"What happened when you got there?"

I automatically shook my head and tried to pull away from him. But then he brushed his lips over mine and I stilled. It was over as quickly as it started but the aftermath was brutal. My heart began pounding so hard in my chest that it actually hurt.

"Please tell me, Jonas."

"I met a man who told me he could help me out. He said he knew some people who would give me a job. He seemed really nice." I closed my eyes to try to hold back the tears that threatened to fall. "I was so fucking stupid," I whispered.

This time Mace's lips skimmed the cheek he wasn't holding, and then his lips settled against my ear, "It wasn't your fault, Jonas. Do you understand me?"

I'm not sure if I nodded or not.

"Was it Mateo Santero?"

I wondered how he knew the name and could only assume Cole had told him. I nodded. "He let me stay at his place, got me some new clothes, fed me…when it came time for me to meet the people who could help me find work, he took me to this motel."

My throat seized up and I felt the tears I'd been desperately trying to hold back slide down my cheeks.

"Is he the one who hurt you?" Mace asked.

I shook my head. "Mateo only broke in the girls. It was his brother, Eduardo."

"Fuck, Jonas, I'm so sorry," Mace said brokenly as his forehead pressed against mine. He just kept repeating that he was sorry even as his mouth brushed mine over and over again. I wanted to ask why he was sorry but I didn't want to risk losing the feeling of his lips ghosting over mine. But he never deepened his kisses or forced his tongue into my mouth like so many men in my past always had. And then he was pulling back from me. I managed to grab the back of his neck to prevent his backward motion.

"Please, Mace," I whispered, hating how urgent my voice sounded. But I needed his touch because even now, I could feel the pain unfurling in my stomach and I knew the feeling of his lips on mine would keep that at bay.

He must have sensed my need because his next kiss was longer, heavier, sweeter. I didn't know how long that kiss or the ones that followed went on for, but he never once asked for more. At some point, I'd wrapped my arms around his neck and he'd pulled me flush against his body. The tight hold he had on me should have had me trying to escape but I just wanted more. More warmth, more safety, more him. On the next pass of his lips over mine, I opened my mouth enough to let my tongue slide over his lower lip. Mace tensed against me but instead of shoving into my mouth, he opened his. I went willingly and moaned when his tongue greeted mine. I took my time exploring his mouth but then it wasn't enough anymore and he and I both knew it and when he finally did take my mouth, I felt a rush of air escape me. My back hit the wall again as Mace plundered my mouth and then his hands were all over me, palming my flesh, kneading it, setting it ablaze with sensation.

I'd never really liked kissing but it wasn't until that moment that I realized that the men who'd smashed their mouths down on my mine and thrust their tongues between my unwilling lips weren't kissing me. Not even close. They'd bought and paid for me so they'd taken what they felt was their due. Everything Mace was taking from me, he was giving back a thousand times over, because I'd never felt more cherished in my entire life. From one fucking kiss.

I'd lost all track of time and our surroundings as Mace drove me higher and higher with each burning kiss but when he froze in my arms, I instantly stopped. His hands, which had been gripping my hips, fell away and his eyes opened and then shifted to the right.

I was about to ask what was wrong when I saw what was happening for myself as Mace turned his head. Even in my inexperience, I knew that what I saw pressed against the back of Mace's head was the barrel of a rifle. I swallowed hard as Mace took a few steps back from me but when I saw Cole standing directly behind him, rifle in hand, I literally couldn't move. I couldn't even process what was going on.

For all I knew, I could have been standing there for a minute or a hundred before I finally managed to say, "Cole?"

While I'd been frozen with fear, Mace had managed to turn around, his arms held out. His body wasn't completely blocking mine so I could see Cole and the way he kept his eyes on Mace. There was a long black bag on the floor at his feet and I could only assume it was for the rifle he was holding.

"Cole, what are you doing?" I asked as fear for Mace and myself threatened to consume me.

Cole's eyes never wavered from Mace as he said, "You want to tell him or should I?"

Chapter 12

MACE

I IGNORED COLE'S QUESTION AND ASKED ONE OF MY OWN. "HOW?"

"Frogman," Cole muttered. "You've called me that twice now. Problem is, I never told you I was a SEAL. I never told Jonas either. He only knows I was in the Navy."

I watched as Cole expertly kept my rifle trained on me as he tossed something to the floor at my feet just beyond my rifle bag. I recognized the tracker I'd put on Jonas's car.

"I found this on Jonas's car today."

"What is that?" Jonas asked.

"It's a tracking device," Cole answered.

I heard Jonas suck in a breath behind me.

Cole ignored Jonas and continued. "I followed you after the party."

Which meant he'd seen me drive the van to the garage and then walk to the apartment building across from Jonas's gallery. And since he was holding my rifle, he'd clearly been waiting for me to leave so he could search it. How the fuck had I not even noticed him?

Because I was too consumed with the devastating realization that I'd fucked every part of this job up. It was what had driven me across the street to confront Jonas. My plan had been to question Jonas earlier tonight when I'd followed him down to the barn, but I'd arrived just in time to see Cole and Jonas in an intimate embrace. I'd held my breath as I watched them together and I was actually disappointed they'd been interrupted.

Once it was just me and Cole in the barn, I'd felt an insane need to force Cole into admitting he wanted Jonas, but he'd caught me off guard with his accusation that I was fucking with Jonas's head. And then those devastating words that had been both the answer I was looking for and a truth I couldn't fathom.

Do you even know what he was, Mace? What he was forced to do to survive?

With those words, everything fell into place for me. There was no affair between Jonas and Devlin Prescott, and Jonas hadn't been anywhere near Boston when the sexual assaults had started. Jonas was an innocent victim in a game where I'd been carefully chosen to be his executioner. And I'd been so blinded by my hatred of the monster that someone had worked very hard to make Jonas out to be, that I'd refused to heed what had been staring me in the face the whole time – that Jonas wasn't capable of hurting anyone.

I had no memory of the trip back to the apartment after the party and once I was there, I'd leaned back against the front door and slid down it until my ass hit the grimy carpet. I'd sat there for hours as Cole's words went through me again and again. I already had an idea of what Cole meant but I'd needed to hear the words from Jonas's lips. I'd needed to know exactly what he'd suffered because I didn't deserve to hide from the truth anymore.

I hadn't meant to kiss Jonas but I didn't regret it for a second because as I now stared at Cole, I knew I was about to lose any trust Jonas might have had in me…and I fucking deserved it.

"Cole, what's happening?" Jonas whispered, the confusion in his voice clear. It was the only time I saw Cole flinch.

"Jonas, I need you to check him for weapons," Cole said firmly. "Then I'll explain everything."

Since my eyes were on Cole, I had no idea if Jonas responded in any way.

"Check his back first," Cole said and I saw the warning in his eyes...the one aimed directly at me. A moment later I felt Jonas's hands lifting my jacket. A gasp escaped his lips before he carefully pulled my Ruger from my waistband. He gave me a wide berth as he walked the gun over to Cole, who tucked it into his waistband, and I felt a stab of loss that Jonas already instinctively knew to trust Cole instead of me.

"Now his ankle," Cole said. To me, "You fucking move..."

The threat was unnecessary since I was no longer a danger to Jonas in any kind of way but Cole wouldn't have known that.

Jonas hesitated before kneeling in front of me. "My right leg," I said gently and I saw Jonas's eyes flash up to meet mine briefly before he started working my pants up to reveal my ankle holster. Once he had the gun, he stepped back to stand next to Cole and I felt a wave of pain wrench through me when I saw the betrayal in his gaze. Cole took the gun from him and dropped it into the open bag at his feet. I could see my laptop sticking out of the bag as well as the manila folder where I'd kept all of the paperwork I had on Jonas.

"Talk," Cole barked even as he kept the rifle trained on me. Jonas was standing several feet from Cole and slightly in front of him so I saw every emotion go through him as he started to realize what was going on.

I struggled to figured out where to even begin but I realized that there was nothing I could say to soften the blow.

"Jonas-"

Before I could say anything else, I saw a red spot bouncing around on Jonas's chest. I was already moving when Cole also noticed the laser sight from a gun. I screamed Jonas's name as Cole yelled at him to get down. Pain seared across my upper left arm as I slammed into Jonas and knocked him to the ground. Fear tore through me as Jonas lay unmoving beneath me but I couldn't check on him because Cole was kneeling above us and firing at someone who was using one of the gallery walls near the front door for cover.

"Jonas," I shouted as I shifted off of him enough to roll him over and felt a rush of relief when I saw him open his eyes. But when I saw the blood staining his shirt, I began searching for the wound.

"I'm okay," Jonas managed to say, his voice barely audible above the bullets flying above us.

"Mace!" Cole shouted and then he was tossing the rifle to me. I covered him while he pulled my Ruger from the waistband of his pants, and reached for Jonas and hauled him to his feet. They ran towards the studio as I held back to engage the shooter but when I heard shots coming from the back of the building, I turned and ran towards them, grabbing the rifle bag as I went.

I found Cole and Jonas taking cover behind the wooden table that Cole had turned over to shield them, and saw there was at least one more shooter firing at them from the back hallway that led to the alley behind the building.

"Roof!" I shouted to Cole as I realized we were boxed in. He nodded and jerked to his feet and began firing as I covered the shooter in the gallery.

"Jonas, go!" Cole yelled. Jonas hesitated but then he was moving as Cole and I held the shooters back. Cole followed quickly and then I threw myself over the table and ran up the stairs after them. Cole had overtaken Jonas on the stairs and led the way up to the roof. Bullets began flying again as both shooters followed us up the stairwell and I knew there would be a point where both Cole and I would be out of ammo.

I followed Cole and Jonas out onto the roof and saw Cole running towards the edge. I held my breath as I watched him jump to the neighboring roof. As soon as his feet hit the ground, he turned and began firing in my direction but I knew he wasn't aiming at me, he was covering me.

Jonas had slowed when he saw Cole leap to the next building so I grabbed his arm to get him moving again and yelled, "Don't think about it! Just do it!"

I couldn't gauge the exact distance between the two buildings but I knew it had to be at least several feet. Add in the height factor and I knew Jonas had to be terrified but he didn't slow down. Just like with Cole, I felt a surge of fear go through me as Jonas jumped.

My feet left the edge of the roof just as Jonas was landing on the other side. He hit the ground hard but scrambled to his feet.

"Fire escape!" I shouted and turned to help Cole hold the shooters off until Jonas reached the fire escape.

"I'm out!" Cole yelled as he fired his last bullet.

I threw the rifle bag at him and said, "Go!"

Once I was sure Cole had made it to the fire escape, I followed so that I could cover them if there was anyone waiting for them in the alley below. My revolver was somewhere at the bottom of the rifle bag but I knew Cole wouldn't have time to search it out.

A glance over my shoulder showed the shooters hadn't followed us so I hurried down the fire escape. We'd lucked out because my car was parked at the end of the alley. I tossed Cole the rifle as I pulled the keys from my pocket. I could already hear sirens in the distance so I was hopeful that the shooters had given up and were making their escape.

Once we were inside the car, I tore out into the street as Cole began watching the cars behind us. Traffic was heavy enough that the likelihood that we'd be followed and shot at while on a busy Brooklyn street were slim, and I eased my foot off the gas so I wouldn't draw any unnecessary attention to us. I glanced at Cole who seemed to be relaxing as well as the immediate danger subsided. When I looked in the rearview mirror to check on Jonas, I saw him sitting frozen in the backseat, his eyes staring at nothing in particular.

"Jonas, are you hurt?" I asked.

Jonas didn't respond so Cole leaned between the seats and cupped Jonas's chin in his hand.

"Jonas," he said gently.

The tone seemed to snap Jonas out of it and his eyes settled on Cole as if seeing him for the first time. "Are you hurt?" Cole asked.

Jonas shook his head.

"There's blood," Cole pointed out as his fingers skimmed a large stain on Jonas's shirt.

"It's…It's not mine," Jonas managed to say. I knew he was in shock but was helpless to do anything about it.

"Were you hit?" Cole asked me.

"Grazed," I said with a nod. The burning pain in my arm continued to build as I felt blood trickling down my arm. "They could be tracking us," I murmured. "I've got extra ammo in the trunk," I added.

I felt Cole's eyes on me and then saw him take his phone out of his pocket and turn it off. "Jonas, I need your phone," he said softly as he turned his attention to Jonas. Jonas still seemed out of it but he complied and handed his phone to Cole without question. Because he trusted him...

"Now yours," I heard Cole say.

I had no doubt that he wouldn't have been okay with me keeping the phone after I turned it off, so I handed it over without argument. After all, I had no plans to call anyone since my trust in my own team had been shot to hell the moment I'd realized I'd been set up to take out an innocent man.

"We need to check the car," I said. Cole didn't respond but he didn't argue when I pulled over at a gas station. I got out and began going over the car looking for any tracking devices. Cole worked the other side and we met up at the front of the car.

"We need some supplies," I said as I began checking the engine. But when Cole didn't move, I glanced at him.

"I'm not leaving you here with him," he said coldly.

I ground my teeth together and then shoved past him and headed into the small store and began grabbing some food and drinks. I kept my eyes on Cole as he checked the car and by the time I got back outside, he was closing the hood.

"We need some place to lay low," I said as I handed him the bags.

"I know a place," Cole said and then he shoved the bags back at me and held out his hand expectantly. I forced back the urge to tell him to fuck off and handed him the car keys.

Jonas didn't say a word as we climbed back in the car and I was seriously starting to worry that the shock was affecting him worse than I'd thought. "Drink this," I urged as I handed him a can of soda. He didn't look at me, didn't even acknowledge that I was speaking to him.

I gave up and remained silent as Cole drove us out of the city and headed north towards the Catskills. It took more than three hours to reach the destination he had in mind and by the time he pulled onto a narrow dirt road that led up to a darkened farmhouse, my arm felt like it was on fire. Motion activated lights on the house went off, flooding the inky blackness with light.

"Whose place is this?"

"It belongs to a guy I served with. We used to come up here a lot between deployments to do some fishing."

"What if he comes up here?"

"He won't," was all Cole said as he got out of the car. As I got out, I saw Cole open the back door to gently pull Jonas from the seat. I went around the car and reached for Jonas in the hopes that I could get him to talk to me but Cole stepped between us and shoved me back against the car.

"Stay the fuck away from him!" he snapped. "The only reason I haven't put you down yet is because you owe us some fucking answers!"

"I don't owe you shit!" I snarled.

I wasn't surprised when Cole took a swing at me. The blow caught my jaw but I managed to stay upright and then I decked him. Cole hit the ground but his recovery was quick and he was on his feet and coming after me within seconds. His arms went around my middle as he tackled me and we landed in a heap on the wet ground.

Cole's fist felt like a battering ram against my sides but I reveled in the pain. I'd take Cole's punishing blows over Jonas's bitter withdrawal any day.

"You think you're innocent in all this?" I snapped as I shoved Cole away and staggered to my feet. I slammed my fist into his jaw and watched him stumble back. "At least before you came along he could fucking sleep! Did you even stop and think what you were doing to him when you asked him to dredge up that shit with your sister? Were you the one who had to sit by helplessly and listen to him screaming and crying out in his sleep night after night because you needed fucking answers?"

Rage mottled Cole's features and then he was on me like an animal. For every punch I gave, I got one back in equal measure. Neither of us held back as we turned our fear and frustration on each other. I had no idea how long the battle raged on for but it ended just as quickly as it had started when the sound of a gunshot pierced the silence. We instinctively jumped apart and searched for our mutual enemy but when I saw where the threat was coming from, I stilled.

Because it wasn't one of our unknown attackers that had tracked us down to finish what they started. No, the threat was aimed solely at me and it was Jonas who was looking down the barrel of the gun that was pointed directly at my chest.

Chapter 13

COLE

BLOOD TRICKLED OUT OF MY NOSE AND DRIFTED OVER MY LIPS AND into my mouth but I didn't dare move my arm to wipe it away. Even though the gun wasn't aimed at me, I could see Jonas was shaking violently and I was afraid that if I startled him, he'd inadvertently fire. As much as I hated Mace in that moment, I didn't want this.

"How long?" Jonas asked, his voice uneven. "How long have you been watching me?"

Mace didn't seem as concerned about not moving because he did use his arm to wipe at the blood streaking down his face where my fist had torn into the flesh near his eye.

"Five weeks," Mace said quietly.

I didn't think it possible but Jonas paled even more. "Did you listen to me?" he whispered in disbelief.

Mace nodded. "I planted a listening device in your apartment the first day we met."

Anger surged through me at that but Jonas just looked completely devastated. I glanced at Mace and saw that he wasn't unaffected either.

"Why?" Jonas asked hoarsely. His pain radiated off of him and I actually began moving but Mace beat me to it. I held my breath as I watched Mace stride right up to Jonas until the gun was pressed against his chest.

"Jonas," he said softly. "Let's go inside and I'll tell you everything-"

"No! Now! Tell me now!" Jonas yelled.

Mace swallowed hard and then closed his eyes. "I was supposed to kill you."

Even though I'd already suspected why Mace had been watching Jonas, it still tore me up to hear it confirmed. I couldn't even imagine what Jonas was suffering.

Jonas didn't say anything but he didn't have to because it was written all over his face. Disbelief, terror, betrayal.

"Why?" Jonas managed to whisper.

Mace stepped back. "There's...there are some papers in my bag...they'll explain everything."

But when Mace made a move towards the car to get them, Jonas yelled, "No! You tell me! I want to hear you say it."

I hadn't had a chance to look at the contents of the manila envelope in great detail after I'd broken into the apartment Mace was using to watch Jonas but I could tell by the look of horror on Mace's face that whatever was in there was pretty bad. I could also tell that Mace didn't want to have to speak the words aloud.

"I work for a group that delivers justice when the law can't," Mace began. "Your...your name came up in one of our investigations."

"What investigation?" Jonas asked when Mace didn't continue on his own.

Mace lifted his eyes so he could watch Jonas when he said, "We had information that you were a suspect in the sexual assaults of three little boys and the disappearance of a fourth."

Jonas didn't seem to register what Mace was saying at first but once he did, his face contorted in agony and his free arm wrapped around his stomach as if trying to stem some wound.

"You think...you think I raped..."

Jonas couldn't even finish the statement before he leaned over and vomited.

"Jonas-" Mace cried brokenly as he stepped forward to try and support Jonas.

"Don't you fucking touch me!" Jonas screamed, waving the gun in his hand. "Don't you ever touch me again!"

More retching followed and then Jonas sank to his knees and wiped his mouth with his sleeve. "I didn't...I wouldn't-"

"I know, Jonas," Mace said. "I know you'd never hurt anyone. I knew it the first time I met you, but I couldn't get past the proof."

Tears were coursing down Jonas's face and I knew he was done. I was walking towards him when he asked, "Is there anything else?"

I glanced at Mace and then came to a halt when I saw his face fall. Fuck, how the hell could there be more?

Jonas lifted his eyes to meet Mace's. His face was streaked with grime and tears and I wanted to beg Mace not to say anything else.

"I was given emails between you and Devlin. They suggested... they were intimate. They suggested you and he had been in a relationship from the time you were a teenager and that it was still going on."

Soft, guttural cries tore from Jonas as he dropped the gun to the ground. He didn't fight me when I put my arm around him and pulled him to his feet. His body felt cold against mine despite the warm evening and violent tremors tore through his body. I managed to get him up the porch stairs and held him against me as I searched out the spare house key that was stashed under a decorative planter.

Once we were inside, I flipped on the lights. Jonas shoved away from me and wiped at his face. The move hurt but I didn't try to touch him again.

"The bedrooms are upstairs," I said gently. "You can get cleaned up and rest," I suggested.

Jonas didn't respond but he did step around me, giving me a wide berth as if he was afraid to have any kind of contact with me, and went up the stairs. I turned back to the door to see if Mace was behind me but saw that he hadn't moved at all. The flood lights turned off, burying Mace in a cloud of darkness. The fact that they didn't come on again right away was telling. I had no doubt that Mace was suffering because I'd seen it in his eyes when he watched me help Jonas to his feet. I still didn't have the answers I needed but I had the most important one…the one that had me leaving the front door open. Mace wasn't a danger to Jonas anymore…my guess was that he hadn't been for a long time.

⁕

I SPENT THE NEXT HALF AN HOUR GOING THROUGH THE HOUSE AND stripping off the dust covers on all the furniture and checking the kitchen for supplies. There was nothing in the fridge but the freezer was stocked with food and the pantry wasn't completely bare so I knew we'd be okay for at least a few days. Geoff, my friend who had inherited the house after his parents died in a car accident, had used this place as an escape from the real world in between deployments. It was isolated so I knew that we wouldn't be getting any visitors investigating the gunshot Jonas had discharged earlier. The property was more wooded than I would have liked, but my hope was that there was no way for anyone to link me to the property and we wouldn't be followed. And since Geoff hadn't had any family left, I knew there wouldn't be anyone coming to check on the house. Even with Geoff's death at the hands of a sniper in Afghanistan last month, I suspected it would take a while for whoever was handling his estate to get around to checking on the remote property.

I still hadn't heard Mace come inside so I closed the front door, but left it unlocked and went upstairs to check on Jonas. There were four bedrooms on the second floor and I checked each one. I'd expected to find Jonas asleep or at least resting in one of them but he wasn't. I finally heard running water in the bathroom attached to the bedroom that had belonged to Geoff as a child, but the door was locked and there was no light showing from underneath the door. Concern went through me as I knocked and called Jonas's name.

When there was no answer, I stepped back and gave the door one good kick, breaking it down. I flipped on the lights and slid the shower curtain back. My heart broke as I saw Jonas huddled on one side of the large tub, still fully dressed with water raining down on him.

"Jonas," I whispered as I reached down to push his wet hair off his face. He was ice cold and I realized he'd run out of hot water at some point and hadn't noticed or hadn't cared. Jonas didn't acknowledge me in any way, so I turned the water off and reached down and wrapped my arms around and lifted him to his feet. His clothes soaked through mine and I cringed at how bitterly cold it felt.

"Jonas, I need to get these clothes off, okay?" I said softly. He didn't answer me even when I gently cupped his face to force him to look at me. The emptiness in his gaze terrified me, so I focused on the task at hand. I wasn't sure if he would stay standing on his own so I sat him down on the closed toilet and knelt down to pull his shoes and socks off. His shirt went next and I grabbed a towel and ran it swiftly over his hair and upper body. He made no move to help me in my efforts so I pulled him to his feet and put my arm around him so I could get him to the bedroom. After I sat him down on the edge of the bed, I made quick work of his pants and underwear and then pulled him back into a standing position so I could push the comforter out of the way.

Once I had him settled beneath the covers, I didn't think too much about what I was doing when I stripped my own shirt off. My pants were damp but not soaked through like my shirt, so I left them on since I didn't want to frighten Jonas when he came around, only to find himself in bed with a naked man. I climbed in bed next to him and pulled him against me and got us both covered with the comforter. Jonas's skin felt like ice against mine and his shivering body had me tightening my arms around him. He still hadn't acknowledged my presence, so I didn't bother speaking to him. I just kept stroking my hand up and down his back as I tried to work some heat into his system. It took a good hour before I finally felt his body relax against mine and when I looked down, I saw his eyes had drifted shut.

I knew at that point that I should leave him, but I found

myself needing the comfort that his body draped over mine brought. I'd been on an adrenaline rush from the moment I'd broken into Mace's apartment and found his rifle, and the impending crash was hitting me hard. I actually didn't even realize I'd fallen asleep until I heard Jonas screaming next to me. At first when his fist slammed into my chest, I thought he was attacking me but then I realized he wasn't even awake. His whole body thrashed on the bed as he begged his unseen attacker to stop.

I'd managed to get a hold of the arm Jonas had hit me with but in his terror, I couldn't prevent him from kicking at me as his other fist struck me in the head. I heard the door to the room crash open and then light flooded the room. I looked over my shoulder to see Mace standing in the doorway and then he was moving. I was sure he was going to rip me off of Jonas thinking I was the one responsible for his screams, but instead he went around the bed to Jonas's side and gently grabbed his flailing arm.

"Jonas," he called out.

Jonas's eyes snapped open and he looked wildly around until he settled them first on Mace and then on me. Awareness returned to him and then he closed his eyes and began to cry. He tugged his arm free of Mace's hold, but instead of turning away from me, he rolled against my chest and wrapped his arms around me as sob after sob rattled through him. I laid back on the bed and held him as I whispered soothing words against his head and stroked his back. I spared Mace a glance who was watching us with such a pained expression that I wanted to reach out to him too. Mace took several steps back from the bed but instead of leaving, he turned the lights off and then sat down in a chair in the corner and watched us. I remembered his comment about having to watch Jonas do this night after night and some of my anger towards Mace receded a little. And was replaced with guilt.

What if what Mace had said was right? What if I had caused this by making Jonas relive Carrie's murder and subsequently his own past?

"Don't," I heard Mace say so softly I barely heard him. I looked over at him. "Don't put this on yourself," he said quietly. "This is on me. Just me."

I didn't know what to say to that but I knew he was wrong. Because we'd both done this. And come tomorrow, Mace and I were going to figure out how the hell to fix it.

Together.

Chapter 14

JONAS

WHEN I HEARD THE BEDROOM DOOR OPEN, I CLOSED MY EYES IN THE childish hope that my visitor would think I was asleep and leave me alone. I hadn't been – not in any of the endless hours since I'd woken up to find myself pressed against Cole's chest, my lips just a breath away from his nipple and my arm wrapped around his waist. The room had been dark, but I'd been able to tell by his even breathing that he was asleep and I'd carefully extricated myself from his hold so I could escape his touch. I still wasn't one hundred percent sure what Cole's role in all of this had been, but it hadn't mattered because in that moment, I couldn't stand his touch. My skin felt like something was trying to crawl out from beneath it and even the soft comforter had made me want to scream in agony. But I'd known pretty much right away that I was naked beneath the stifling blanket so I'd had no choice but to leave it on.

I'd rolled away from Cole but had felt my heart stop at the sight of Mace sitting in a chair in the corner of the room. Even without light, I'd known he was awake and watching me. I'd felt the bile creeping up the back of my throat as he'd watched me and I'd had no choice but to bury my face in the too soft pillow beneath my head in the hopes of quelling the nausea that rolled through me. A moment later the bedroom door had softly shut but it had taken me several moments to garner enough courage to open my eyes to see that Mace had indeed left.

I'd felt Cole leave the bed a couple of hours later as light started to filter through the curtains but I didn't move and I was glad when he didn't speak to me. I hadn't moved after that, not even when my body began to cramp from the position I'd pulled myself up into. My brain was still struggling to process the events of last night after Mace's bone-melting kiss, but I hadn't been able to give much thought to anything other than knowing what vile things Mace had thought me capable of doing. The idea that he'd believed I was like the monsters who'd preyed on me the moment I stepped off that bus in Chicago nine years ago was abhorrent to me, and all I really wanted to do was wake up from what had to be another one of my many nightmares.

"Jonas."

I flinched at the sound of Cole's voice but when he sat down on the bed behind me and settled his hand on my shoulder, I jerked away from him until there was no room on the bed for me to escape to.

"You need to eat something."

I forced myself to sit up, keeping my back to him. "I want my phone," I said.

Cole didn't answer me but I felt his weight shift off the bed. I closed my eyes when I sensed him come around to my side of the bed and sit in the chair Mace had been sitting in last night. I hated that part of me wanted him to try to touch me again.

"We can't risk turning it on. Someone could be tracking it," Cole said gently. "There's no land line here but we'll get some burner phones as soon as we can, okay?"

I nodded. "Is he still here?"

"Yes."

"I don't want him here." Even as I said the words, I knew that Cole wasn't the only one to hear them because I felt a chill go up my spine. I forced my eyes open and glanced over my shoulder to see Mace standing in the doorway, his shuttered eyes watching me.

He turned away before I did and I heard his footsteps on the stairs.

"Jonas," Cole said as he reached for my hand.

"Don't," I whispered as I pulled my hand from out of his reach. "I don't...I can't..."

I didn't look at Cole as I spoke but heard him settle back down in the chair. "We need to figure out what's going on," Cole said. "Like it or not, Mace is the only one who might have some answers."

I managed a nod. "Do you...do you believe the things he said about me?" I forced myself to ask.

The bed next to me shifted and I felt Cole's thigh brush against mine through the blanket. I tried to pull away but his hand snaked around to grab the back of my neck to hold me still.

"Look at me," Cole said, the soft order leaving no room for argument.

I opened my eyes even as I tried to hold back the pain that bloomed in my chest. "I don't believe one fucking word of it," Cole said angrily. "And neither does he...not anymore."

Not anymore.

I knew he'd meant the words to comfort but they didn't – they just reminded me of the lie I'd been living in from the moment Mace had walked into my gallery. I remembered the hatred in his eyes when he'd first looked at me and a shiver went through me.

"I saw it that first day," I whispered.

"Saw what?"

"He wanted to hurt me. I was afraid of him but then he helped me. Some wood fell in the studio and he stopped it from hitting me." I shook my head. "Why would he do that?"

Cole's fingers began massaging my neck and I had to admit, it felt good.

"Because he knew on some level that whatever that shit someone told him you did wasn't true. He was watching you long before he met you, Jonas. He probably had a lot of chances to hurt you but something held him back."

My whole body began to shake as the reality I hadn't even dealt with hit me. Mace was a murderer. He'd been hired to kill me which meant he'd likely done it before.

"I need a little more time, Cole," I managed to say.

Cole nodded, his hand on my neck tightening just a little bit. And then he did something I hadn't been expecting. He leaned forward and brushed his lips over mine. The contact was brief but it left me reeling. He released me the second his lips left mine and then stood.

"I left some breakfast on the nightstand," I heard Cole say as he moved towards the door. "Come down when you're ready."

I nodded but didn't look at him. As soon as I heard the door close, I lifted my fingers to my mouth which was still tingling. Cole kissing me was almost too much for me to handle. Almost. Because even though I couldn't process what it meant, the warmth that spread through me afterwards helped chase some of the coldness away and I managed to climb to my feet.

As I made my way to the bathroom, I saw a cup of coffee sitting on the nightstand next to a plate stacked high with pancakes. I ignored the food and drink and went to the bathroom. I noticed the busted door but couldn't remember how it had gotten that way. I didn't remember much after climbing in the shower and letting the hot water wash over me.

I managed to find a new toothbrush in the cabinet under the sink and scrubbed my teeth and then got dressed. My clothes had been sitting on the end of the bed and I could see that they'd been freshly laundered. I eyed the food again but couldn't stomach the idea of trying to force it past my lips. I took a couple sips of the coffee in the hopes that it would take away some of the exhaustion I was feeling. The coffee was sweeter than I'd expected and I wondered if Cole had made the assumption I liked it that way, or if Mace had had a hand in it since he knew I only ever ordered flavored lattes when I went to the coffee shop down the street.

The reminder of my daily coffee runs had me remembering the studio as bullets had started flying and tearing into the walls around us as we'd huddled on the ground. Only I hadn't huddled when the first bullet had torn through the space – Mace had used his body to push me out of the way and shield me. And at some point, he'd gotten shot in the process.

I shouldn't care. I didn't.

Frustration tore through me as my inner voice called me a liar, and it nagged me even as I left the room and walked down the stairs as images of the blood that had stained my shirt washed over me. Mace's blood.

I didn't hear anything once I reached the first floor but the layout of the house was pretty simple and I found the kitchen with little trouble. But as I walked through the entryway, I spied motion to my right and saw Mace sitting at a small table in the alcove that the owner of the house used as a dining area. Cole stood next to Mace and I felt a little sick as I realized what he was doing. Mace's flesh was torn open on his left bicep and Cole was in the process of stitching it closed. Mace didn't even make a sound as the needle pierced his skin repeatedly but when his eyes caught mine, he flinched and then dropped his gaze. I couldn't remember any time that Mace had actually looked afraid of me, not even last night when I'd held the gun on him, but that was exactly how he looked now. Like he wanted to be anywhere else.

Cole noticed me and then motioned to the chair at the opposite end of the table. I didn't want to be so close to Mace but I knew I didn't have a choice. The sooner we figured out what was going on, the sooner I could get away from both men. I'd already made a plan to call Devlin and Casey the first chance I got. As much as I liked being able to do things on my own like starting my studio, I had absolutely no qualms about relying on Devlin's power and connections to help get me out of whatever mess I'd been tossed into.

Cole kept stitching as he said to Mace, "Tell us, Mace. Everything."

It felt strange to not have Mace's eyes on me when he spoke since he'd always been so direct with how he looked at or spoke to me in the past.

"The group I work for…we monitor a lot of different channels to pick out potential marks."

I swallowed hard at the term but held my tongue.

"But we mostly use the Deep Web," he said.

"What is that?" I interjected.

"It's the internet beneath the internet so to speak," Cole said as he continued to drive the needle through Mace's skin before tying off the thread. "There's a lot of illegal shit there including black markets for everything from stolen credit cards to body parts to child pornography."

I found myself wanting to throw up again. Mace lived in a world where looking through that kind of shit was normal?

"You found my name there?" I said in horror.

"Our tech guy, Benny, has algorithms that look for certain crimes," Mace said quietly. "From there we look at police reports, trial transcripts, whatever we need to determine if we should step in. Crimes against kids are high on our list. We also look for people who are trying to hire hitmen to take out a spouse or a loved one and we step in and stop it."

"You kill them? The people you decide are guilty?"

I saw Mace flinch at that but then he stiffened. "We do what it takes get the innocent victims justice."

Let Justice be done.

The tattoo on Mace's chest made sense now but I wondered if I would ever be able to consider it beautiful again. And then I realized the direction of my thoughts. Did I even want to see it again?

"What did you find on me?" I managed to ask.

Mace motioned to a large manila envelope sitting in the middle of the table that I hadn't even noticed. I noticed that my fingers shook as I reached for it.

The first few pages I skimmed after I'd removed everything from the envelope contained basic information about me as well as my lease on the gallery. Next were several pictures of me but they weren't any I remembered someone taking. I finally realized they were surveillance pictures and most had been taken while I was doing inconsequential things like getting coffee or buying groceries. Except the last one.

The last one was a mug shot of me. I was holding up some kind of board that showed it was for the Boston Police Department and there was a date and a bunch of numbers beneath it. It was dated a year earlier.

"What is this?" I croaked. "I've never been arrested," I stammered. "The only time I was ever in Boston since my parents kicked me out was when Devlin's plane had to divert there because of weather."

"From Paris, you mean?" Mace asked.

I nodded and then realized the date of that flight was within a few days of the date on the board the picture version of me was holding.

"My finger..." I whispered as I looked at the mug shot more closely. "I'd flown in for Casey's birthday and I cut my finger while I was helping her in the barn. I had to get stitches," I said as I lifted my finger to show off the scar on the outside of my pointer finger. "There aren't any stitches in this picture," I said as I flipped the photo to show them.

"Someone doctored it," Mace muttered.

"What...what was the arrest for?" I asked even though the question sounded odd even to my own ears.

"The cops were looking for the man who kidnapped a nine-year-old boy whose body has never been found."

It was little consolation that Mace didn't refer to me as the one the cops were supposedly looking at. I flipped to the next page and then covered my mouth when I saw the images of four little boys looking back at me. They were all the kinds of pictures kids had taken at their schools. I felt like I was going to be sick as I skimmed the names written along the bottom of each picture. The page right after the pictures listed each boy's statement and as I began reading the first one, I felt my stomach roll violently as I saw my first name listed when the boy was asked if he knew the name of the person who'd hurt him.

The nausea was so intense that I knocked the chair over in my attempt to get up and find a bathroom. I managed to make it to the half bath I'd spied near the front hallway but all that came up were the few sips of coffee I'd taken and then I was dry heaving. A hand settled on my back and then handed me a dampened washcloth.

"I'm okay," I said, my throat burning as I spoke. It was Cole who was standing behind me watching me with concern but then he nodded and pulled some mouthwash from a small cabinet next to the sink and left the bathroom. I splashed some cold water on my face and rinsed out my mouth with the mouthwash before I returned to the kitchen. The stack of pages was still on the table in front of my chair but all the boys' statements had been set aside and turned over.

I kept my eyes glued to the pages in front of me as I returned to my righted chair because I didn't want to know what Mace and Cole thought of me for my pathetic show of weakness. But all of that fled my mind as I began reading the first few lines on the nondescript page.

I need you, Devlin. I need to taste you, to feel you inside of me. Can you sneak away tonight? --Jonas

Revulsion went through me and I let out a hoarse shout and shoved the offensive papers away from me.

"Who did this?" I yelled as I stood up and tried to get a hold of myself but the fury kept rolling off me in waves. I lashed out at anything in my path and that meant several mugs sitting on the kitchen counter went flying, their contents spraying over the white cabinets. Seeing the destruction actually made me want more, and I began grabbing up every dish I could find and throwing it against the wall.

When Cole's arms wrapped around me from behind, pinning me so I couldn't move, I struggled violently against him for several long seconds but he was too strong. When the rage finally started to seep out of me, I could feel Cole's warm breath against my ear as he spoke.

"We're going to figure this out, Jonas. I promise you."

"Devlin's one of the best men I know, Cole. He doesn't deserve this."

"We'll prove it's a lie, Jonas. This will never touch Devlin or Casey."

I managed a nod. "I need to take a break," I whispered. "Can I go outside?"

"Just stay in sight of the house, okay?" Cole said gently. When he released me, I bent down to start cleaning up the mess I'd made but Cole grabbed my wrist and said, "I'll take care of it." My skin automatically tingled where he touched me and I remembered the sweet kiss he'd brushed over my lips. I wanted another one but I didn't know how to ask for it. Hell, I didn't even know if Cole was gay.

But Cole must have seen something in the way I looked at him because he leaned down and sealed his mouth over mine. The kiss was still relatively tame since he only lingered for a moment but I felt it in my bones.

Just like Mace's…

At the reminder, I glanced over to the table to see if Mace had witnessed the kiss but he was gone. I cast Cole another look and then left the kitchen. I only went as far as the porch because I was too afraid to wander away from the house despite my intense desire to escape this whole situation. I sat on the porch swing that hung from two long chains. The rocking motion very quickly became soothing, and I finally took the deep breath I felt like I'd been holding from the moment Cole had pointed the rifle at Mace the night before.

My anger with Mace had started to ease after seeing the so called proof he had against me. Both the mugshot and emails looked so real that I wondered how many people would have known they were fakes. I knew the answer…only the people who really knew me would know I wasn't capable of something like that. And that translated to Casey and Devlin. Because I'd never let anyone else close enough to know me.

Until Mace.

The anger may have started to fade but the hurt was front and center. And I had no one to blame for that but myself. Because I'd trusted Mace. I'd wanted to connect with him. I'd wanted…him.

The object of my thoughts rounded the house and began climbing the porch stairs when he saw me and stopped. My eyes settled on the rifle in his hand and how easily he held it. Like it was an extension of his body.

"I was just checking the perimeter," he said quietly. His gaze raked over me and I felt an intense longing – the same longing I'd felt last night when he'd kissed me and I'd needed more.

Mace shifted his eyes from me and then reached for the screen door.

"Was it all a lie?" I found myself asking even though I hadn't meant to.

Mace's hand froze on the door handle and I could see the knuckles were turning white from how tightly he was holding it. He didn't say anything at first, and I regretted the question because I knew I wouldn't be able to believe anything he said to me anyway.

"Our kiss last night…" he whispered and I flinched because I'd wanted more than anything to believe that his kiss had been real. "The last time I kissed someone was my wife, the day we lost our son…eight years ago."

With that, Mace disappeared into the house and I could only sit there in mute silence as I tried to grasp the enormity of what he'd just told me.

Chapter 15

MACE

My whole body shook as I entered the house. I hadn't meant
to tell Jonas that, but I knew he'd never have believed me if I'd
answered him with a simple "no."

I didn't notice Cole until I was practically on top of him and I
knew just from looking at him that he'd heard what I said to Jonas. I
hated the look of pity I saw in his eyes but I realized it didn't matter.
Whatever tension had and still existed between us didn't matter
because he would walk away with everything I wanted. He was
everything I'd once been a lifetime ago before one careless oversight
destroyed my entire world. Before I'd drowned myself in liquor, sex
and the quest for vengeance.

I'd seen Cole kiss Jonas as I was heading out of the kitchen,
because I'd been too disturbed to watch Jonas's meltdown, knowing
I was the cause of it. Their kiss was everything I'd expected it to
be...beautiful, perfect, devastating. With one achingly sweet kiss,
Cole had taken away a little bit of the pain I'd heaped on Jonas. It
was the only measure of comfort I took from the whole situation.
Even if Cole was straight, I could see by the way he looked at Jonas
that he wasn't using Jonas out of some need to test his sexuality. Not
like I'd used him...

"Perimeter's clear," I said as I handed the rifle to him. "I'm going to go take a shower."

"Mace-"

I ignored Cole and hurried up the stairs and found an empty guest room that had an attached bathroom. I hadn't had a chance to clean up the night before because just minutes after I'd finally forced myself to go into the house after the brutal confrontation with Jonas, I'd heard him screaming. After helping Cole subdue him, I'd stayed in the room in case he had any more episodes. Seeing the two of them lying together had done something to me, though. It was the same thing I'd felt when I saw Jonas hug Cole in the studio the day after they'd met...I was on the outside looking in on something I wanted to be a part of. It was a startling realization that I wanted them both. Initially I'd brushed off the attraction I had towards Cole as just that – attraction. But there was something about Cole that drew me in – his strength probably. He gave me something I hadn't really even realized I needed, just like Jonas did.

But I knew now that nothing about what I was feeling was simple. I didn't understand it but seeing them together somehow felt...right. My world felt right when I was around both of them at the same time. Even with things as fucked up as they were, I took comfort in seeing them together.

I cursed the ridiculousness of my thoughts as I stepped out of my clothes and climbed into the shower. Cole had covered the wound he'd stitched up for me with a waterproof bandage so I didn't have to worry about not getting the stitches wet.

That was something else that had surprised me. I'd expected another confrontation this morning when Cole had come into the kitchen. But instead of railing at me or shooting questions at me as I sat sipping coffee at the kitchen table, he'd simply poured himself a cup of coffee and made pancakes from a box of mix he'd found in the pantry. We'd eaten in silence and then he'd made a batch for Jonas and disappeared upstairs. I'd made the mistake of following him so I could see for myself how Jonas was doing but then I'd heard Jonas say he didn't want me around so I'd gone back to the kitchen, the pain of Jonas's hatred making my insides bleed.

When Cole had come back down, he'd tossed a first aid kit down in front of me. But it wasn't just any first aid kit when I'd opened it. There'd been an array of scissors, scalpels and needles. I'd had to assume the kit belonged to the owner of the house and while he cleaned my wound, I'd prepared the needle. The only time he'd spoken was to warn me just before he pushed the needle into my skin.

After my shower, I hunted around under the vanity, unearthing a spare toothbrush and a bottle of mouthwash. I made use of both and then crashed on the bed with the intention of just grabbing a few minutes to try and gather myself together. The plan was to go downstairs and finish this thing with Cole and Jonas, since the sooner we figured out who'd set all this up, the sooner I could fuck them up and then get the hell out, but I ended up falling asleep and didn't wake until it was already dark outside.

I found Jonas and Cole working side by side doing dishes from whatever meal they'd prepared for dinner. They worked in silence but I could see them occasionally looking at each other.

Jonas was the first to notice me, and I was glad to see he didn't look away from me like he had earlier this morning when he'd seen me watching him and Cole sleeping.

"Dinner's in the microwave," he said quietly before returning his attention to the dishes.

"Not hungry," I murmured as I went to the table and sat down. "We need to figure out our next steps," I said.

"The guys last night – were they yours?" Cole asked.

I shook my head.

"How do you know?"

"Because my guys wouldn't have missed," I said simply. "They also would have had the patience to wait until Jonas was alone to take him out."

I immediately regretted my words when Jonas stilled in the process of putting a plate away.

"Can you trust your guys?" Cole asked as he dropped down in the chair next to me.

I hated needing to do it but I shook my head. The only thing that had kept me from pulling the trigger was some instinct...some pull Jonas had on me. I knew that most of the members of my team wouldn't have felt the same thing. And even if they had, they certainly wouldn't have spent weeks trying to figure it out. They would have accepted the solid evidence that had been presented to them and done their job and moved on.

"The only people I currently trust are in this room," I admitted. "We're on our own," I added.

I heard the chair on the other side of the table scrape across the floor and I lifted my eyes long enough to watch Jonas sit down, a dish towel twisted between his fingers.

"The stuff in that file...is it real?" Jonas asked. "I mean, I know the arrest isn't real but do the police really believe I did those other things? That one statement had my name in it."

"I don't think so," I said as I held Jonas's eyes. "The boys might be real victims but whoever went through the trouble of setting you up would have changed their names and added yours in place of the real suspect. But they would have risked exposing themselves if they tried altering the actual records."

I forced myself to voice a truth I didn't want to have to admit was a possibility. "Whoever did this could have been someone on my team," I said. "Any one of them would have had the skill needed to alter the police reports and create those emails."

"You think one of your guys wants Jonas dead?" Cole asked.

"That or they were setting me up."

Cole straightened in his chair. "What do you mean?"

"If one of my guys just wanted Jonas dead, they could have just as easily done it themselves. But they went through a lot of trouble to make Jonas out to be a pedophile because they knew I'd be the one assigned to take him out."

"How...how would they know that?" Jonas asked, his voice shaky.

I pinned him with my gaze and said, "Because a pedophile murdered my son."

Chapter 16

COLE

"Mace..." I heard Jonas whisper in disbelief at Mace's admission. I could see that Mace was barely holding it together because his fists were clenched on the table and his jaw was tight with agitation.

"I'll head back down to the city tomorrow...maybe I can find something at Jonas's studio," Mace said, ignoring both mine and Jonas's concerned looks. "It'll give me a chance to get online to see what I can find out."

"You're not going back to the gallery," I said firmly. "It's an unnecessary risk."

"Don't worry, I'll make sure I'm not followed back," Mace quipped as he stood. "Besides, it'll give you two some alone time," he added, but I recognized the jab for what it was and grabbed his arm to keep him from leaving the kitchen.

"You are not going back there."

I felt the tension in Mace's body and I knew it wouldn't take much to push him over. We were both still bruised and battered from our fight the night before, but I didn't give a shit. If what he needed was a fight to defuse whatever rage was rolling through him because of the admission about his son, I'd give it to him.

"Was his name Evan?"

Mace froze at Jonas's question but then nodded.

"How old was he?" Jonas asked gently.

"Seven," Mace said, his eyes now on the place where I was holding on to his arm.

"It wasn't your fault," Jonas said softly. I had no idea if Jonas knew something about Mace's son that I didn't, or if he was just guessing, but the question got a reaction from Mace, because he yanked his arm free of my hold and took several steps away from both of us.

"I'm going to go check the perimeter," he said, his tone clipped. I saw him shutting down and withdrawing from both of us, so I hurried after him when he left the kitchen and I reached for the rifle that was sitting next to the front door before he grabbed it. I stepped in front of the door and wasn't surprised when he grabbed me by the throat and slammed me back against the unforgiving wood.

"Get the fuck out of my way!" he snarled, his desperate anger reminding me of a wounded animal.

"Mace, please just talk to us," Jonas said from doorway leading to the kitchen.

Mace released me and jerked his eyes towards Jonas.

"Whatever happened, it wasn't your fault," Jonas repeated.

"Fuck you!" he snapped at Jonas. "Fuck both of you."

He started heading towards the back door but Jonas stepped in his path. He grabbed Jonas like he had me but even from where I stood, I could see that his hold was loose and gentle and seemed more about keeping Jonas back rather than moving him out of the way.

"Tell me," Jonas whispered as his hand came up to rub up and down the arm that was holding on to his neck.

"I overslept," Mace suddenly whispered, his voice barely a croak. "I was supposed to pick him up from school but I forgot to set my alarm clock. I'd worked a double shift the night before and Shel had left that morning to visit her parents in Miami."

"Was Shel your wife?"

Mace nodded. "Shelby."

"What happened to Evan?"

"He must have decided to walk home on his own…we only lived a few blocks from the school. They found his body two days later."

Mace dropped his arm and I could see tears running down his face as he stepped back until his back hit the opposite wall near the staircase.

"I slept through my son being raped…through him being beaten and then strangled with an extension cord, and through his body being dumped in the woods less than a mile from my own house." Mace suddenly let out a howl of pain and then began slamming his head back against the wall. I quickly put the rifle down and hurried to Mace's side and slid my hand behind his head to keep him from hurting himself.

"You couldn't have known," I whispered.

"I was his father!" he shouted and then he grabbed my arms in a painful hold. "I can hear him calling for me, Cole! He needed me and I fucking wasn't there!"

"I'm sorry," I said as I gripped Mace's face with my hands. "So sorry," I repeated as I pulled him forward and began kissing away the damp tears that still flooded his skin. He quieted under my ministrations and the bruising hold on my arms eased but he didn't release me. I could feel his soft breath against my lips as I reached his mouth and we both held there for several long seconds until I finally slanted my mouth over his.

Like with Jonas, I'd meant the kiss to be brief and comforting but I knew Mace needed more when he automatically opened for me. I let my tongue brush his before I gently explored every surface of his mouth. I knew he was vulnerable so I didn't deepen the kiss any further and when I pulled back, I waited to see if he would lash out at me. But he didn't. Instead, he wrapped his arms around me and drew me close and then buried his face against my neck. I held him as tight as I could until I felt a hand settle on my back.

Jonas.

Guilt went through me that Jonas had witnessed the kiss but I couldn't make myself regret it. Nor did I regret kissing Jonas. I didn't know what to make of that, but I didn't have to think on it for too long because the second Mace relinquished his hold on me, Jonas reached up to stroke his hand over Mace's face before pulling him down for a kiss. It was nothing like the passionate one I'd witnessed between them the night before in the gallery, but it was just as intense.

"Let's go lay down for a bit, okay?" Jonas said to Mace even as his hand closed around mine. Mace managed a nod as he wiped at his face. As I followed Jonas and Mace up the stairs, I knew I was crossing a line I wouldn't be able to come back from. Not only had I taken the leap into the deep end in terms of exploring my sexuality this morning when I'd kissed Jonas for the first time, I was building a connection with not one but two men and I had no idea what that meant for any of us. I knew what was about to happen between us wasn't about sex since Mace was way too vulnerable for that but that almost made it worse because what we were seeking in each other wasn't about pleasure – it was about so much more.

We ended up in the master bedroom which had a king sized bed. None of us removed any clothes other than our shoes and Jonas urged Mace to get under the covers before crawling in next to him. I went around to the other side of the bed and climbed in. Mace and Jonas were both lying on their sides facing each other and Mace had one arm under Jonas's head and the other wrapped around his waist. But as soon as I pressed up against Mace's back with my front, his hand sought out mine and then he was pulling my arm around his chest. I linked my fingers with his and pressed our connected hands against his sternum and rested my head on his shoulder. I felt Jonas's hand settle on the arm I had wrapped around Mace and I smiled because with the one move, Jonas had made sure we were all connected.

Just like we were supposed to be.

Chapter 17

MACE

THE FIRST THING I NOTICED BEFORE I EVEN OPENED MY EYES WAS the smell of cinnamon. The second thing was the warm body pressed up against me. Only problem was that there was just one and I really didn't like how empty and cold one side of my body felt. I wanted last night back. I wanted to be surrounded in heat and soothing touches.

"Your coffee will get cold if you don't wake up," I heard Jonas say softly against my shoulder where his head was resting.

"Don't want to," I responded.

"Why not?"

"I don't want this to be a dream."

I felt Jonas shift and I was sure I'd lost him but then I felt his mouth brush mine. "Only way to find out is to open your eyes."

I did just that and was rewarded with Jonas's silver eyes watching me. "Morning," he whispered before he kissed me again. I let him control the kiss but I couldn't keep from wrapping my arm around his back as his tongue slid over mine. I was painfully hard when he finally released me and lowered himself back down to my shoulder.

"Where's Cole?" I asked.

"Gone," Jonas said. My heart constricted painfully in my chest at that. "He left a note that he needed to check on some things and that he'd be back tonight."

Anger and fear went through me at the same time.

"He'll be okay," Jonas said quietly but his statement sounded more like a question. I shifted so that Jonas was flat on his back and I was hovering above him.

"He's strong, Jonas. Smart. He knows how to take care of himself," I said even though the words didn't ease my own fears for Cole's safety.

The feel of Jonas beneath me turned the pleasant warmth inside me into a full on inferno of need and I leaned down to kiss him. I kept the kiss light because I didn't know where I stood with him. What if last night had only been about comforting me? What if daylight meant we had to go back to him hating me?

"Why?" I whispered as I brushed my thumb back and forth over his jawline. "Why did you give me that last night?"

Jonas's fingers were brushing over my bicep but he kept his eyes on me. I could feel his erection pressed against mine and as thrilled as I was by that, I needed to know why he'd given me what he had the night before.

"Why did you stop that wood from hitting me when we first met?"

The question surprised me but it also answered my question.

"Because I needed to," I said simply and then I settled more of my weight on him and sealed my mouth over his. I felt him shift his legs beneath me and I groaned when he opened them to make room for me. I took my time exploring his mouth as I let one of my hands travel up and down his side. When Jonas dragged his mouth from mine so he could catch his breath, I kissed my way down his neck but I didn't go any farther. My body felt like it was on fire but I forced myself to just hold Jonas as I fought for control of my raging need. It took several minutes before I felt calm enough to shift back up and brush a chaste kiss over his lips.

"Do you want this, Jonas? Do you want to see what this thing between the three of us is?"

"You mean sex?" Jonas asked tentatively.

I hesitated with my next words because I knew the weight they carried. I knew that saying them would change the trajectory of my life forever.

I shook my head. "It would be so much more than that," I admitted. "I can't speak for Cole but I want everything with you, with him."

Jonas reached up to sift his fingers through my hair. His silence frightened me...maybe I had misread the events of last night. What if Cole and Jonas had merely pitied me in that moment and nothing more? What if they didn't feel the completeness that I'd felt when we were wrapped around each other?

"I want it," Jonas suddenly whispered and then he was urging me down. His kiss was gentle at first, teasing, exploring. Then his hunger took over and he stole into my mouth with vicious intent. As much as I wanted to wrap myself around Jonas and never come up for air, I knew something was missing. Not something... someone. I allowed myself one more taste of him before pulling back.

"I want us to wait for Cole," I said. I didn't know how to explain that despite my intense need for Jonas, it didn't feel like enough. But when Jonas nodded, I knew he got it.

"Me too," he whispered.

I smiled as relief flooded my system. I had no idea what the hell was happening between the three of us but I wanted it. I wanted all of it.

"Mace," Jonas said as I began to pull back from him.

I stopped and looked down at him.

"I...I don't know if I'll be able to..." Jonas's voice dropped off as he struggled with whatever he was trying to say. I let my fingers trail up and down his arm before I linked our fingers together.

"I haven't been with anyone since Casey and I left Chicago. I tried once in Paris but it didn't go well..."

Understanding dawned and a bone-crushing sadness settled in my chest but I kept my expression soft. "Nothing happens that you don't want," I said.

"I want to try...I want to be a part of whatever happens," he said, his voice shaky. "I just don't want you and Cole to be disappointed if I can't let you-"

I kissed him before he could finish because I didn't want him to end his sentence with "fuck me." It was too crude of a word to describe what I wanted to do with Jonas.

"I can guarantee that nothing you do or don't do would ever disappoint us," I said against his lips. I kissed him gently a few times until I felt the tension ease from his body. I levered off of him and sat up enough so I could reach for the coffee. I was thrilled when Jonas adjusted his position so he was still laying against me.

"How did you know so much about construction work?" I heard Jonas ask.

I let my fingers sift through his hair as I spoke. "My dad owns a construction company. I worked for him all through high school and for a little while after I left the force."

"You were a police officer."

"Yeah, for almost ten years. I left after...after Evan," I said. I had trouble controlling the tremor in my voice when I said my son's name.

"Are your parents still alive?"

"They are. They live in Philadelphia. That's where I grew up."

"Do you see them a lot?"

When I didn't answer right away, Jonas sat up and shifted so he was facing me. I couldn't call the words forth so I just shook my head. My throat hurt as I recalled the last time I'd talked to my mother and father.

"After we lost Evan, I wasn't in a good place. I guess I needed to punish myself because they wouldn't. Neither would Shel. I hated them for that..."

"What happened to your wife?"

Pain lanced through me at the thought of Shelby. "She remarried a few years ago. She had a baby last year."

"You keep in touch with her?"

I shook my head and dropped my eyes. "I go there sometimes to check on them. Her and my parents."

"But you don't talk to them?"

"No," I said. I lifted my eyes and spoke before Jonas could ask his next question. "I did some really shitty things, Jonas. Things you can't just come back from."

I was glad when Jonas merely nodded and then leaned forward to give me a kiss before he climbed out of bed. "Is it safe enough to take a walk?"

I nodded.

"Great. Cole said there's a lake nearby. Let's go check it out."

I USED MY FOOT TO GENTLY ROCK THE PORCH SWING BACK AND forth as my eyes surveyed the end of the driveway for any sign of headlights. I had the rifle resting across my lap as my eyes slowly adjusted to the falling darkness and I began tightening my grip on it as my fear for Cole began to increase. As the tension within me began to build, I forced myself to focus on the events of the day instead.

Somehow my admission to Jonas that I wanted to explore a relationship with him and Cole had brought down some of the walls that had stood between us and as we'd explored the property, he'd been more relaxed than I'd ever seen him. He'd joked with me and shared stories about the culture shock he'd experienced when he'd first arrived in Paris. I'd also heard countless stories about many of the rescue animals he and Casey had worked with during the years they'd spent running the small animal shelter after they'd left Chicago. But as the day went on and Cole hadn't returned, I'd sensed the same worry in him that was going through me.

It was how I knew I was in love with both of them. I'd known pretty quickly that my feelings for Jonas ran deeper than just simple fascination or attraction so admitting that I was in love with him was easy. What I felt for Cole was unexpected, especially considering the short time we'd known each other for. But the second he'd confronted me last night, refusing to let me walk away from both of them after my admission about how Evan had died, I'd realized the truth. I was completely and utterly in love with two men at the same time and I couldn't and wouldn't be able to choose between them.

I automatically reached for my rifle when I saw headlights flash at the end of the driveway. Relief was my first reaction when I saw my car come into view but it quickly turned to anger. And it didn't help when Cole barely acknowledged my presence as he strode past me into the house.

I followed him into the kitchen and watched him dump a couple of plastic bags on the table and then he was opening a bottle from the six pack of beer he'd been holding. He took several long drags on it before he glanced at me and snapped, "What?"

"*That's* what you're going to say to me right now?" I bit out as I leaned the rifle in the corner.

"You're not my fucking keeper, Mace." He drained the beer and reached for another one. "Where's Jonas?"

"Asleep," I said. "Between the nightmares last night and him worrying about you all day, he was worn out."

Cole stilled in the process of opening the second beer and I knew he was remembering the two episodes Jonas had had the night before. The first had been similar to most of the ones I'd witnessed and Cole and I ended up positioning Jonas between us in the middle of the night as he'd fought off his unseen attacker. He hadn't completely awoken and having both Cole and me soothing him with soft words and touches had seemed to help bring him out of it. The second nightmare had been worse because Jonas had started calling out Carrie's name. And while he hadn't gotten violent, his anguished cries as he'd apologized to Carrie over and over had left their mark on Cole.

"Where did you go?" I asked.

"Home. I needed to check up on some things."

"You should have waited to talk to me about it," I said as I watched Cole begin draining the second beer.

"I made sure I wasn't followed," Cole growled.

"That's not what I meant."

Cole ignored me and reached for yet another beer. I stepped forward and snatched it from him. The move flipped some kind of switch inside of him because he used all his weight to shove me back. And then he kept coming at me until my back hit the wall. He pulled his fist back to hit me, the rage in his eyes glittering like diamonds. "Do it," I said quietly.

I didn't know if it was my tone that deflated his anger or something else but he dropped his arm and released his hold on me. But when he didn't step back, I snagged my arm around him and turned us so that it was his back to the wall.

"What happened?" I asked as I gently pinned his arms to the wall.

"I can't stop it," he whispered. "He's going to die and there's nothing I can do about it."

"Who?"

"My father."

"Is that who you went to check on?"

Cole nodded. "You know what he is, don't you? You saw him at the funeral."

I'd suspected but I hadn't said anything. "He's an alcoholic."

Another nod. "I'm trying to get him to go to rehab…"

"But he won't go," I finished for him.

"You should have seen him, Mace - the man he used to be. I don't even know him anymore."

"Men like him need to hit bottom before they'll get help, Cole. Believe me, I know."

Cole studied me for a long moment before saying, "You?"

I nodded. "Six years sober." I leaned in to kiss him. "We'll get him some help when this is over. I promise."

"You talk like you'll still be around when we figure all this out."

I wanted to tell him I wasn't going anywhere but I couldn't because I didn't know what the hell was going to happen. So I kissed him again and felt a thrill go through me when Cole kissed me back. We were both breathless by the time I pulled back and I rested my forehead on his as I tried to recover. "Is this okay?"

Cole seemed to know what I was talking about because he nodded and then kissed me.

"Have you ever been with another man?" I asked.

"No," he admitted as he leaned his head back against the wall. "I'm completely out of my element here, Mace. And that should scare the shit out of me but it doesn't. None of this makes any sense but I want it."

I slashed my lips over his again and sucked, nipped and licked at his mouth until he was desperately rubbing his dick against mine. I tore my lips from his and said, "It has to be with both of us. Me and Jonas. Or not at-"

"Yes," Cole moaned as he tugged his hands free of my hold and grabbed my head so he could plunder my mouth. He switched our positions so it was my back against the wall. This time when we separated, he let his lips hover against mine as he said, "Sorry I left without talking to you."

I nodded, stole a kiss and then said, "This thing between us, Cole, I don't want it to be about scratching an itch. Jonas and I, we're already in too deep for that. I know it's not fair to ask since you're also dealing with the newness of it all..."

"An itch wasn't what kept bringing me back to Jonas. It isn't what had me scared to death when you said you were going back to the gallery by yourself yesterday. Everything about my life is fucked up right now, Mace. Everything I've known has been stolen away from me. You and Jonas...you make me feel a little less lost. I'm not giving that up just because it didn't come in the package I always thought it would."

Cole kissed me thoroughly and by the time we separated, I was riding a high unlike any I'd ever known. "We need to talk about Jonas before this goes any further...what he needs from us if we do this," I managed to say as I struggled to catch my breath.

Cole nodded and put some space between our bodies. I missed the contact almost immediately but we both turned when we heard the floorboards creak. Jonas was standing in the entryway and I could tell from his flushed skin that he'd been watching us...and that he'd liked what he saw.

"I'll tell him," Jonas said to me before he turned his attention to Cole.

Chapter 18

COLE

"LET'S GO IN THE LIVING ROOM," I SAID TO JONAS AS I REACHED out to take his hand. It felt cold and clammy in mine despite how turned on Jonas was as a result of having seen me and Mace together.

I'd had a shitty day from the moment I forced myself to release my hold on Jonas this morning and climb out of bed. I'd known Mace would be pissed at me for leaving without an adequate explanation but I hadn't expected him to actually be worried about me. I also hadn't expected to hear that he shared the same affliction as my father but in a perverse way, it gave me hope. Mace had suffered so many of the same things as my father, but had come through it. Maybe I could still get back the man I'd idolized instead of having to bury the bitter, angry drunk who just this morning had called me some pretty choice names when I'd told him I was going to go see his doctor about getting him into rehab. The answers I'd gotten were on par with what I'd expected. The most I could do was try to get a court to find my father incompetent but since he didn't have any mental issues, it was unlikely any judge would give me the power to make medical decisions for him. Which meant the only way my father was going to get help was if he chose to. And that was looking more and more like a pipe dream.

I led Jonas to the living room and sat on the couch, pulling him down next to me since I didn't want to relinquish the contact between us. I turned my body so that I was facing him and was pleased when Mace took up a similar position on his other side. Cushioned between us like he was, I hoped that it would be a little easier for him to say what he needed to say. I already had a good idea of what he needed to share with me considering his childhood, but I didn't push or rush him in any way as he twisted his hands. But when he didn't speak after several minutes, I leaned forward and kissed him. My plan was to keep it short and sweet but when he opened his mouth on a moan, I couldn't resist taking a taste of him. It took everything in me not to continue the molten kiss and when I released his mouth I said, "Nothing you tell us changes anything between us. Nothing."

Jonas nodded and sucked in a deep breath. His hand searched out mine.

"You asked me if I worked for Mateo, do you remember?"

I nodded.

"I did for a little while when I first arrived in Chicago. I met him at the bus station."

I felt my heart clench as I remembered how Jonas had stepped in to try to stop Carrie from the same fate.

"His brother...his brother was the one who got me ready to meet with customers. They were planning to sell my services online and then have me meet with the johns in motels. Eduardo kept me for almost a week before he said I was ready."

Jonas's voice shook but I resisted the urge to tell him he didn't need to say anything else. Instead, I began stroking his palm with my thumb.

"I hated it," Jonas whispered. "Them," he added. "Eduardo always went with me when I met clients so I couldn't get away. But this one client liked to drink and do drugs while he was fucking me so one night I kept urging him to drink more and more till he passed out. I climbed out of the room through a bathroom window."

"Did Eduardo or Mateo find you after that?" I asked.

Jonas shook his head. "I took the client's money when I ran. It wasn't much but I was able to get a room to stay in. I tried finding a regular job but no one was going to hire a fourteen-year-old kid. I knew I'd have to keep doing what I'd been doing. I thought if I was in control then maybe it wouldn't be so bad."

I knew listening to Jonas would be hard but I hadn't expected the full-on rage that took over me. I wanted to track down every man who'd ever touched Jonas and rip him to shreds. I managed to keep my grip on Jonas gentle but that was only because my eyes connected with Mace over Jonas's shoulder and I saw the silent message there. Jonas didn't need me to be angry for him, he just needed me.

I let my fingers drift up to his wrist while I waited for him to continue but when I felt the raised flesh beneath my touch, I dropped my eyes to look at what I was feeling. A long, ugly scar ran the width of his wrist.

"I did it about a week after I got away from Eduardo," Jonas said softly as he watched me caress the healed wound. "The first few times that I was on my own, a couple of the guys I'd been with took more than they'd paid for and one didn't pay at all…he had a knife. I thought I was going to die and when he was done, I wanted to."

Jonas shook his head. "I was just really tired, you know?" he whispered as he lifted his eyes to meet mine.

"I know, baby," I responded as I closed my hand around his and pulled his fingers up against my lips.

"I met Carrie about nine months later. After I got away from Eduardo, I didn't go to the bus station at first because I knew it was one of Mateo's favorite places to find new girls. But picking up johns on the streets was more dangerous because you'd have to get in their car or go to motels. At the bus station, the johns were in more of a hurry and there was this spot behind the building where people couldn't see what was happening but they'd hear if you started calling out."

Jonas's voice dropped off for a moment before he seemed to collect himself. "I kept a low profile whenever I worked the bus station and if I saw Mateo or one of his guys, I took off. I saw him talking to Carrie one night and I saw the way she looked at him... desperate, hopeful. I knew I couldn't leave her there. You know the rest."

"Jonas, you said there was someone in Paris," Mace said softly and I saw his hand rubbing gentle circles over Jonas's shoulder.

"Um, yeah, Victor. I met him my first year in school. He wasn't a student. He was a few years older than me. We met in a café and started dating. I was attracted to him but I was having trouble letting him get close to me. We didn't even kiss until our seventh date. I could tell he was getting frustrated with me so I told him the truth about my past."

Jonas fell silent again and I could see tears shimmering in his eyes. "What happened?" I asked, knowing he needed to finish his story so he could start finding a way to be free of it.

"He said he understood, that we could take it slow. We were hanging out one night in his apartment just watching TV. He had a lot to drink and started kissing me. It was okay at first but then he wanted more. I told him I wasn't ready and he got pissed. Started calling me a cock tease. He pinned me down on the couch and began unbuttoning his pants. I begged him to stop but he kept saying I should be good at sucking cock since I was a professional. He was having trouble getting his pants loose so he had to release me and I hit him. I was able to get away...I never saw him again after that."

I struggled to find the right words and finally settled on just kissing Jonas. "I'm in awe of you, Jonas," I whispered against his mouth. "Thank you for telling us."

Jonas nodded. "I don't know if I'll ever be ready to be with you like that."

"Just having you with us is enough," I said. Jonas glanced over his shoulder and saw Mace nod in agreement.

I could see Jonas's nervousness increasing as the silence grew between us so I said, "Did you like watching us?"

"You guys are beautiful together," he said softly, a small smile gracing his lips. I returned his smile and then covered his mouth with mine. He opened to me almost instantly and as I swept my tongue into his mouth, I gently eased him back so that his back was flush with the couch cushions. I let my hand rest on his belly as we kissed but didn't move it. As soon as I pulled free of the searing kiss, Mace's mouth took the place of mine and I felt my dick swell at the sight of them consuming each other. Then it was my turn. I welcomed Mace as he took my mouth over and over again. Jonas had a perfect view of us since he was still between us and I could hear his breathing increase as Mace made love to my mouth. Fingers curled over my thigh and since one of Mace's hands was at the back of my head and the other was supporting his weight as he leaned over Jonas to reach me, I knew the hand belonged to Jonas and a thrill shot through me that he felt comfortable enough to participate.

When Mace released me, I turned my attention back to Jonas and kissed him as I let my fingers rub over the tight muscles of his abdomen. I sensed Mace moving but I didn't know what he was doing until his body appeared in front of me. His hands settled on my knees and gently shifted my legs open. It wasn't until he dropped to his own knees that I understood what he was planning and a shot of trepidation went through me. As much as I wanted what was about to happen, the knowledge that it would be a man's mouth bringing me pleasure was still something I had to adjust to. I didn't know if Jonas sensed my nervousness or not but he suddenly became the one stealing my mouth in a series of heart stopping kisses and his hand began stroking all over my chest. When Mace pushed my shirt up just a little, Jonas grabbed the hem and pulled it all the way up so that he could get it off me.

His lips were back on mine as Mace worked my pants loose. The feel of Mace's fingers pulling my cock free of my underwear had me gasping and dropping my head back on the couch. Within a few strokes, he had me rock hard and I wasn't even sure I'd have to worry about having his mouth on me since I'd probably come long before his lips ever reached me. Jonas's hands continued to stroke over my skin and I just languished in the differences in how they touched me. But I wasn't even a little bit surprised to find that

Jonas's inexperienced and tentative touches stirred the same level of lust in me that Mace's knowing caresses did.

I still had my eyes closed when I heard a zipper open. Since mine was already down, I assumed it was Mace's but when I opened my eyes, I was thrilled to see that it was Jonas who had opened his own pants. His eyes were on Mace as he stroked himself in his jeans.

"Show us," I heard Mace whisper as his passion-filled eyes held Jonas's gaze even while his fingers continued to torment my now leaking dick. Jonas hesitated for a moment and then pulled up his shirt until it was tucked under his armpits and then he pushed his jeans down enough to release his cock. We both watched him stroke himself and I held my breath when Mace settled one of his big hands on Jonas's jean clad thigh. Jonas didn't stop his tugs on his dick and to my amazement, he used his free hand to cover Mace's. Then everything went into overdrive because Jonas turned his head to seek out my mouth at the exact same time that Mace swallowed me down.

Jonas absorbed the curse that spilled from my lips and then I had to rip my mouth from his so I could watch Mace work me. I hadn't expected the sight of Mace's wet lips stretched around my dick to be as beautiful as when it was a woman, and I'd been right. Because it was so much more than that. It was fucking epic because I could see and feel Mace taking his pleasure from my body at the same time that he was giving it back to me. His eyes shone with such emotion that I couldn't hold back my orgasm and it slammed into me before I could even warn Mace so he could pull off. But as my semen flooded his mouth, he swallowed over and over and each time he did it, he milked more of my release from me. I heard Jonas cry out next to me and turned just in time to see white ropes of come spraying over his chest and abdomen. I was so overwhelmed by the beauty of watching Jonas bask in his pleasure that I crushed our mouths together so I could drink down his whimpers as his release crashed through him.

I felt Mace release me and looked down to see some of my cum clinging to his lips. He shifted up but instead of seeking out my mouth, he took Jonas's in a blistering kiss that left me reeling. I expected him to kiss me next but I could only watch in stunned silence as he lowered himself to lick up some of the fluid from Jonas's chest and belly. Jonas tensed momentarily but then relaxed just as quickly. I knew even as I watched Mace what his plan was and as soon as he lifted his head, I grabbed him and yanked him forward and drank down the proof that Jonas had been with us every step of the way. The salty, bitter taste coated my tongue before slipping down my throat and as I adjusted to the unfamiliar flavor, I reveled in the knowledge that I'd get to taste it again soon enough.

My body felt completely relaxed as I sat back against the cushions but one look at Mace's flushed features and I knew he hadn't sought his own relief. I leaned forward and began to put my hand on his crotch but he grabbed my wrist and said, "I want to come when you're inside me," he said stiffly. "Will you fuck me, Cole?"

I couldn't speak. Not even a syllable. So I nodded and grabbed his hand and yanked him upright as I stood. My sated body was already starting to stir again as I reached my other hand down. Jonas grabbed it without hesitation and then I was leading them both towards the stairs.

Chapter 19

MACE

AS HARD AS I WAS AND AS MUCH AS I WANTED TO TAKE THIS NEXT step with Cole and Jonas, the idea of bottoming terrified me because I'd only done it on a few occasions and it had either been a painful, humiliating experience or I'd been too drunk to care either way. I also knew that this would be Cole's first time with another man but I wasn't sure if he'd had anal sex with women. But Cole must have sensed my trepidation because as soon as we reached the bedroom after a quick stop in the kitchen to grab the lube and condoms he'd bought while he'd been out, Cole said, "Same rules apply to you...nothing happens that you don't want."

I nodded. "Just go slow because it's been a while for me."

Cole's response was to kiss me long and slow and deep. "I can still taste him," Cole whispered against my mouth and we both turned to eye Jonas who'd gotten stuck near the doorway. Cole shifted us so that Jonas could see everything we were doing and then his hands went to work just learning my body. I was still fully dressed but Cole was shirtless, so I took advantage and began exploring the rigid muscles of his abdomen. He had a slight smattering of chest hair that descended down his middle and disappeared into his pants which he'd left unzipped but had secured the button to keep them up. I rubbed my palm over his cock which was already starting to harden again but Cole grabbed my wrist and forced it and my other hand above my head. As soon as he was satisfied that I would leave them there, he reached for the hem of my shirt and pushed it up and off of me. His eyes fell on my tattoos and I realized he hadn't seen them before then.

"Beautiful," he muttered and then he was skimming his lips over my ink. My head fell back at the feel of his silky smooth tongue tasting me but I let out a moan when his fingers flicked my nipple piercing. When they grazed my other nipple he said, "I think you should get this one done too so Jonas and I can play at the same time."

I heard Jonas suck in a breath at that and I settled my hand on the back of Cole's head as his tongue laved my unpierced nipple. "I think he likes that idea," I murmured as I maintained the eye contact with Jonas. He still hadn't moved from the door but his eyes hadn't left us even once. I hated whatever it was that held him back from us despite the longing in his gaze but I resisted the urge to ask him to join us.

"Does he?" Cole asked knowingly. I knew even as Cole stepped around me and put his hands on my waist what he was doing and I was more than happy to go along with it. He turned me so that I was facing Jonas and then stood behind me and began kissing the top of my shoulder as his hands reached around me to play with both of my nipples at the same time. The contact felt so good that I leaned my head back against Cole, exposing my neck in the process and his mouth instantly closed over my thrumming pulse. He continued to play with my unpierced nipple but let his other hand slowly glide down my chest and abdomen before dipping inside of my pants. I groaned as soon as he fisted my cock.

"Open your eyes, Mace," Cole breathed into my ear. "See what you do to him."

I did as Cole told me and sucked in a breath at the sight of Jonas playing with himself. His position mirrored mine only it was his own hands bringing him pleasure. Jonas watched everything that Cole did to me but I saw the instant something inside of him changed, because his eyes softened and his hands stilled. At first I thought we'd somehow pushed him too hard but when he stepped forward, I wanted to cry out in relief. There was no hesitation when he reached me. He simply pulled my head down for a kiss and then his hand was joining Cole's in my pants. I cried out at the exquisite pleasure that rippled through me as they both played with me but it wasn't enough.

Jonas released my mouth only to seek out Cole's and I reveled in the sight of them loving each other over my shoulder. I didn't know which one ended the kiss but Jonas's next stop was my nipple – my pierced one - and he didn't even play around. He just grabbed it between his teeth and gently tugged before biting down on me. The sting of pain amped up the pleasure and his soothing lick a second later just drove me higher.

"I'm not going to last," I had to admit as both men continued to bathe my body with their blend of sensual torture. Jonas was the one who led me to the bed. He kissed me as his fingers worked my jeans open. I managed to kick off my shoes just before he pushed my pants and underwear down. But I nearly swallowed my tongue when he reached for his own clothes and began peeling them off. He was considerably leaner than me and Cole but had good muscle definition. I wanted to touch him to see if his skin was a smooth as it looked but I didn't dare. I saw him hesitate when he reached for his pants but it only took a moment and then he was shoving them down along with his briefs. He stood in front of me, his earlier tension back but he held his ground.

"Would you touch me, Mace?" he asked.

They were the words I'd been waiting to hear but once he said them, a tremor of uncertainty went through me. What if I did something that scared him? What if I fucked up the only chance Cole and I had with him?

I felt Cole's hands on my back again but they weren't doing anything but resting there. He was giving me this moment…this first with Jonas.

I bent my head to kiss Jonas as I settled my hands on his neck. I used my fingers to rub gentle circles into his skin as I moved my hands slowly down his chest. I kept my exploration confined to his upper body and it didn't take long for Jonas to respond and recipro- cate. And then something seemed to switch inside him again because he became the aggressor. His mouth teased every muscle and plane on my chest as his fingers settled on my hip. I felt Cole's hands moving again but it was to urge me to lie down on the bed. Jonas followed me down as did Cole and they took turns kissing me and exploring my chest. And in between, they tasted and pleasured each other. By the time Cole rolled me on my side so that I was face to face with Jonas, I was desperate for relief. When I accidentally shifted my hips so that my cock brushed Jonas's, I stilled at his gasp but it only lasted a second because then Jonas was doing the exact same thing.

I was so focused on Jonas that I didn't even feel Cole's finger until it pressed against my entrance. I jerked at the contact and then slid my eyes shut as Cole began massaging the sensitive skin. The lube felt cold compared to how hot I felt everywhere else. My whole body was tense as I waited for Cole to push his finger inside of me but when he just continued to tease me, I began to relax and focus on Jonas who'd started playing with my piercing again. Cole's lips settled at the back of my neck but it wasn't enough and I turned my head and sought out his lips. As his tongue greeted mine, I felt his finger bear down on me and I automatically pushed back. The sting of his entry stole my breath for a moment but it shifted over to a wonderful burn that began to radiate throughout my entire ass and then my whole body.

"More," I urged against Cole's mouth. He obliged me and sank his finger all the way inside of me. My body adjusted quickly to the intrusion and when he pulled his finger back before plunging it back in, I was sure I was going to come before I got the part of Cole I really needed.

Cole teased me with a couple more twists and turns of a single finger before he added a second. I flinched at the bite of pain that accompanied the addition.

"Okay?" Cole asked. He'd stopped kissing me at some point but I was so wound up that it didn't matter. Jonas was lying in my arms, his light eyes watching me intently. It was a heady feeling – being watched by these two men whose only concern was my pleasure.

I nodded. "Don't stop, please," I begged as the pain receded. Cole must have heard how close I was because he twisted his fingers in my body a few times before he withdrew them. I felt the head of his condom covered cock slip between my ass cheeks and bump up against my entrance and all the tension Cole had managed to work out of me came back. As his body began to breach mine, I felt Jonas's fingers briefly ghost over my face. He didn't need to say anything because it was written all over his face.

As my body fought to accept Cole's cock, I felt his and Jonas's hands clasped together on my outer thigh and I reveled in the feeling of completeness that went through me. My body finally gave up the fight once Cole pushed past my outer muscles and when he bottomed out inside of me, I felt tears sting my eyes. Cole didn't move at all except to lever himself up enough so that he could lean over me and kiss me long and hard.

"So fucking perfect, Mace. It's so fucking perfect." He kissed me again and then he and Jonas were kissing. As Cole slowly withdrew from me, I dragged Jonas to me and sealed our mouths together. He took every grunt and groan I gave him as Cole began a steady pace of gliding in and out of my willing body. But when long fingers fisted around my cock, I nearly cried out in relief. I knew whose hand it was because I'd already memorized the nuances of each man's touch.

"You don't have to," I said against Jonas's mouth.

"I know," was all Jonas said before he kissed me again. And then he shifted his hips forward and our cocks brushed as he held both of them at the same time. Jonas began thrusting his hips to match Cole's rhythm and I moaned as they fucked me in nearly perfect unison. And I could do nothing but lie there as they shared my body and worked together to send me higher and higher. Cole's fingers bit into my thigh as he began to hammer into me, and Jonas frantically began jerking us off. Sweat clung to my body as the orgasm began to build and roll over me in sweeping waves.

I was so close but I couldn't speak – I couldn't do anything to beg them to send me over. But Jonas heard me anyway because he bit gently down on my piercing and I felt it everywhere – my ass, my balls, my dick. A flood of sensation rocketed through me and I screamed as I was flung off the precipice. I felt Cole's cock pulse inside of me and then he roared in my ear as his arm wrapped around my chest to hold me as close to him as he could. Jonas let out a ragged moan as my come shot all over both of us and then his release followed a moment later. He kept pumping our dicks together to draw out the orgasm before he gently released his hold on both of us.

The only thing I processed after that was Cole's withdrawal from my body and Jonas's gentle kisses on my neck and jaw. And then there was just blackness and my last conscious thought was that I had to find a way to make sure I never lost this second chance at perfection that I'd been given.

✸

"YOU OKAY?" I HEARD COLE ASK AS HE CAME OUT ONTO THE porch. The sound of the screen door creaking seemed loud in the night air.

"Yeah," I said and I wasn't surprised when he came and sat down next to me on the porch swing. "Was thinking we should start taking turns taking watch."

"Okay," Cole said, though I could tell from the way he said it that he didn't really believe me. His entire body pressed against mine and I both loved and feared how it settled the agitation rolling around inside of me.

"Jonas still asleep?" I asked, more to fill the silence than anything else since it was two o'clock in the morning and Jonas hadn't stirred even once as I'd extricated him from my arms.

"Yeah," Cole murmured. "Mace, I didn't hurt you did I?"

I looked over at him. There was enough moonlight flooding the front yard for me to see his concerned expression.

"Are you kidding me?" I said with a laugh. "You fucking slayed me, Cole."

I saw his whole body relax at that.

"If I hadn't known better, I would have guessed you'd done that before."

"I googled it," Cole said.

"What?"

Cole chuckled. "While I was at home checking on my father, I googled a few things so I'd know what to expect."

I couldn't help but laugh and it felt so good that I leaned over to kiss Cole. "That must have been quite educational," I said as I drew back.

"It was. I saw some things I don't ever want to see again but a few things I think we definitely need to try."

My laughter died in my throat as a whole host of images flashed through my brain. The things I wanted to do with my men...

Except they weren't my men.

"Hey," Cole said softly and I turned my focus back to him. "We're going to figure this out."

I shook my head and looked out over the moonlit yard. "You know what I am, Cole. What I've done. You're saying you're okay with that?"

Cole was silent for so long that I was tempted to get up and leave so I wouldn't have to endure his unspoken answer.

"A few weeks ago, I would have said no. I would have made the argument that we have laws and rules for a reason. But when I think about what those men did to my sister, to Jonas, what they're still doing...they're no better than the terrorists who steal countless innocent lives in the name of a religion they've distorted and twisted to meet their own needs."

I felt Cole's eyes on me. "We're not so different, Mace. The things I've done may have been sanctioned by our government but I've still killed to protect the innocent...to get justice for the fallen."

I didn't know what to say to that.

"Why are you really out here?" Cole asked softly.

I drew in a deep breath. "Because I'm fucking terrified that the more time I spend with you and Jonas, the harder it's going to be when I lose you."

I knew what Cole was about to say so I cut him off. "Don't tell me I'm not going to lose you, Cole. Because I wasn't supposed to lose Evan either. I wasn't supposed to shit all over my marriage by cheating on my wife more times than I can count, and I sure as hell wasn't supposed to beat up my own father because he tried to take my car keys away when I was too drunk to drive!"

I shoved myself off the swing but Cole stood just as quickly and used his body to force mine back against the porch column. "Don't run from me…us," Cole whispered and then he kissed me. "You're not that man anymore."

"I can feel him, Cole. Right there under the surface. One wrong step…I won't survive it this time," I said with a shake of my head. "I tried, too," I whispered, needing to tell this man who'd so quickly become a part of my everything the truth of who and what I'd been.

"Tried what?" Cole asked gently as his hands began stroking up and down my arms.

"What Jonas did," I said since I couldn't force the actual words from my lips.

Cole stilled. "You tried to take your life?"

I swallowed hard and nodded before I took Cole's hand in mine and sifted his fingers through my hair until they found the scar on the side of my head. "My hand jerked at the last second. The doctors kept saying how lucky I was."

Cole gently probed the raised flesh before dropping his hand to my cheek.

"Lucky," I whispered.

"What happened after?"

"They institutionalized me for a while until they said I wasn't a danger to myself or others. As soon as I got out, I picked up where I'd left off. Bought another gun, made plans to get it right the next time around. Then I met a man who offered me something I wanted more than my next drink." I hesitated for a moment before I said, "You still sure I'm not that man anymore?"

"I'm sure," he said with a nod as he brushed a soft kiss over my lips. "Because that man wouldn't have given one thought to whether the man he saw through the scope of his rifle deserved to be there or not."

The next kiss Cole laid on me both eased and terrified me at the same time. Eased me because I could feel that Cole was in just as deep as me and terrified me because he'd just validated my greatest fear...that there would be no coming back for me a second time if I lost this.

Chapter 20

JONAS

As I listened to Cole and Mace kiss, I felt my heart start pounding as I realized I'd been right the night before as I'd watched them making love to each other. I was in love with both of them. And I was scared to death at what that meant.

I'd woken up alone just a few minutes earlier and the emptiness I'd felt had been crushing, because it was a sign of how quickly Cole and Mace had changed everything I'd thought about myself…everything I'd spent years coming to accept. Even with my inattentive parents, I'd still known as a kid that I would someday meet the man I was supposed to be with. I'd dreamed of what that man would look like, sound like. I'd envisioned him being the suit and tie type who'd come home after a long day of work and not care that when I greeted him, it was with paint stained fingers. He'd be attentive and open with a wicked, teasing sense of humor and he'd want the same things as me – kids, dog, white picket fence.

One night of Eduardo's "lessons" changed all that. I knew the second he stole what remained of my childhood that he was stealing the man, the kids and the white picket fence too. The men that came after took what was left, and it was only by sheer lack of knowledge that I hadn't lost everything else after dragging the razor blade across my wrist in one smooth glide as I'd sat on the dirty floor of my bathroom.

Casey had managed to give me back a piece of myself by showing me that being family didn't necessarily mean sharing blood, but I hadn't been foolish enough to think I'd find a version of the man from my childhood fantasies. Victor had been proof that I'd been right because he'd been everything I'd wanted – patient, sweet, understanding. Until one night when he wasn't. When he became one of the many men who took rather than gave.

There'd been several men since Victor who'd shown an interest in me, but I hadn't even considered trying again. And it wasn't just the fear of sex that held me back. It was the fear of losing that one last piece of myself to someone else…that piece that had made me get up off that dirty bathroom floor and reach for a towel to stem the flow of blood from my wrist, instead of picking up the shiny razor blade so that I could finish what I'd started.

But I knew now that Mace and Cole didn't want to take that from me. The only things they wanted to take were things I would have gladly given up willingly if I could have…the pain, the darkness, the memories. But they'd done the next best thing. They'd lanced the part of my soul where those things festered and then they'd given me what I needed most…a choice.

I'd been sure I wouldn't be able to be a part of their lovemaking the night before so I'd stayed by the bedroom door so it would be easier to walk away when it became too painful to watch them together. I hadn't expected them to include me so completely without even touching me. And in that instant that they both watched me as they loved each other, my childhood version of my perfect other half dissolved and morphed into the two men in front of me. After that, it had been easy to walk forward, straight into Mace's arms.

Now as I sat on the stairs just out of view of the screen door, I listened to my men as they murmured a few more things to each other that I couldn't make out, and then went back up to the master bedroom and crawled into bed. I heard their footsteps on the stairs a moment later and I closed my eyes. Not because I wanted to hide from them but because I didn't want Mace to know I'd heard his painful admissions. I knew he'd tell me when he was ready.

The bed shifted beneath their weight as they got in next to me. I knew Cole was at my front because I could smell his unique, woodsy scent as he pulled me against his chest. Mace's lips skimmed over the back of my neck in a feather light caress and then I felt his warm breath fanning my skin as he settled there, his arm wrapping around my waist.

My last thought as I drifted off to sleep was that tomorrow I was going to start giving back to them just some of what they'd given me.

❋

THE NEXT TIME I WOKE UP, IT WASN'T DARK ANYMORE AND I certainly wasn't alone. Lips and hands were exploring my body but never once strayed below my waist. At some point, I'd flipped so that I was facing Mace so his were the first eyes I saw. He didn't say anything, he just watched me as his thumb came up to stroke my cheek. I was the one who pulled him down for a kiss and then I was reaching behind me to seek out Cole's mouth. Mace rolled me to my back as Cole kissed me.

"Can we touch you, Jonas?" Cole asked, his lips hovering just above mine.

My throat felt too tight to speak because I knew what he meant. Fear skittered up my spine but I pushed it away. All it would take from me was one word and I knew without a shadow of a doubt that they would stop.

I nodded.

Cole kissed me again and then began working his way down my throat. They left no part of me untouched except the part that needed their touch the most and by the time they both reached my mouth again, I was ready to beg them. Only I couldn't force the words past my lips.

And then blessedly, Mace's hand wrapped around my painfully hard cock and the feel of his rough skin on my sensitive flesh had me arching off the bed. As Cole kissed me, Mace used the fluid leaking from my tip as lubricant and began heavy drags up and down my shaft. The torture didn't last long because he released me and began fondling my balls.

"Has anyone pleasured you with their mouth?" Cole asked me between kisses. I wanted to tell him that that was exactly what he was doing at the moment but I knew he wasn't talking about my mouth.

Mace's torment had slowed so I was able to speak. "One of my regulars liked to do it to me but I didn't…"

"You didn't like it," Cole supplied. When I nodded my head, Cole asked, "Will you let Mace show you?"

I cast my eyes at Mace and then shifted them back to Cole. "Will you both show me?"

I saw a hint of fear in Cole's eyes and I guessed it would be his first time touching a man in that way. "You don't have-"

Cole stole my words with a kiss. I felt Mace shift his body and I couldn't help the tension that overtook me. I could feel my erection wilting as my fear began to increase but before I could call the whole thing off, I felt Mace's tongue lick over my crown. The sensation caught me off guard and I held my breath to see if it was just some anomaly as I waited for Mace to do it again. But he didn't just lick me. He sucked the head into his mouth and used the tip of his tongue to tease the slit. The hot, wet heat of Mace's mouth felt so good that I instinctively shoved my hips up. He took more of me inside of him and then added such an intense level of suction as he dragged his mouth back up, I bowed off the bed and dug my nails into Cole's arm.

After that, I lost all sense of everything except being engulfed in white hot heat and the coil of need in my body that drew tighter and tighter. I managed to open my eyes long enough to see Cole's head bobbing up and down on me just before he pulled off and joined Mace in licking my entire length from root to tip over and over again. I came with almost no warning and I didn't know whose mouth I shot into as I screamed Cole and Mace's names. I couldn't even tell who'd taken my load when they each kissed me because I tasted myself on both of their tongues. Which meant I'd missed the kiss where one had shared my release with the other.

When I next woke up, it was under far less pleasant conditions because Cole was shaking me awake and I tensed when I saw the rifle in his hand.

"Jonas, someone's here, we've got to move."

I yanked on my jeans and snatched my shirt off the floor but didn't bother with anything else and then Cole grabbed my hand and dragged me down the stairs. I tried to look out the front door but it was closed. I was about to ask where Mace was when Cole led me to the back door and handed me the revolver I'd held on Mace just a couple nights ago. "I need you to watch the back and tell me if anyone heads towards the house."

I swallowed hard but managed a nod.

"I need to cover Mace but I'll hear you if you call out," he said as he headed towards the front door and yanked it open and then aimed the rifle.

I need to cover Mace.

I wanted - no, needed - to know what was going on, but Cole needed me to do this. Mace needed me to do it. So I forced myself to turn my back on whatever was happening up front and started methodically scanning the backyard.

Chapter 21

MACE

I held my Ruger loosely by my side as I watched the car come to a stop next to mine. I already knew who it was but that didn't change my stance at all. But when I heard the front door of the house open behind me, it took everything in me not to take my eyes off of Ronan as he got out of the vehicle.

"Cole-" I said without looking behind me.

"Mace, don't waste your breath telling me to go back inside. I've got Jonas covered," Cole said coolly. I wanted to tell him that my worry wasn't only for Jonas, but I needed to keep my attention on the man in front of me.

Ronan was wearing his standard issue black slacks and perfectly pressed white shirt but he'd foregone his usual suit jacket, probably so I could see he wasn't armed. In fact, he wasn't wearing the double shoulder holsters he typically wore. He kept his hands by his sides instead of holding them out, despite my gun and the rifle I had no doubt Cole was holding on him.

Ronan always had been a cocky son of a bitch. But I knew it wasn't for show – he was exactly what he portrayed himself to be.

"How?" I asked. I kept my eyes on him and hoped like hell Cole was able to scan our surroundings to watch for any forthcoming attacks.

"Jonas's watch," Ronan said.

Fuck, I hadn't thought to check Jonas's watch for a tracking device.

"How did you get his watch?"

"He takes it off when he washes his hands. I swapped it out when he went to the bathroom in the coffee shop he goes to every day."

I shook my head at my own stupidity. Ronan clearly hadn't believed me when I'd said I'd followed through on the assignment after he'd provided the so-called proof of Jonas's supposed affair with Devlin Prescott.

"You knew I'd take him and run."

Ronan shrugged. "It's what I would have done."

I wasn't sure if I should take that as a compliment or not. "You're not getting him," I said. "Even if you get past me, you won't get past him," I said motioning to Cole.

Ronan's eyes never left mine. "I've known where you were from the moment you left the city. You really think I would have waited all this time if this was about a job?"

"Then what are you doing here now?"

"There've been some developments you need to know about."

"You think I'd believe any of your bullshit? You fucking set me up. I know it. You know it," I bit out. I hated the disappointment that went through me that Ronan's betrayal actually hurt. I started backing up towards the house so that I'd be next to Cole if we needed to make a stand.

"It wasn't about you," Ronan said. "It was about Jonas. It still is."

I stopped moving at that but didn't respond otherwise.

"He used you. He used all of us," Ronan admitted and I was actually surprised by the thread of disappointment I heard in his voice.

"Who?" I asked.

"Benny."

I couldn't school my reaction to that. Benny was one of the most trusted members of our group.

"Look Mace, can you just check me for weapons and let me in so we can talk about this? I've been running my ass ragged for three days trying to figure out what the hell is going on."

I studied him for a moment and then finally backed up until I reached the porch stairs. I reached my gun behind me and Cole took it without hesitation. Ronan held out his arms as I approached him and I took my time searching him. I searched his car next.

"Grab the folder on the front seat," Ronan said.

I got the folder and then searched the car as best I could for any tracking devices but figured it was pointless since Ronan would have told his backup where he was going.

"I swear, Mace, it's just me," Ronan said as I came around the car. "You trusted me once," he added.

"The stakes are too high now," I said. "Talk."

"Jonas will want to hear this," Ronan said.

"Cole," I called out.

"Kitchen," he responded without hesitation. "We can cover the front and back yard from there."

I motioned to Ronan and followed him to the house. Cole was already in the kitchen and he had Jonas at his back. I could see my revolver tucked in the waistband of Cole's jeans.

"Sit there," I said as I pulled a chair out and put it near the front window so that I could watch both Ronan and the driveway at the same time. Cole moved to the window overlooking the back yard. I kept Jonas between us as I glanced down at the folder in my hand.

"Benny set this up?" I asked.

"Isn't that your tech guy?" Jonas asked from behind me.

"He was," Ronan said and I didn't miss the fact that he used past tense. I knew what that meant in Ronan's world. "After the shootout at your gallery," Ronan said as he looked at Jonas, "I began looking at what we had. They weren't any of my guys, Mace."

I nodded because I'd already figured that. Ronan's men would have had all the exits covered, but the men who'd shot at Jonas had left the roof unguarded. We wouldn't have gotten out of there if they'd been Ronan's men.

"Open it," Ronan said as he motioned to the folder.

I flipped the folder open and the first page I saw was very familiar. It was a picture of one of the boys Jonas had been accused of assaulting. The statement the boy provided was exactly the same except for the part where he named his attacker. The same suspect was named on all three statements and listed as the person of interest in the case file on the missing boy. I handed the pages to Jonas so he could see for himself.

"Those are the real reports, Jonas," Ronan said. "Benny pulled them from BPD's servers and changed the suspect's name to yours."

"So no one else saw the other reports? The ones with my name on them?" Jonas asked.

Ronan shook his head. "Your name isn't linked to any investigation anywhere."

I didn't need to look at Jonas to feel his relief.

"The emails between Jonas and Devlin?" I asked.

"Also fakes. He spoofed Devlin's email address to make them look real and he hacked his expense reports to get information about what hotels he stayed at and when and then he dated the emails to line up with those hotel stays."

"Why?" I bit out.

Ronan shifted his gaze to Jonas. "Did you know Mateo Santero was appealing the plea deal he made in the murder of Cole's sister?"

"What? No...no, the D.A. said he wouldn't be able to do that once he took the plea deal," Jonas said quickly.

"He's arguing ineffective counsel."

"Ineffective how?" Cole asked, the anger clear in his voice. He obviously hadn't been kept in the loop about his sister's case either.

"He's saying his lawyers failed to discover that Casey Prescott's biological father is a U.S. Senator who used his political connections to influence the investigation into the attack on Casey, as well as Carrie's murder."

I glanced at Jonas who was shaking his head. "He didn't!"

"Whether he did or didn't is irrelevant," Ronan explained. "It's the perception that matters. And it seems to be working because the judge in Wisconsin already threw out the plea deal. But he went a step further and dismissed the case with prejudice – that means the D.A. can't charge Mateo again for the attack on Casey."

"But he did it," Jonas whispered.

"What about Carrie's murder?" I asked Ronan.

"The hearing is scheduled for next week. Chances are high that the plea deal will be overturned but because of the seriousness of the crime, the judge probably won't dismiss with prejudice like the one in Wisconsin did. That means the D.A. can re-file charges…"

"And Jonas would have to testify," I said grimly as it all came together.

Jonas was visibly upset, so I ushered him to one of the kitchen chairs to sit. Like me, Cole had sensed that Ronan was no longer a threat to us and he joined Jonas at the table and covered his hand with his.

"What was Benny's role in all this?" I asked.

"There's a contract out on Jonas," Ronan announced.

Cole tensed up and Jonas looked like he was barely holding it together.

"Benny found the contract but instead of reporting it to me, he accepted it and then set Jonas up to make it look like he was a pedophile. My guess is he knew you'd get the assignment and that you wouldn't see past your hatred to notice what was really going on."

I swallowed hard because I almost hadn't. If Jonas hadn't been who he was or if I hadn't been drawn to him for some inexplicable reason, I would have done exactly what Benny had expected me to do.

"Why did he do it?" Cole asked.

Ronan shifted his attention to Cole and said, "The contract is worth a quarter of a million dollars. Benny's excuse was that he had gambling debts."

An excuse that had fallen on deaf ears if I knew Ronan.

"Where does a lowlife pimp get that kind of cash?" I asked.

"Mateo didn't put out the contract. His brother did."

I heard Jonas gasp and I took my attention off of Ronan long enough to lean down and put my lips next to Jonas's ear. "It's going to be okay," I whispered. "He won't ever touch you again."

Jonas nodded but then his fingers bit into my hand where I'd draped it against his chest. Instead of straightening, I took the chair Ronan offered me after he stood up. I saw a flash of something go through Ronan as his eyes studied Jonas but it was gone just as quickly.

When Jonas had settled, I gave Ronan a quick nod.

"Eduardo took over things when Mateo went to prison but he's doing more than just dealing in drugs and prostitution. He's built quite a name for himself in the world of human trafficking and it looks like he wants his baby brother back to help him run the business."

"Does Casey know?" Jonas asked.

Ronan actually seemed reluctant to answer Jonas's question and when he glanced at me first, I knew whatever he was going to say was going to make things even worse than they already were.

"I called Devlin after I learned about the contract on your life. Although we didn't find one for Casey, there's the possibility Eduardo will put one out on her if the D.A. decides to call her as a witness in Carrie's death. He may have held off because Mateo's lawyers could easily discredit her based on who her father is and the fact that her own case was dismissed."

"Oh God," Jonas whispered.

"Devlin had just learned about the dismissal. They were preparing to come back to the States when Casey…"

Jonas straightened and released my hand. "What? She what?"

"There were some complications with the pregnancy. She and the baby are fine but the doctors are worried about the stress she's under so she's on bed rest. Probably for the remainder of the pregnancy. She can't fly home."

Jonas paled. "I have to talk to her," he said, automatically jumping up.

Cole grabbed him gently and said, "She's okay, Jonas. We'll call her as soon as we're done here."

Jonas hesitated and then nodded and lowered himself back down. I could tell he was checking out so I turned my attention to Ronan.

"They need protection."

"Devlin's already hired some people. I sent Hawke to keep an eye on things."

I nodded. Michael "Hawke" Hawkins was one of Ronan's best men. I knew next to nothing about him but I'd seen him in action on more than one occasion. All of Devlin Prescott's wealth couldn't have found him a better man.

"What happens next?" Cole asked, though his eyes were on Jonas.

"If the plea is overturned next week, the D.A. will seek to re-indict and he'll want Jonas to testify in front of the Grand Jury. That's probably why Eduardo hired other guys to go after Jonas the other night…Benny was taking too long to get the job done."

I nodded and then stood up and moved closer to Ronan. I spared Cole a glance and saw understanding in his gaze. He knew what needed to happen. My eyes shifted to Jonas who seemed to be in a daze.

"Can you get me whatever you've got on Eduardo?" I said to Ronan.

Ronan didn't question my request. He simply nodded. "I'm looking into what can be done about Mateo."

"What?" Jonas said, his voice uneven. I heard his chair scrape back and then he was shoving between me and Ronan. "What are you doing?"

"Cole," I said but as soon as Cole stood, Jonas put his hand out to stop him.

"No!" he said firmly. "No, you are not doing this. I won't let you."

I settled my hands on Jonas's upper arms but he shrugged them off. "I said no!"

"Jonas…"

But he whirled on Ronan and shouted, "Do you even give a shit about him?" Ronan looked caught off guard by the attack but he didn't even get a chance to respond. "Did you really think you were saving him when you offered him a job where he fucking killed people?"

"Jonas," I said, grabbing Jonas's arm.

Jonas shoved me off but turned back to me. "I heard you and Cole last night. He's the one, isn't he?" he asked as he slashed his finger at Ronan. "The man you said offered you something you wanted more than anything else."

I nodded because I was too overwhelmed to speak. I'd meant to tell Jonas about my past when I was stronger...when I no longer had to worry about losing him over the betrayal I'd inflicted on him.

"He used you, Mace! He used your grief and turned it into something cruel and ugly. Because the man I've come to know and love doesn't enjoy going around killing people! If he'd cared for you even a little, he would have helped you find a way to live with your loss instead of exploiting it!"

I hadn't missed Jonas's indirect admission of love but I couldn't focus on it so I said, "Jonas, I knew what I was signing up for-"

"How could you? You were so filled with hate and anger and pain that you couldn't have known what it would do to you."

I felt my whole body go tight at Jonas's words. He couldn't know the toll my work had taken on me over the years. He couldn't know the same darkness that had consumed me after Evan's death had started to bleed back into me little by little with each life I took.

But he grabbed my face and said, "I get it, Mace. You wanted to protect kids like Evan and you did it the only way you knew how. But you're not like that monster who took Evan from you. You don't take pleasure in taking a life...any life!"

"I need you to be safe," I whispered.

"And I need you to be whole."

I closed my eyes to try and get my bearings but all I saw was the red laser sight bouncing on Jonas's chest as we'd stood in the gallery. If I'd been looking somewhere else or if my reflexes had been even a millisecond slower...

I steeled myself as I opened my eyes. I closed my hand over one of Jonas's wrists where he continued to gently cup my face. "I love you too much not to do this," I finally said.

Jonas's face fell and he dropped his hands. "And I love you too much to let you." With that, Jonas left the kitchen and I heard his footsteps retreat up the stairs.

Chapter 22

COLE

I ONLY HALF LISTENED AS MACE AND RONAN DISCUSSED THE PLANS for finding Eduardo. While I was glad to finally have a name to go with the threat against Jonas, I couldn't help but wish the three of us could stay in our little bubble for a little while longer.

I knew I was in love with both men. I'd suspected it when Mace and I made love to Jonas and I'd known for sure the second I saw the unknown car driving up the driveway. Mace had been doing a perimeter check and I'd been torn between checking on him and making sure Jonas was safe. I'd managed to do both but it was my fear that had made me realize that what I felt for Mace and Jonas went beyond attraction, beyond just being thrown together by highly charged circumstances.

For every mission I'd ever been on in my eleven-year career in the Navy, I'd never once let my emotions control anything I did in the field. The moniker of Ice Man had been borne of my complete and total focus, decisiveness and self-control. But they were the same qualities that now eluded me as I considered the pain and hurt Jonas and Mace were inflicting upon each other. As devastated as I was at the prospect of my sister's murderer going free, I was more worried about the impact it was having on Jonas and what would happen if Mace followed through on his plan to kill Eduardo and Mateo.

Because I knew deep down that Jonas was right. You never walked away unscathed after you ended a man's life. Never. It didn't matter who the man was.

As I got up from the kitchen table, Mace gently grabbed my wrist to stop me from leaving. I saw the unspoken question in his eyes and I nodded. We were okay.

"I'm just going to take the phone to Jonas so he can call Casey."

Mace nodded but he held my hand for a second longer before releasing me. I grabbed the burner phone off the counter and went upstairs. I expected to find Jonas in the small bedroom that he'd spent the first night in but he wasn't there. He was in our bedroom.

Ours.

God, I needed that in my life. I needed to share everything with Mace and Jonas. I didn't want to ever go back to it being just me. And as much as I loved each man individually, I needed it to be all three of us. I knew logistically it would be a challenge for the three of us to build a life together. People would pass judgement on us and even the most open minded ones would question how three men could have what we did. And if by some miracle I managed to get my father back to a lucid state, I wasn't sure he would accept my men. Hell, I didn't even know how he'd react to me being with even one man. My parents had always been accepting of homosexuals and had supported their fight to be treated as equals, but it was different when it was your own son.

The door to the master bedroom was closed, but I didn't bother knocking. Jonas was sitting on the edge of the far side of the bed, staring out the window.

"Here," I said as I handed him the phone. "Make sure your friend is okay."

"Thanks," Jonas murmured as he took the phone. I was glad to see he hadn't been crying but he looked so heartbroken that he may as well have been.

"He'll be okay, Jonas."

"I won't," Jonas whispered.

I tilted his chin up to force him to look at me. His eyes were shrouded with so much pain that I knelt down in front of him and put my hands on his hips. "Talk to me, baby."

"I can't be the reason he loses a little more of himself," Jonas said. "I want Eduardo and Mateo to pay for what they did. I want them stopped. But I don't want him to be the one who does it."

I didn't really know how to respond since I understood what Jonas was saying. But I also knew that even if Mateo and Eduardo both ended up behind bars, they could still reach Jonas.

Jonas must have sensed my hesitation because he said, "I need to call Casey."

I nodded and released Jonas and stood. I told myself all this would right itself once Mace had eliminated all the threats against Jonas, but as I looked over my shoulder and saw Jonas still sitting exactly as I'd left him, head hung, phone lax in his hand, I started to seriously wonder if any of us would be able to come back from this.

By the time I got back downstairs, Ronan was gone and Mace was sitting in the same spot at the kitchen table. But I stilled when I saw the bottle of beer sitting in front of him on the table. It was still full and capped but the way he was looking at it…

I sat down in the chair next to Mace and watched him as he studied the bottle of beer.

"My friends used to make fun of me in high school because I refused to even take a sip of alcohol at parties," Mace said quietly. "I saw what it did to some of them – how it made even the smartest guys do the stupidest things. I didn't want to do anything that would jeopardize my chances of getting into the academy so I never even tried it."

"The police academy?" I asked.

Mace nodded. "I knew when I was a little kid that that's what I was going to be when I grew up. Perfect childhood, perfect job, wife, kid…I did everything right and it paid off."

"How did you meet your wife?"

"I arrested her," Mace said with a chuckle.

"Really?"

"Yeah. She was part of an animal rights protest outside this lab where they did animal testing. She and a bunch of others had chained themselves to the front door so no one could get in or out. When I arrested her, she called me some pretty choice names. Even took a swing at me. I knew right then that she was the one for me."

I laughed at that. "What happened?"

"She came by the precinct to apologize. She actually asked me out before I even got the chance. A year later we were married and Evan was on the way." Mace looked up at me. "What about you? Was there anyone special?"

"No," I said, shaking my head. "A couple girls here and there in school. Lots of women between deployments but those were more about convenience," I admitted.

"No guys?"

I laughed. "No. This" – I motioned between us – "was a complete surprise. What about you? Did you always know?"

Mace nodded. "I knew when I was maybe twelve or thirteen that my attraction to guys was just as strong as it was to women, more so even. I fooled around with some guys in high school but it was always in secret. I finally told my parents when I was eighteen and I wanted to bring my first serious boyfriend home to meet them. We'd met in the academy. The relationship didn't last but my parents barely even blinked. They were just as welcoming to him as they'd been to the girls I'd dated."

"And Shel?"

"She knew I was bi. It didn't bother her – she knew she was it for me."

I hated even needing to ask but the not knowing was killing me. "Are you still in love with her?"

Mace didn't even hesitate when he said, "I still love her but I'm *in* love with you and Jonas."

I sucked in my breath at that because I hadn't expected the admission. At least not for me.

"It's the same, if you're wondering," I heard Mace say and I forced my eyes up, not even realizing I'd dropped them.

"What is?"

"What I feel for you. It's just as strong as what I feel for Jonas. I wouldn't be able to choose between you. I won't," he added firmly.

Something tight deep inside of me released. I *had* been worried that I was the odd man out in our relationship.

"Me too," I said and then I leaned over and kissed him. "I love you too," I said against his mouth.

A pent up rush of air fled Mace's lips and I realized he'd been struggling with the same feelings. I sealed my mouth over his and kissed him until we were both breathless before I released him and sat back down. As much as I would have liked to revel in this new development, I knew I needed to try and figure out how to mend the rift between Jonas and Mace.

"Mace, how did you meet Ronan?"

Mace began toying with the bottle of beer. "It was a year after Evan's death before the cops finally found the guy who did it. I'd taken a leave of absence from the force after we lost him and I'd started drinking every day to try and deal with it. The news that they had him helped snap me out of it but when the trial finally rolled around, everything went to hell and I just lost it."

"Was he acquitted?" I asked.

Mace nodded. "His attorney got this rookie cop to admit he'd fucked up the chain of custody with the DNA evidence. Fucker smiled at me and Shel when he walked out of the court room a free man. Told us he was sorry for our loss."

"I'm sorry, Mace," I said as I covered his hand with mine.

"Nothing mattered after that. Not my marriage, not my job, nothing. I drank until I blacked out. I fucked anything that moved and didn't even try to hide it. I stole money from Shel and my parents to buy booze and if anyone got in my way…"

"Your dad?" I asked, remembering Mace's admission about striking out at his father.

"He tried to take my keys away from me after he came to my house to check on me. Shel had already left me by then and I was stumbling around in the garage trying to get in my car." Mace choked up and his fingers laced with mine and squeezed hard.

"I left him there on the floor of my garage covered in blood. I didn't even remember doing it until I saw him the next day, his face all bruised up. I left after that. Never spoke to him or my mom again. I started staying in shitty motels and drinking myself into a stupor every night. When it got to be too much, I bought a gun off the streets. I met Ronan a couple weeks after I was released from the psych ward."

"How'd you meet?"

"He found me. No idea how. I was just sitting in this bar and there he was. He asked me all sorts of questions about my past, my job as a cop. I finally told him to fuck off. When he wouldn't stop hassling me, I took a swing at him. Then the cops showed up and I spent the night in the drunk tank. A cop I used to work with told me the news the next morning when he released me."

"What news?"

"My son's killer was murdered the night before. Shot execution style in his own house."

"Fuck," I murmured.

"The cop said if I hadn't been in the drunk tank, I'd have been their first suspect."

I shook my head in disbelief. "Ronan set you up so you'd have an alibi."

Mace nodded. "The guy raped another boy a few months after he was acquitted. The kid survived but had brain damage from lack of oxygen. The fucker had strangled him and left him for dead but some hikers found him in time."

"So Ronan took him out."

"He approached me a few days later. Offered me a chance to make sure what happened to Evan didn't happen to other kids. He got me sober and then gave me a reason to stay that way."

Mace looked at the beer in front of him. "I like testing myself," he said as he fingered the label. "I like knowing I'm still stronger than it." Mace twisted the top off the beer and then rose and went to the sink and dumped it out.

"Jonas was right, wasn't he?" I said.

Mace leaned against the counter but didn't look at me. "They were just monsters to me at first. I only saw the face of the man who killed my son when I looked through the scope of my rifle. I only heard Evan calling out for me when I pulled the trigger. Then I started seeing everything else. Their wives, their kids…the people who loved them because they didn't know the evil that lay beneath the suit and tie or the high powered job or the charming smile. The way my parents and Shel and Evan loved me."

"You're not like those men, Mace," I said.

"You sure about that, Cole? Because I wonder every time I pull that trigger if I'm doing it to protect future victims or if I'm doing it to avenge one past one."

I got up and went to stand behind Mace who was still leaning over the sink, his fingers gripping the edge. I wrapped my arms around him from behind and said, "Then don't do this, Mace. We'll find another way."

Mace's hand came up to cover one of mine. "He'll never be safe, Cole. You know that."

Mace turned around to face me. "One last job and I'm out." Mace kissed me before pulling free of my hold. "I'm going to go get some air."

I watched him leave the kitchen and heard the front door open and close. I went on autopilot after that and started preparing the dinner that I knew no one would eat.

❖

WHEN I OPENED THE DOOR TO THE MASTER BEDROOM, I WAS pleased to see two things. One, that Jonas had eaten a little bit of the dinner I'd left on the nightstand while he'd been in the shower and two, that he'd found the sketchpad and pencils I'd left on the bed for him. He was so engrossed with whatever he was sketching that he didn't even notice me until I stopped next to the bed.

"Thank you," he said as he lifted the sketchpad just a little. I nodded and climbed on the bed next to him and leaned back against the headboard. I'd bought the sketchpad the day before when I'd gone to check on my father. With all that had happened, it felt like a lifetime ago.

"The guy at the store picked out the pencils since I didn't know which ones would work."

"They're perfect," Jonas said and he leaned over and kissed me. I could tell that drawing had relaxed him because his whole body seemed more at ease. Unfortunately, his eyes still looked haunted.

"Did he leave?" Jonas asked, his fingers working furiously on whatever he was drawing.

"No. He just needed some time to clear his head. I saw him walking down the driveway an hour ago."

Jonas nodded.

"How are Casey and Devlin doing?"

"Okay considering what's happened. They were both really scared about possibly losing the baby but the doctors are sure she'll be able to carry it to term if she doesn't get too stressed. They wanted me to come out there to stay with them but I told them it wasn't safe."

He fell silent as he focused on his work.

"Can I see?" I asked.

He nodded and handed me the sketchpad. He leaned back against the headboard next to me so he could watch me flip through the pages. The first page had a picture of the horse from Casey and Devlin's barn as well as drawings of Ryan and Isabel Prescott. The second page had a picture of me and Mace lying in bed, my front to Mace's back, my head resting against Mace's neck. Mace's eyes were closed but mine were open. I knew exactly when the picture was from – it was from the night before when Jonas and I had made love to Mace and he'd fallen asleep between us. Jonas and I had just stared at each other as we listened to Mace's soft breathing.

"You knew it before I did," I said as I studied the expression on my face. I was a man at peace...a man who was exactly where he was supposed to be. I looked up at Jonas. "I didn't fully admit to myself that I was in love with both of you until this afternoon when Ronan arrived."

Jonas didn't say anything. He just took the pad from me and placed it on the nightstand on his side of the bed and then shifted until he was straddling me. I let my hands settle on his hips as he leaned down to kiss me. All the kisses Jonas had instigated with me had always started off tentative, as if he was unsure of what my reaction would be. This kiss…with this one he went straight in for the kill because by the time his tongue was done mating with mine, I was desperately rocking my hips up against him in an effort to ease the ache in my dick. I sat up so our bodies were flush and wrapped my arms around his waist as I took everything he gave me. When he was done, he pulled back and rested his forehead against mine.

"I always wondered what would have happened if things had been different. If I'd begged my parents to let me stay. If I'd picked some other city besides Chicago. If I'd pushed down on the razor blade just a little bit harder. I've stopped wondering because all those things led me to you. To this moment. It was all worth it," Jonas said, his voice breaking. "It was all fucking worth it." Then he kissed me again until we were both shaking.

"I love you, Cole," Jonas breathed against my lips. His fingers fisted in my hair as he ate at my lips and when my hands slid to his ass, he began rubbing against me, his erection brushing mine. When we separated again, his skin was flushed and his hands trembled as he cupped my face.

"Promise me you won't leave him," Jonas whispered. "You're strong enough to bring him back from wherever he has to go inside of himself to do this."

Jonas didn't wait for my answer. Maybe because he knew it was a promise I wasn't sure I could make. His fingers skirted over my sides before he lifted my shirt and dragged it over my head. He put just enough space between our bodies so he could pull his own shirt off and then he wrapped himself around me again. "Can I make love to you, Cole?"

My heart stuttered to a stop at the words. I'd been mentally preparing myself for this moment but I hadn't expected Jonas to take the initiative. And although I was terrified of the unknown, I still wanted it. I wanted that moment where I gave myself over to someone else's keeping. Where all I had to do was feel.

I hadn't even realized I hadn't responded in any way until Jonas suddenly stammered, "I'm sorry, maybe Mace should, since I've never-"

I silenced him with a kiss. "I want it to be you. I want us to have these firsts together."

Jonas was panting hard and I could already feel his soft skin slickening with sweat. I loved knowing how badly he wanted me. Our kisses quickly turned frantic and I could feel Jonas's fingers tugging desperately at the button on my jeans but before he could finish the task, we both heard the door open.

Jonas stilled as his eyes connected with Mace's and I felt all the tension return to his body. Mace wasn't faring any better because his eyes skimmed us with longing and then he was turning around.

"Mace," Jonas whispered.

Mace stopped but it took him a long time to turn around. When he finally did, he looked like he was preparing to hear the worst. But Jonas didn't say anything at all. And he didn't move off my lap. What he did next had my love for him flaring up in my chest.

He held out his hand to Mace.

And poor Mace just stared at Jonas's extended arm like he didn't know what it was. Then his face fell and I could see the relief there. Once he reached the bed, he took Jonas's hand in his and then leaned down to kiss him. It was soft and sweet and full of apology and while I knew it did nothing to solve the underlying issues between the two men, it was a truce of sorts. Mace cupped his hand around the back of my neck and kissed me in much the same way.

There were no words after that. Everything that was said was done with a look or a touch.

While Mace worked his shirt off, Jonas shifted his attention back to my pants. I tried to control my raging desire by forcing deep breaths into my lungs but then Mace was shifting me so that he was able to push my upper body flat on the bed. He unfolded his long body so that it was lying next to mine and he began teasing my lips with shallow kisses while Jonas scooted farther down my legs to pull my now open pants down. His hands coasted up my thighs at the same time that Mace began teasing my nipples with his calloused fingers. And then I felt Jonas's hand slide over my hardness with only the fabric of my underwear separating us. He gave me a few experimental strokes and then his fingers grabbed the waistband of my briefs and tugged them down and tossed them to the floor.

Mace's mouth had started exploring my jawline but I felt him still against me and I knew we were both focused on Jonas as he stared at my flushed, leaking cock. He looked so torn that I wanted to open my mouth to tell him that he didn't need to do this but Mace's fingers subtly pressed into my side. Whatever internal struggle Jonas was dealing with went on for several long moments. I wanted to curse my own dick for the way it twitched under Jonas's perusal. Jonas suddenly lifted his eyes up to mine and held there for a moment before he lowered his upper body and placed his nose against my groin and inhaled deeply. And when his fingers closed gently around the base of my dick and his tongue flitted over the crown, I nearly wept at the relief that flooded through me. After that, they showed me no mercy. Mace sucked my tongue into his mouth repeatedly as his hands roamed over every part of me he could reach. At one point, he took over stroking my dick with his hand when Jonas began licking my balls before sucking them into his mouth.

I couldn't stop the moans that fell from my lips and the only thing that kept me from bucking wildly beneath Jonas's teasing tongue was Mace's upper body pressed over mine. When Jonas sucked me deep into his mouth, I groaned against Mace's lips. "I can't, Mace. It's too good."

Mace smiled against my mouth. "He's just getting started, baby." Mace leaned back and dragged me up against his chest, supporting my shoulders so that I could watch Jonas work me over. But nothing prepared me for the sight of Jonas reaching his left hand up my thigh to my stomach so that he could twine his fingers with Mace's hand as it rested there.

"Jonas, I'm going to come," I warned as the pressure in my balls kept building and my skin drew tight across my body. Every tug of Jonas's lips had electricity shooting up my spine but it wasn't until Jonas's finger slipped between my cheeks and stroked over my hole that I exploded. I expected Jonas to pull off as I came but he began

SLOANE KENNEDY

swallowing me down. I heard Mace groan at the sight of my come spilling from between Jonas's lips and as my orgasm crested, I watched Mace drag Jonas up to us so he could crush their mouths together. Jonas's jeans scraped over my sensitive dick and I moaned as another tremor went through me. I tasted come as someone kissed me but I was still too overcome with the sparks that were still firing through me to know who it was.

Jonas's weight disappeared off my body and I managed to come back to awareness long enough to watch Jonas and Mace undressing each other, stealing kisses as they went. Once Jonas was naked, he crawled back on top of me and sought out my mouth again. I still felt sated from the orgasm but every time his tongue swept over mine, I could feel my body trying to find the energy to command my dick to respond. When the mattress dipped next to us, I heard Mace whisper in my ear to roll over. I didn't know what his plan was and I didn't care since the position meant I got to have Jonas beneath me. Although I could feel Jonas's erection between us, I still paid attention to his breathing and his body to make sure I wasn't scaring him. But his kisses remained as hungry and as needy as mine and he kept his arms locked around my neck.

I felt the bed move as Mace shifted farther down it but when his hands closed around my hips, I tensed. I hadn't realized I'd stopped kissing Jonas until I felt his fingers skirt through my hair and give me a gentle tug. "He's going to get you ready for me," Jonas whispered. "It's going to feel so good being inside you," he said as his tongue licked my lower lip before tugging it between his teeth. This sexy, confident side of Jonas had me intrigued and well on my way to rock hard again.

Mace lifted my hips until I was on my knees but he spread my legs wide and kept his hand on my back to keep me pressed up against Jonas. His rough palms began kneading the globes of my ass but when he split me open, my whole body locked up tight. Mentally I knew what went into preparing me to take Jonas inside of my body but the unknown of how it would feel was messing with my head.

180

"Talk to me," Jonas said softly as his hands roamed over my back.

"I'm nervous," I admitted.

"That it will hurt?" Jonas asked.

"Nervous that I won't be able to give this to you," I admitted. Because I knew even if there wasn't much pain, I might not like the act, no matter how gentle Mace and Jonas were with me.

"You and Mace have already given me enough firsts to last a lifetime, Cole," Jonas whispered.

I didn't get a chance to respond because at the exact moment I opened my mouth to speak, I felt hot, wet heat slick over my hole. I gasped first in surprise, then in pleasure as sensation flooded my nerve endings. I knew without a shadow of a doubt that it wasn't a lube covered finger pressing against me.

"Fuck," I groaned as Mace's tongue repeated the move and I managed to look over my shoulder to see Mace's face buried between the globes of my ass, his big hands holding me open. Another gentle lick had me hanging my head and I felt Jonas's fingers teasing a sensitive spot behind my ear. My knees began to shake under the strain of trying to hold my weight up and when I felt Mace begin licking me in long, heavy drags that started at my taint, drifted over my hole and slid up my crack, I gave up and dropped my weight on Jonas. Mace's sinful mouth only left me for a moment before it was back. I could feel his arms on the backs of my thighs so I knew he'd shifted his position so he was lying behind me.

A couple more licks had me rubbing my hard dick against Jonas's shaft but when Mace applied suction, I let out a hoarse shout. I knew I needed to distract myself or I'd come so hard that there'd be no way I'd be able to recover before Jonas could get inside of me so I lifted myself off of Jonas and said, "Slide up."

Jonas hesitated for only a moment before he did what I asked. I was glad the bed was king sized because it gave us plenty of room to maneuver until Jonas's beautiful, flushed shaft was beneath my hungry mouth. My body shook every time Mace licked me but when I felt his tongue press inside of me, I let out a string of curses. My whole body felt so tight, I was sure it would snap in two. I managed to look up at Jonas who had pushed up on his elbows. I knew he could probably see what Mace was doing to me because his mouth was parted and he kept licking his lips. I kept my eyes on him and smiled when I saw his eyes jump to me as soon as I drew the tip of his cock inside of my mouth. Since I'd done this just this morning to Jonas, the newness of it didn't frighten me anymore but I knew better than to try to take too much too fast. So I made up for my inability to deep throat him with intense suction.

Jonas thrust up into my mouth and I forced my throat to relax enough to take more of him in. Mace continued to torment my ass as I licked and sucked Jonas's cock until he was fisting my hair to hold me in place but I couldn't help but freeze when I felt cold lube replace the heat of Mace's mouth on my hole. Jonas seemed to sense the change because he gently pulled himself free of my mouth and moved so that he was lying pressed up against my chest as he rolled me to my side.

"Cole," I heard Mace say and I turned to look at him. He was on his knees, his glistening cock standing proud against his abdomen. "Do you want to keep going?" he asked.

"Yes," I said and then I looked at Jonas. "Yes," I repeated. Jonas smiled and kissed me. I focused on his mouth as Mace's finger began to press against me. I flinched as my outer muscles gave way under the incessant pressure and the sting that followed had me inhaling sharply. I was glad when neither man asked me how I was doing because I was too ashamed to admit that I was struggling to adjust to Mace's intrusion. How the hell was I ever going to manage it when it was Jonas's cock?

Mace had stopped moving as he waited for me to get used to the feel of him and I actually felt my body start to relax as the burning sensation eased somewhat. It flared up again as soon as Mace began moving again but I rode it out until I felt his hand press against me and I knew he was as deep as he could go. Jonas was running his hand up and down my side but I barely noticed because Mace pulled his finger almost all the way out before pushing it back in. I flinched as a spear of pain filtered through me but as Mace continued his gentle plunges and withdrawals, the lube began to ease his movements and I felt a spark of sensation start somewhere deep inside me. I finally noticed that Jonas's hand was slowly stroking my cock back to life, his drags matching the rhythm of Mace's finger. And when Mace pulled his finger free a moment later, I actually felt a pang of loss. But it didn't last long because then Mace was breaching me again, only this time with two fingers.

I groaned as another round of pain went through me but it was momentary and not as intense as the first round. Mace's plunges grew in intensity and then he curled his fingers inside of me. The added pressure messed with the rhythm I'd just started enjoying but then Mace hit something inside of me that sent fireworks directly to my dick. I knew enough from my very thorough internet search on anal sex to know that he was massaging my prostate but nothing had prepared me for the pleasure that ripped through me over and over at the contact. My erection was back in full force and I actually had to press my mouth against Jonas's chest to stifle the endless grunts and groans that kept spilling from my lips.

Mace straightened his fingers and began gliding them in and out of me and adding in a twisting motion. Every few strokes, he'd strike my prostate so I was always on the edge, even as Jonas gently pushed me onto my back and reached for a condom that someone had tossed onto the mattress at some point. I watched him through hooded eyes as he rolled the condom down his length and slathered some lube over the smooth latex but I was enjoying Mace's ministrations too much to worry about what would come next.

But when Jonas finally moved into position as Mace pulled his fingers free of my pliant body, I felt my unease come back. I did my best to keep my anxiety from my eyes but I didn't miss the way Jonas hesitated as Mace pushed my legs up. I watched as Mace dropped his lips to Jonas's ear and whispered something and then they kissed. Whatever Mace had said got Jonas moving and one of his hands opened me while I felt his cock nudge my hole. Mace eased down next to me and settled his hand on my chest.

"Just feel," he breathed against my mouth just before he kissed me. So that's what I did. I felt the smoothness of Mace's tongue as he explored every inch of my mouth. I felt the burn of Jonas's entry into my body as one of Mace's arms wrapped around my leg to pull it farther up, opening me for Jonas. I felt Jonas's eyes on me as he slowly worked his way past my resistant muscles. And I felt a sense of relief when my hole collapsed and my body stretched to accommodate his length.

But what I felt most was the perfection of what these two men were giving me. And I knew in that moment that I would do anything to keep it. Anything.

There was no pain as Jonas slid all the way inside of me, only a sense of fullness and a desperate need for him to move, to give me the exquisite friction Mace had stirred up in me. But instead of moving, Jonas leaned over me until his lips were right above mine. "I love you so much, Cole." He kissed me then and seconds later he was telling Mace the same thing and stealing his exhale of breath into his mouth. And then he reared back and began moving. Exquisite agony burned through me as he glided in and out of me with ease, his balls slapping gently against my ass. His arms were holding my legs open to take the burden off of me and I watched as Mace's hand trailed down my chest, past my cock and around my leg to where Jonas and I were joined. Jonas let out a sharp breath at whatever Mace was doing to him and then it was my turn because Mace's finger slid inside of me on top of Jonas's cock. The added pressure had me closing my eyes and reaching for my cock but Mace beat me to that too because his mouth licked over my length before sucking me deep.

I had no doubt that Jonas was suffering with the same raw need that I was as Mace pleasured us, because Jonas began slinging into me desperately, his fingers biting into my thighs where he was holding me. I couldn't speak or move as they controlled every aspect of what I was feeling. I managed to keep my eyes on Jonas as his eyes widened and his cock began to pulse inside me. I felt Mace's finger slide out of my body and his hand replaced his mouth at the exact moment that Jonas released my legs and dropped all his weight down on me as he began to hammer into me uncontrollably. Mace's hand was still stuck between us and he was jerking me off at the same frenetic pace that Jonas had set. Jonas's mouth seized mine as his orgasm hit him and I went over at nearly the exact same time. Jonas swallowed my shout of pleasure and he continued to hump into me as aftershocks hammered us both. I heard Mace let out a groan and felt his come splash against my ass cheek.

As we each came down, we ended up in a tangle of limbs and touches and kiss after kiss was speared across my mouth and I had no idea whose were whose and I didn't really care, because each and every kiss was perfect.

Fucking perfect.

But less than eight hours later, my perfect world shattered.

Because Jonas was gone.

Chapter 23

JONAS

I COULDN'T HELP BUT KEEP LOOKING OVER MY SHOULDER TO SEE IF the two burly men that the District Attorney had assigned to protect me were still standing outside the office door. Seeing their outlines through the glass of the upper half of the door made me feel marginally better, but I knew I wouldn't feel a hundred percent safe again until I was with Mace and Cole.

Since I couldn't bear to think of the way I'd left Cole and Mace in the pre-dawn hours two days earlier, I turned my attention back to the well-dressed man on the other side of the desk. Kyle Ridgefield was a good looking guy who had an air of confidence about him that said he knew his job and he knew it well. There'd been a brief moment when I'd first met him that I'd actually been reminded of the dream man I'd always pictured myself with when I was a kid, but as quickly as the thought entered my mind, it disappeared again because I already had my dream men. I just needed to hope that they would still want me after all this was over.

"So do you have any questions about tomorrow?" Kyle asked as he closed the file in front of him and clasped his hands over it.

I shook my head. Testifying in front of the Grand Jury about Carrie's murder would be easy compared to the day I would have to face Mateo in court and tell the world what he'd done. I'd just been relieved to learn that as soon as Mateo's plea deal had been tossed out, he'd been re-arrested for Carrie's murder before he could even walk out of the courtroom. But if the Grand Jury failed to hand down an indictment tomorrow, Mateo would be a free man.

"Well, if there's nothing else..."

"What about Eduardo?" I asked.

Kyle shook his head. "Unfortunately, we don't have enough to file charges against Eduardo and since the statute of limitations for what he did to you ran out several years ago, I'm afraid there's not much we can do at this point."

I shook my head. "It's not right," I said. "He shouldn't get to keep profiting from what he did to me."

Frustration went through me as I stood but the attorney put up his hand. "Wait, what do you mean by 'keep profiting'"?

"He showed me once how much money he made in just one day from one of the videos he made of me. Those plus the pictures... those aren't ever going to go away."

"Jonas, did he post the videos and pictures on the Internet?"

I nodded. The knowledge that even now there were men out there getting off on watching me being raped over and over again made me feel ill. I expected Kyle to tell me how sorry he was that that had happened to me but to my surprise, he actually smiled and then reached for his phone.

"Distribution and possession of child pornography is a federal crime. There's no statute of limitations," he said excitedly.

"But I don't have proof."

"Your affidavit would be enough to get us a warrant. We can check his computers, his financials."

I only half listened as he made a call to someone to discuss the next steps. My thoughts drifted back to where they'd been in the two days since I'd left Mace and Cole wrapped in each other's arms in the old farmhouse. Mace had actually woken up as I'd crawled over his big body and I'd been forced to make up a lie about needing to take a shower and then starting breakfast. He'd looked at me with such contentment in his eyes that I'd leaned down and kissed him and told him to go back to sleep before I could change my mind. I'd gone into the bathroom long enough to turn the shower on while I tugged on my clothes.

By the time I'd come back out, Mace had rolled against Cole's chest and had wrapped his arm around Cole's waist. I'd wanted nothing more than to crawl back in between them and go back to sleep. *Almost* nothing. And it was that one thing that I did want more that had had me hurrying down the stairs, taking Mace's car keys as well as all the cell phones and climbing into his car. The only thing I'd left behind were the guns and my sketchbook. I'd also left my watch behind since Cole had told me it was how Ronan had found us.

I'd known it wouldn't take long for Mace and Cole to make it to the nearest town or even to a neighboring property, but I'd hoped the few hours lead I had on them would be enough time for me to connect with the District Attorney in Chicago who was handling Mateo's case. Kyle had been thrilled to hear from me since he'd been looking for me for nearly a week. He'd taken care of the arrangements to fly me to Chicago and as soon as I'd arrived, I'd been swept off to a nondescript hotel on the outskirts of the city.

I'd half expected Mace and Cole to arrive at some point to try and drag me back out of harm's way but when they hadn't shown up last night, the self-doubt had started to trickle in and wreak havoc with my head. Maybe they hadn't really meant what they'd said when they'd whispered their words of love to me. Maybe I was just too damaged and not worth the effort of having to deal with my hang-ups. Maybe they just needed each other…

Asking Cole to let me make love to him had been an impulse and as soon as I'd done it, I'd feared that I wouldn't be able to make it perfect for him. When Mace had come into the room, I'd been torn between wanting him with us and wanting to force him to promise that he wouldn't go after Mateo and Eduardo. But then I'd seen the loss in his eyes and I'd known that I'd take any moment I could have with him and Cole, because I'd already known at that point it could very well be my last. Because I'd already decided what I would have to do to make sure Mace didn't lose any more of himself to the brutal world he'd relied on to stem the pain of losing his son.

"Okay, let's go ahead and get your statement written up," Kyle said, snapping me out of my reverie.

It took another hour to get everything down on paper and I struggled to keep my emotions in check as I described the sordid details of the many times Eduardo had committed my torment to film. When we were done, all I wanted to do was take a shower and try to rid myself of the filth the memories had left behind.

Kyle shook my hand and then escorted me back to the guys who'd been assigned to keep me safe. I couldn't remember their names and they didn't speak to me other than to tell me what to do as they escorted me from place to place. Both men flanked me as we walked towards the elevator.

"Jonas!"

At the sound of my name, I felt my heart soar at the same time that my stomach crashed. They'd come.

My bodyguards immediately shoved me behind them as we all turned and I could only get glimpses of Mace and Cole striding towards us. I saw Ronan at the end of the hallway but he stayed where he was.

A mix of emotions went through me at the sight of my men. I was thrilled that they'd come for me after all, but I knew they wouldn't understand why I'd done what I'd done, and we'd be back where we'd been two days earlier.

"Sir, I'm going to need you to stop right there," I heard one of the bodyguards say as he reached for his gun.

"No, no," I said quickly. "They're with me, they're friends," I said. "I want to talk to them."

The bodyguard didn't remove his hand from his gun but he kept it holstered. But neither man moved as Cole and Mace reached us.

"Get the fuck out of our way," I heard Mace growl.

"Sir, if you want to speak with Mr. Davenport, you'll need to arrange it with Mr. Ridgefield."

Shit, this was bad. No way Mace and Cole were going to let me go without talking to me. At least a dozen people were milling about in the hallway and many of them were stopping to watch the confrontation.

"Please," I said, grabbing one of the bodyguard's arms. "Just a couple minutes."

The man glanced down at me and then finally relented with a nod. He moved enough to let me pass by him but when he and the other bodyguard only took a few steps back, I knew my men and I were going to have an audience whether we liked it or not.

"What the fuck were you thinking?" Mace bit out as he dragged me into his arms. Since my answer would take a lot longer than the few minutes I'd been granted, I remained silent and just held on to him. His hold bordered on painful but I loved it. And then Cole was wrapped around me and while the hug wasn't as tight, his lips settled against my neck and I heard a long rush of air brush over my skin, like he'd been holding his breath in for a really long time. Guilt went through me as I realized how much my disappearance hadn't just hurt them...it had scared the hell out of them.

"Sorry," I murmured against Cole.

I felt Cole nod and then he was kissing me, not caring who watched. "Don't ever do that to us again."

I nodded. I turned my attention to Mace and grabbed his hand. "Please, please don't go after him," I whispered so my bodyguards wouldn't overhear. "The D.A. thinks he has enough for a warrant."

"Mr. Davenport," I heard one of my bodyguards call.

I gave him a quick nod and then turned back to Mace. "Promise me," I said harshly, desperately. I knew it was unfair to ask him to make that kind of promise but I didn't care.

"I promise," Mace finally said.

I could only hope he was telling me the truth because his eyes were hooded. I reached up to pull him down for a kiss. "Everything's going to be okay," I said against his lips.

Mace gave me a nod but I was the one who had to tug my hand free of his as I turned to go because he refused to release me. I'd gone a few steps when I turned to give Mace and Cole another quick look and I saw both of them turn their attention on a young, well dressed woman walking past us. Then everything was a blur.

One of them shouted my name as the woman turned towards me and then a hard body slammed into me as a gunshot rang out. I managed to see Mace wrestling with the woman who was holding a gun. He hit her hard enough to knock her down.

I knew it was Cole on top of me but I was having trouble getting my bearings since I'd hit my head on the floor. But that only lasted for a few seconds because I knew instantly something was wrong when Cole didn't move. And then I felt it – something warm and wet seeping into my shirt.

"Cole!" I shouted and gently pushed him off of me. "Oh my God," I whispered when I saw that the entire right side of his shirt was covered in blood. I sat there in stunned silence for a split second and then my instincts kicked in and I leaned over him and jammed my hands down on the hole that the blood was seeping from.

"Cole," I said desperately as I tried to get him to focus on me. His eyes were open but he was staring straight up at the ceiling so I didn't know if he was aware of me. "You're going to be okay," I said frantically. "Just stay with me, okay?" Cole finally looked at me and his lips parted like he wanted to say something but nothing came out.

"Mace!" I screamed. And then I just kept screaming Mace's name as I watched Cole's glassy eyes close.

Chapter 24

MACE

I HAD MY KNEE ON THE WOMAN'S BACK TO HOLD HER DOWN WHEN I heard Jonas shouting my name. The bodyguards had finally reached me and one began cuffing the woman as the other took possession of the gun that I handed him. But one look at Jonas had me scrambling off the woman and shoving past the bodyguard.

Jonas was covered in blood. Cole's blood.

"Call an ambulance!" I screamed to anyone who would listen as I reached Cole's side.

"Cole, hang in there, okay?" I said even though his eyes were closed. Jonas's hands were soaked in blood where he was pressing on the hole in Cole's side but when blood starting pooling beneath Cole on the floor, pure panic flooded through me.

Jonas kept saying my name but I knew I couldn't fix it. I couldn't do anything except watch the life blood of one of the men I loved seep out of him while the other man I loved begged me not to let it happen.

"Mace, you need to move back," I heard someone say. I knew in the back of mind before I even turned that it was Ronan but I couldn't comprehend what he wanted. And then he was grabbing me by the chin, his hold gentle. "Mace, let him go so I can help him," Ronan whispered.

Ronan never whispered. He never touched anyone unless it was to inflict pain.

I moved back and watched as Ronan pushed Cole up onto his side. Blood soaked through the back of Cole's shirt. "Mace, help Jonas keep pressure on his front. We need to slow the bleeding."

Ronan spoke with such calm authority that I found myself moving to Cole's other side. I put my hands on top of Jonas's and pushed as hard as I could. I felt Cole's body being pushed against us as Ronan applied pressure to Cole's back. People were running around us crying and shouting but all I heard was Jonas's harsh breathing. I couldn't look at him because I knew I wouldn't be able to hold it together if I did. But even when the paramedics arrived and pushed us both out of the way, I didn't want to touch Jonas.

Because I'd failed him.

I'd failed Cole.

I'd failed.

Again.

◉

It was Ronan who rode in the ambulance with Cole because he'd somehow managed to stem the worst of Cole's bleeding and had refused to release his hold on Cole even when the paramedics arrived. In fact, he was the one who'd begun barking orders at them and I knew from the things he'd said that he'd been holding out on me. I'd just assumed he had some type of law enforcement or military background but from the moment he'd taken charge of Cole's care, I knew he was much more than that.

I'd managed to snap out of my cocoon of paralyzing fear as soon as the ambulance had pulled away from the building. One of Jonas's bodyguards had directed us to a car and I'd climbed in back with Jonas. We hadn't touched or spoken at first because we'd both been too numb from the shock but when Jonas's fingers finally linked with mine, the contact unlocked my brain and I pulled him against me. I could feel his hot tears against my neck and I had no doubt he could feel mine as well.

Ronan was nowhere to be found when we arrived at the hospital, but a nurse directed us to a private exam room so Jonas and I could wash our hands while we waited for someone to tell us what was going on. While I logically knew we'd only been in the room for a few minutes, it felt like hours and as each minute dragged by, I grew more frantic that Cole was already gone and the doctors were just trying to get up the nerve to tell us.

I'd given up on trying to stand still and began pacing the small room as Jonas leaned back against the wall, his arms wrapped around himself.

When the door finally opened, I felt the bottom of my stomach drop out. Ronan stepped into the room, his face grim and I automatically reached for Jonas's hand and drew him next to me.

"He's alive," Ronan said. The words should have brought relief, but it was the way Ronan said them that had me biting so hard into my lower lip that I felt blood coat my tongue.

"He's in surgery now. The bullet hit his liver and he's losing blood as quickly as they can get it into him. If he survives the surgery, it will be touch and go for a while. You need to prepare yourselves."

I felt Jonas turn into me just before a sob engulfed him. I automatically wrapped my arms around him but any words of comfort I wanted to offer escaped me because I couldn't get past Ronan's last statement.

You need to prepare yourselves.

How the fuck were we supposed to do that? The only thing we were supposed to be preparing for was figuring out how to make a life for ourselves...a life we'd been given a glimpse of in our secluded little farmhouse in the middle of nowhere.

"I brought you guys some scrubs to wear," Ronan said uncomfortably before he put them on one of the chairs. "I'll be outside if you need me."

Jonas was shaking violently against me and I knew I wasn't faring much better. I pushed him gently back and lifted his chin so he had no choice but to look at me. "He's strong, Jonas. He'll pull through this."

"I'm sorry, Mace. I thought I was doing the right thing. It...it should have been me."

His words infuriated me and I shook him hard. "Don't you say shit like that to me, do you hear me? This is not your fault!"

But I knew Jonas didn't believe me. And I knew in that instance if we lost Cole, Jonas would never forgive himself.

Just like I had never forgiven myself.

And as I drew Jonas back against my chest, I knew what I needed to do.

Chapter 25

JONAS

I'D LOST ALL SENSE OF TIME AND MY SURROUNDINGS AFTER THE shooting. The only thing that registered for me was whenever Mace spoke to me, which wasn't often, and whenever a doctor or nurse appeared to give us updates on Cole's condition. We'd spent hours waiting in the Surgery waiting room before a doctor finally came out to tell us that Cole was still hanging on and that they'd had to remove part of his badly damaged liver. They'd finally gotten the bleeding stopped but not before Cole's heart had arrested on two different occasions. While the news that they had started the process of closing Cole up was positive, the doctor hadn't held back any punches when he said that Cole might not survive the night.

As we waited for Cole to be moved to the ICU where we would be able to see him, I felt Mace's fingers wind through mine where my hand rested on my thigh. I struggled to accept his touch because I didn't deserve it. I didn't deserve any kind of comfort because it was my actions that had put us here. It was my body that should have been lying on the operating room table, my insides exposed, my tired heart struggling to keep me alive.

I was glad when Mace's hand released me a moment later but when I heard a woman's soft cry, I looked up and saw an older couple standing a dozen feet away, their hands clutching each other's as they stared at Mace who'd risen from his chair. The woman had her free hand pressed against her mouth and tears were streaking down her face. I guessed the couple to be in their late sixties or early seventies. I knew instantly they were Mace's parents because the man looked so much like Mace that it was eerie. Mace's mother was tiny compared to the man she was standing next to. Her black hair was streaked with generous shades of silver and she was wearing a pair of white slacks with a floral print blouse.

If I hadn't felt so numb inside, I would have taken pleasure in watching Mace walk slowly up to his parents before wrapping his arms around both of them. It was a moment I'd hoped for since Mace had admitted to me that he hadn't spoken to his parents in years but I couldn't find the strength to share it with him.

I dropped my eyes back to my hands and felt the need to wash them again even though I knew no trace of Cole's blood lingered on my skin. I could still feel it though, hot and slick and relentless as it seeped past my fingers.

"Jonas, baby," Mace whispered as his big hands settled over mine. He was kneeling in front of me but I couldn't make myself look up. He did it for me by putting his fingers under my chin and lifting my head.

"I need to go and get Cole's father. He needs to be here in case..."

In case Cole didn't make it.

I managed a nod even though the idea of facing Cole's father and admitting I'd failed both his children made me want to throw up.

"Jonas, I'm so fucking scared," he whispered suddenly. His admission and the pain behind his words had my eyes filling with tears.

"Me too," I managed to say.

"I need to know that if the worst happens, that I won't lose you."

I swallowed hard. I couldn't fathom a life with Mace that didn't include Cole. But I also couldn't stomach a life without Mace either.

"If you still want me after all this is over…"

Mace leaned in to kiss me and whispered, "I will always want you, but that isn't what I meant. I can't lose you to yourself."

I dropped my eyes because I understood what he was asking and I couldn't promise that.

"I need you whole, Jonas."

I flinched as my own words were flung back at me. He wanted for me what I'd wanted for him. He needed me to forgive myself. And I knew that no matter what happened to Cole, he would want that for me too. Because they both loved me even when I couldn't love myself.

I nodded and then forced my eyes up. I didn't know if I could manage it but I owed it to him and Cole to try. I owed it to myself.

"You won't," I said firmly. "Go get Cole's dad."

Mace smiled and then he was dragging me into his arms. "Love you," he whispered against my ear as he clung to me. We held onto each other like that for a while and then he said, "Come meet my folks."

❋

MACE WAS ABLE TO SEE COLE FOR A FEW MINUTES BEFORE HE HAD to leave for the airport to catch his flight to New Haven. We'd known that Cole wouldn't be able to talk to us but the sight of him lying in the hospital bed, still as death, his pale skin almost as white as the thin blanket that covered him, was frightening. But nothing scared me more than the sight of the ventilator. Somehow the idea of knowing Cole couldn't breathe on his own scared me even more than all the blood that had poured from his body.

Mace had kissed me gently before he left and then he'd leaned over Cole and whispered something into his ear before kissing him on the forehead. That had been almost four hours ago. The nursing staff had brought Mace and me some chairs to sit in, and I'd drawn mine up as close to the bed as I could get it, and then covered Cole's hand with one of mine while I let my eyes settle on the up and down motions of his chest. The whooshing sound of the ventilator was strangely soothing and I didn't realize I'd fallen asleep until a hand settled on my shoulder.

"Cole?" I said hoarsely as my eyes flew to his face only to see he was still out.

"Sorry," Ronan murmured as he settled in the chair next to me. "I got you a latte from the coffee shop downstairs," he said. "They wouldn't let me bring it in here so I left it out at the nurse's station for you if you want to take a break."

I shook my head tiredly. "Did you help them find me?" I asked after I settled my hand back over Cole's.

"Yeah. They called me from a resort a few miles from the farmhouse. They weren't sure if you'd left with a certain destination in mind or just left," Ronan said.

I looked over at him in surprise. Had Mace and Cole really thought I'd left them because I didn't want to be with them?

"I kind of figured it was the former so I had one of my guys hack the airlines' databases until they found you. Once we realized you were in Chicago, I figured I'd tag along to make sure they didn't get themselves into too much trouble getting you back. They aren't the most...diplomatic when it comes to you," Ronan said with a slight smile.

"How did you know what to do to help Cole?"

The smile disappeared and Ronan actually dropped his eyes to his hands. He began tapping the pads of his fingers together one by one. The nervous gesture seemed so out of place for such a brash, confident man.

"I used to be a trauma surgeon," he finally admitted.

The answer surprised me and I wanted to ask how he'd gone from saving lives to taking them, but I doubted he'd answer me.

"Thank you for what you did," I said. "He wouldn't be here if you hadn't stepped in," I said softly and I placed one of my hands over his still jittery ones. He froze at the contact but didn't jerk away from me like I would have expected. But he clearly didn't like to be touched so I withdrew my hand.

"I do give a shit about him," Ronan said, his voice so low I struggled to hear him over the noisy machines surrounding us. It took me a moment to realize Ronan was talking about my accusation that he hadn't cared about Mace and that he'd used and exploited his vulnerabilities to get Mace to work for him.

"Ronan, I was upset…"

Ronan shook his head. "I didn't offer him the job to take advantage of him. I could have found dozens of guys willing to do what he did for the right amount of money. I knew he wasn't going to forgive himself for what happened to his son so I gave him another outlet for his hate. It worked for me so I figured it would work for him."

Ronan's statement was telling. He'd clearly suffered some unimaginable loss just like Mace had. "*Did* it work for you?" I asked.

But Ronan didn't answer me so I turned my attention back to Cole. "I'm going to take a few sips of that latte," I said as the exhaustion began to settle over me again. "Would you stay here with him?" I asked Ronan.

Ronan nodded.

I started to pass Ronan but then stopped and did something I knew he wouldn't like but that I felt compelled to do. I leaned down and wrapped my arms around Ronan and hugged him. "Thank you for saving both of them."

Ronan felt as stiff as a board in my hold so I quickly released him and left the room without looking back. I found the latte at the nurse's station and took a few sips but as I was putting it down, the top popped off and some of the warm liquid splashed all over my hand. I grabbed some tissues from the end of the counter and cleaned up the mess I'd made but I knew the stickiness on the back of my hand would bother me until I cleaned it off so I looked around for my bodyguard to let him know I was going to the bathroom. Only one of the men had stayed with me after the shooting. The other one had presumably stayed behind to work with the police to deal with the shooter who'd started shouting almost immediately that she'd done it because Eduardo had threatened to kill her if she didn't.

I finally spotted the big man talking on his cell phone at the far end of the hallway. I waited for him to turn around but figured it would take just as long to get his attention as it would take for me to go and wash my hands so I walked down the opposite hall until I reached the men's room. There was only one other man in there when I entered and he nodded at me as he walked out. I washed my hands and then leaned my face over the sink so I could scrub my face. The cold water worked wonders to soothe my tired, pained eyes.

I was in the process of wiping my face with a paper towel when I noticed someone approach me from behind. The man, presumably a nurse or orderly based on the scrubs, didn't move to one of the other sinks, and before I could move out of his way, my head was slammed forward against the mirror. Pain exploded behind my eyes at the contact and then a hand wrapped around my throat, and I was dragged back several feet until my back hit the wall at the far end of the bathroom. Blood dripped over one of my eyes but I was still able to make out Eduardo's face with the other.

The man didn't look any different than he had nine years ago when he'd held me down and told me to be a good boy for him and it wouldn't hurt as much. His long, greasy black hair was slicked straight back and his pockmarked face made his beady eyes look too small for his face. His putrid breath washed over me even before he started speaking.

"I knew from the first time I saw you that you were going to cause me all sorts of problems, you little shit," Eduardo sneered as his fingers dug into my throat, cutting off my air supply.

Tears stung my eyes as my body began to yearn for air and I tried kicking out at Eduardo. All I managed to get was his shin and he punched me in the stomach with his free hand, stealing what little air I had left in my system.

"Such a shame," Eduardo murmured as he pressed his mouth against my ear. "You were my favorite fuck. A little bit of tears, a little bit of fight. I still get hard every time I watch our movies together…the way you kept begging me not to hurt you."

Eduardo's fingers eased off my throat just a fraction, enough for me to suck in a tiny bit of air.

"Beg me like that again, Jonas. Beg me not to hurt you…"

I wouldn't have said the words even if I'd had enough air to speak so I spit in his face instead. Rage mottled his features and his fist slammed against my cheek. Then both of his hands wrapped around my throat and any scraps of air I'd managed to pull into my lungs disintegrated and I began gasping desperately as I clawed at his arms.

And then he fell away from me and I collapsed into a heap on the floor. As I tried to draw in breath, I saw Ronan striding towards us, a gun in his hand. Eduardo was just feet from me, screaming in pain, holding on to his knee which seemed to be gushing blood. It took me a second to realize that Ronan had shot Eduardo there to force him to release me.

I expected Ronan to hold Eduardo there until help came, but he stepped past the moaning man and came to stand in front of me, his legs blocking my view. I closed my eyes when I heard the gun discharge again. I opened my eyes just in time to see Ronan using what looked like a piece of fabric to place a knife in Eduardo's lax hand and then he was flexing Eduardo's hand around the handle. Then Ronan knelt in front of me and put his hand on my chin as he examined my face.

"It's over," he whispered and then he stood and placed his gun on the bathroom counter and held up his hands. My only thought after the chaos that ensued as security guards stormed into the bath-room, was that I needed to get back to Cole.

Chapter 26

MACE

I ACTUALLY STUMBLED WHEN I WALKED INTO THE PRIVATE ROOM that the police officer had pointed me towards. The cops had told me what had happened when I arrived at the hospital, but they hadn't fully prepared me for the damage that Eduardo had inflicted upon Jonas. A large gash that had already been stitched was just above his left eye and his left cheek was bruised and swollen. Bruises also covered almost his entire neck. When he saw me, he stood on shaky legs and it took every effort not to embrace him too hard because I didn't know if there were other injuries I couldn't see.

"Cole?" Jonas asked.

"Still out," I said quickly. "My parents are with him. His father too."

"Just a couple more questions, Mr. Davenport, and we'll be done," the police officer who'd been questioning Jonas said.

Jonas sat and I wrapped my hand around his as I pulled up a chair next to him. The cop had only agreed to let me in the room with Jonas if I didn't interfere with the interview.

"When you say Mr. Santero threatened you, did he have the knife out?"

I felt Jonas squeeze my hand hard before he said, "I...I don't remember. It all happened so fast. I couldn't breathe. I saw it when he went after Ronan."

"And Mr. Grisham shot Mr. Santero in the knee first?"

Jonas nodded. "Ronan came up to me to make sure I was okay and that's when I saw that Eduardo had the knife."

The police officer nodded. "Thank you," he said as he stood.

"Officer, Ronan saved my life."

"The arrest was standard procedure. This was a clear cut case of justification. I'll talk to the D.A. as soon as I get back to the precinct and I'm sure we'll have Mr. Grisham out of there in a few hours."

As soon as the police officer left, I stood and drew Jonas into my arms. "Are you hurt anywhere else?" I asked.

Jonas shook his head. "He saved my life, Mace."

I forced some air into my lungs. Knowing I'd come so close to losing both of my men today was threatening my ability to stay upright. I'd been going on adrenaline from the time I'd heard Jonas call my name and seen Cole covered in blood and I knew when I did crash, it was going to be mind-numbing.

"Did Eduardo cut you anywhere else?" I asked as I examined the wound over Jonas's eye.

Jonas stilled. "There was no knife," he whispered. "Ronan planted one on him afterwards."

"You told the cops-"

"I get it now," Jonas interrupted. "Men like Eduardo...they don't stop. They never stop. He would have kept coming after me. Ronan knew that."

I leaned down to press my lips against Jonas's head. "Are you okay with covering for him?"

I felt Jonas nod against my chest. "I need to see Cole," he said.

I nodded and took his hand and led him out of the room.

"How's Cole's dad?"

"Struggling," I admitted. "I was lucky enough to find him relatively lucid when I got to their house."

The encounter with Cole's father had been an ugly one. Mostly because I hadn't been content for Cole's father to just agree to come to Chicago with me to see his son. I'd shown the man no mercy when I ripped into him for putting his grief and his need to drink above his own son. If he'd been drunk, I knew I never would have gotten through to him, but he'd been aware enough to hear my words and when I warned him that he stood a good chance of losing his son today, I'd gotten a glimpse of the man I knew Cole had idolized.

"I need to talk to the staff here and see if they can help him detox so he can be near Cole as much as possible while he recovers."

Jonas tugged me to a stop. "He agreed to get sober?"

"He agreed to try," I clarified. "I think it's the most we can hope for."

I got us moving again and when we got to Cole's room, I was disappointed to see there'd been no change. My parents both stood as soon as we entered. Calling them had been one of the hardest things I'd ever had to do, but I'd known that if I expected Jonas to find a way to get past the punishment he was inflicting upon himself for what had happened to Cole, I needed to do the same. And truthfully, I'd needed them. As much as I needed to be strong for Jonas if the worst happened, I needed them to be strong for me.

As soon as my dad had answered the phone and I told him who it was, he began crying and I heard him call my mother's name. There'd been lots of shuffling of the phone as my dad put me on speaker, and then my mom had said my name and the familiar sound had washed over me, and I'd had to sit down in one of the waiting room chairs because my knees had gone weak. To my parents' credit, they hadn't asked a lot of questions when I said I needed them. They had just asked where and then they'd told me to hold on, that they were on their way. I hadn't told them I was involved with two men but I'd figured they had probably come to that conclusion themselves by now considering I told them the man I loved had been shot and then a minute later they'd seen me kiss Jonas.

"There's been no change," my father said as he embraced me and gave me his seat. My mother enfolded Jonas in her arms and asked him if he was all right. Jonas hugged her back and I couldn't help but think how right he looked there...he'd needed a mother for so long and he finally had one. My parents left us with the promise that they would be in the waiting room since there was a limit to how many people could be in Cole's room at once.

Cole's father had pulled his chair up as close to Cole's head as he could get and was stroking his son's hair. He kept repeating, "I'm here now," every once in a while. I could see his hands shaking and I knew I would need to talk to the staff sooner rather than later, but I needed a moment to drink my fill of Cole. While he hadn't necessarily improved since I'd left, he hadn't gotten worse and the doctors had assured us that that was a good sign. I knew Cole was a fighter and I knew he had a lot to fight for. I just hoped it was enough.

I had my answer an hour later when Jonas shook me awake and I saw Cole's eyes were open and looking straight at us.

※

"ARE YOU SURE YOU'RE UP FOR THIS?" I SAID TO COLE AS I HELPED him out of the car.

"How many more times are you going to ask me that?" Cole groused even as he leaned heavily against me until he got his balance. I helped him up onto the curb and Jonas immediately took his hand. I managed to close the car door without releasing my hold on Cole and I didn't remove my arm as we began the short walk up the path.

"You can let go now, I'm good," Cole said.

"I know you are," I responded but I didn't remove my arm. Cole shook his head and smiled.

In the four weeks since Cole had been released from the hospital, he'd gotten used to Jonas and me hovering over him. He'd complained about it at first but when he'd realized it was mine and Jonas's way of making sure he was still really with us, he'd relented and let us mother him.

We'd ended up moving into Cole's parents' house after leaving Chicago because it didn't have a lot of stairs and because we knew

Cole's father could use the support. The man's discipline and drive had been exactly like his son's, and while he'd struggled terribly during his withdrawal period, he'd never wavered and he'd managed to visit Cole on multiple occasions while he remained in the ICU. We'd stayed in Chicago for the two weeks that Cole remained admitted and I'd taken Cole's father to daily AA meetings. Once we'd gotten back to Connecticut, we'd found Cole's father an outpatient rehab program that would help him deal not only with his alcoholism, but with his grief over the loss of his wife and daughter as well.

Cole's father had admittedly struggled to understand that his son was involved with two men, but he'd come around quickly as he realized what Jonas and I meant to Cole and he to us. But living under the same roof with Cole's father had put a moratorium on sex even after the doctor had given Cole the all clear. Whenever we started sniping at each other for even the most trivial of infractions, Cole and I would head down to Jonas's studio where he'd go during the day to paint and insist he take a break. His bed was a tight fit for the three of us but that only forced us to try a bunch of new positions.

Jonas's safety had continued to be a concern in the days that followed Eduardo's attack, especially after Mateo was released from jail since the D.A. had had to postpone the Grand Jury hearing until Jonas was in a position to testify. I'd called Ronan the day we'd learned that Mateo had gotten out and asked him if he could spare some men to help me watch Jonas, but he hadn't answered. After several hours with no word from Ronan, I'd been in the process of calling Mav and some of the other men I was on a first name basis with to see if they would help me off the books when I got a text from Ronan that simply said, *It's done.* I had an idea of what he'd meant but it wasn't confirmed until I watched the news that night and saw the story about the pimp who'd been released from prison only to be shot and killed a day later in a drug deal gone bad.

I hadn't known that Ronan had stayed in Chicago after he'd been cleared of any charges relating to Eduardo's death, so I hadn't had a chance to thank him. I'd finally managed to reach him a few days after Mateo's death, but he'd brushed off my efforts to thank him for everything he'd done. I'd ended the call by telling him I was out and he'd simply said, "I know," and hung up on me.

"Down here," I said as we reached the third row of grave markers. Jonas turned into the row and led us down it until I told him where to stop.

I drew in a deep breath at the sight of my son's headstone. It was the first time I'd seen it since the funeral and while the pain of his loss radiated through me, it no longer felt as insurmountable as it once had. Jonas released Cole's hand and stepped forward to place a bouquet of flowers in front of the headstone and then he came around to my other side and wrapped his arm around me. It was my favorite position – me between the two of them.

Jonas had only ever wanted me to be whole but I knew now that whole for me meant being a part of them.

"Happy birthday, Evan," I said quietly as I reached into my pocket and pulled out the Matchbox car and stepped forward to place it on the top of the smooth marble headstone. I let my fingers linger there for a moment before stepping back. Jonas leaned his head against my shoulder and Cole wrapped his arm around me as they gave me the moment of silence I needed to remember my little boy. I didn't bother to imagine what Evan would have been like at fifteen, just like I no longer dwelled on how or why he'd been taken from me because the what ifs of life served no purpose. I focused on the time I'd had with him and as I began accepting my loss, I started sharing those memories with Cole and Jonas.

"Mace?"

I turned at the sound of my name and felt a wave of heat pass through me at the sight of Shelby standing at the end of the row, a baby in her arms.

"Shel," I breathed.

Although I'd started rebuilding the relationship with my parents, I hadn't yet had the courage to reach out to Shelby. While the things I'd done to my parents were horrendous, my treatment of Shelby had been so much worse because I hadn't been there to grieve with her when she needed me. I'd also thrown all her words of forgiveness for my part in our son's death back in her face.

Shelby smiled widely and began walking towards us. She was more beautiful than ever with her long blonde hair tied up in a sleek ponytail. Her yellow sundress flowed around her legs as she picked her way down the walkway towards us.

I stepped past Jonas once she reached us and wasn't surprised when she pulled me against her for a hug. "I've been so worried about you," she whispered.

"I know, I'm sorr-"

Shelby put her fingers over my mouth to stop my words and then she leaned in to hug me again. "Welcome home, Mace."

I sighed and wrapped my arms around her, mindful of the baby between us. "Shel, I have some people I want you to meet," I said and then I pulled back enough so I could introduce her to my men.

Chapter 27

COLE

"I THINK IT'S PERFECT," I SAID AS I SAT DOWN IN THE BAY WINDOW and looked around at the clean walls and polished hardwood floors. "When can we move in?" I asked Mace as he closed the closet he'd been checking.

"As soon as we stop at the furniture store and order a bed," Mace said as he came up to me and leaned down and covered my mouth with his.

I shuddered at the feel of his tongue sweeping over mine and when he finally let me come up for air, I said, "I'll pay for the same day delivery charge."

Mace chuckled. "I think we need to break it to your father first," he said.

It was my turn to laugh because somehow the tables had turned in the three months we'd been living with my father. "After last night, I don't think he'll have a problem with it."

Mace looked at me as he settled down on the bench next to me. "Mrs. Pellano, again?"

I nodded. "Caught them making out on the living room couch like a couple of teenagers. I think I permanently damaged my eyes."

As Mace laughed, I marveled over the change my life had taken since the day I'd walked into Jonas's studio to find out why my sister had been stolen from me.

My father's journey to sobriety hadn't been an easy one but he'd been diligent in working his program and on the occasions where he'd been close to breaking, Mace had recognized the signs and went with him to AA or got him in touch with his sponsor. He'd also started seeing a therapist to deal with the brutal way Carrie had been taken from us, and I'd accompanied him on more than one occasion.

After waking up in the hospital, I'd been confused by what was happening and how I'd gotten there. I remembered nothing of the shooting and I'd struggled to understand not only my injuries but the ones I'd seen on Jonas's face. But the hardest part was the guilt I'd seen in Jonas's eyes as he told me how sorry he was for what had happened. I'd been prepared to lay into him for blaming himself but then Mace had leaned over and kissed me and then whispered, "He's working on it," in my ear. That was enough to silence me.

Having my father at my bedside had torn me up because I could see how he was suffering as he struggled through his withdrawal symptoms. But he only left when he physically couldn't bear it anymore and had to be sedated to get through the worst of it.

In recent weeks, he'd started doing some consulting work for the Navy and when Mrs. Pellano had asked him over to her house for dinner, he'd gone. I hadn't initially liked the idea of him with my mother's best friend but when he came back home looking more at ease than he had in a long time, I'd realized that it would take time for me to get used to seeing him with any woman who wasn't my mother. I knew it would be hard to leave my father but his therapist and sponsor had assured me that he was ready and that he had the tools and resources he needed to deal with his addiction.

The townhouse Mace had found was only a few miles from Jonas's studio and I knew that would thrill Jonas since he'd been making the daily commute back and forth from New Haven after Mace had finished the repairs to his studio. He taught daily art classes and spent the rest of his day painting, but no matter how long he worked, he always made the long drive home to be with us.

Mace had started working for a local security firm that specialized in protection training. His relationship with his parents had blossomed and we spent at least one weekend a month with them in Philadelphia. Shelby, her husband and their daughter were constant fixtures at the elaborate family dinners Mace's mother would put together during our visits. My father had come on a few visits as well.

My own job hunt had been trickier since I'd decided against returning to the Navy. As much as I knew Mace and Jonas would have supported my choice to reenlist, I knew that being away from them for extended periods of time wouldn't work for me. And in truth, I'd had enough war to last a lifetime. I was still mulling my options for pursuing a career in law enforcement since I doubted I'd ever be suited for a nine to five office job. Jonas had mentioned how hot I'd look in a uniform, so there was that too.

"We should get going," Mace said as he glanced at his phone. "He should be wrapping up his last class soon."

After a quick stop at the furniture store to pick out our new mattress, we headed to Jonas's studio which was in complete chaos when we arrived. Jonas's students were in the process of being picked up, and most of the eight and nine year olds were showing off their artwork to whatever parent or loved one was picking them up. Most of the action was in the actual studio but a few of the kids and parents were exploring the gallery where a good number of canvases hung. Jonas swapped out the artwork every week and threw elaborate "openings" so the kids could show off their creations to the community. Mace and I had attended most of them and we were never prouder of Jonas than when he was in his element making each and every kid feel special.

As we made our way into the studio, we saw Jonas saying his goodbyes to several kids who were giving him hugs and speaking in rapid fire about what they would be working on the following week when they returned. Jonas gave each child his undivided attention as they spoke, but he did send me and Mace a wink when he spotted us. It took a good twenty minutes for the studio to be completely cleared and locked up for the night.

"I thought your dad was cooking tonight," Jonas said to me as he began cleaning up.

"Change of plans," Mace said.

Jonas paused and then smiled. "Mrs. Pellano again?" he said with a laugh and I groaned. He kissed me and said, "I think they're cute together."

Before he could get away, Mace snagged him by the waist and drew him in for a bone-melting kiss that had me growing hard with need almost instantly.

"We have a surprise for you," Mace murmured against Jonas's lips. "Two, actually," he said. "Can you leave this for tomorrow?" he asked as he nodded towards the canvases that needed to be moved to a back room to dry.

Jonas was breathless from his kiss so he just nodded and grabbed Mace's and my hands and led us towards the stairs. As soon as we were inside his apartment, Jonas and Mace were all over each other and I began stripping off my jacket in anticipation. Then Jonas was in my arms, his tongue greeting mine. "Hi," he finally murmured against my lips.

"Hi," I returned with a smile.

"You mentioned a surprise," Jonas said even as his hand began stroking over my erection.

"Two," Mace corrected. He pulled a piece of paper from his jacket pocket and handed it to Jonas. "Happy birthday, baby," he said before he brushed a sweet kiss over Jonas's mouth.

Jonas's real birthday had been the day after I'd gotten shot but predictably, no one had cared or noticed, least of all Jonas. But it had taken weeks to realize we'd never made up for it so Mace and I had spent the last several months plying Jonas with little gifts here and there and wishing him a happy birthday to make up for it. He'd told us after the first few that it wasn't necessary but he always lit up whenever we did it, so we'd already decided it would be an ongoing thing until his next birthday.

Jonas released me long enough to take the lease and look over it. "It's ours?" he whispered.

Mace nodded. "Cole loved it too, so we signed the lease."

Jonas threw his arms around Mace and then me. "When are we moving in?"

"Our bed will be there tonight," Mace said. "So we have about three hours to kill. Any ideas on how we should do that?"

"I can think of a few," Jonas said as he dropped the lease on the kitchen counter and reached for the hem of his shirt. "Wait, you said I had two surprises," he said.

I smiled and said, "The second one needs to be unwrapped."

Jonas watched in confusion as I moved in front of Mace and turned him so Jonas could watch. I began unbuttoning his shirt after he stripped his jacket off, but I couldn't keep my mouth off him and we spent more time kissing than anything else. One glance at Jonas showed that he'd lost all interest in his surprise too because he was stripping off his own shirt. Jonas's sexual confidence had grown over the weeks and while he still hadn't been ready to give himself to us completely, he'd become a master at working both me and Mace over until we were boneless with need.

I finally managed to get the rest of Mace's shirt unbuttoned and then turned him so he was facing Jonas. I pulled Mace's shirt away as he shrugged it off and then we both waited as Jonas eyed Mace's impressive chest.

"No," Jonas said a second later. His eyes lifted to Mace's and he smiled wide. "You didn't!"

I laughed and watched as Jonas closed the distance between them to get a better look at Mace's newly pierced nipple. Jonas trailed his fingers over it but when he gave it a tug, Mace winced and said, "Go easy, it's still a bit sore." Jonas's response was to bend his head and drag the flat of his tongue over Mace's nipple before circling it with his entire mouth.

"Fuck," Mace muttered.

"Better?" Jonas asked coyly.

Instead of answering him, Mace kissed him and then they came after me.

Which I was perfectly fine with.

214

Chapter 28

JONAS

As soon as I said the words, "I'm ready," Cole and Mace both froze. It would have been comical if I hadn't been so nervous.

Since we'd been reluctant to take our hands and mouths off each other for the time it took to get undressed, it took us several long minutes to finally make it to my bed at the far end of the apartment. Now, Cole was at my back kissing a path down my neck while Mace was in front of me, his hand stroking over my cock. They both stilled their movements and then Mace was gently cupping my face and saying, "You know it doesn't matter, right? What we have is absolutely perfect."

"I know, but I want it all," I said. "I want this, Mace. I've never been more sure of anything in my life." I saw Mace look over my shoulder at Cole and I knew I would never get tired of that. How they were so in tune with each other to make sure I got what I needed.

Since the shooting, I'd struggled with forgiving myself like I'd promised Mace I would, and that made me think of the things Ronan had said to me. Mace had punished himself for so long that he'd needed something stronger than his own self-hatred to be able to make it through each day. Ronan had given him that, but it was the absolution that he'd gotten from the people he'd hurt the most that truly set him free.

It had taken me a while to understand that my own absolution had to come from myself. Because despite all the things Eduardo and the men who had come after him did to me, I hadn't ever truly forgiven myself for believing I'd done something to deserve what had happened to me...that I'd brought it upon myself because of my foolish decision to accept Mateo's help so long ago when I'd gotten off that bus. It was one of the only things Mace and Cole couldn't give me but they'd given me the strength I needed to give it to myself.

Neither of my men said anything after that because they didn't need to. I knew all I had to do was ask them to stop and they would. They both picked up right where they'd left off and by the time Mace dropped to his knees in front of me, I was quivering in desperation for relief. But that only lasted for as long as it took for Cole to run his hands over my ass before spreading my cheeks apart. Because then my nerves came back at full speed and even though I'd seen Mace and Cole do this to each other, had done it to them myself, I still couldn't get past the fear that it would bring back the darkness of my past.

I locked my knees at Cole's first swipe of his tongue over my hole but it wasn't until Mace stood up and kissed me and whispered, "Breathe," against my mouth that I realized I hadn't been doing that. Releasing the pent up air in my system helped. Mace stepped into me so that our bodies were lined up and I felt his hands replace Cole's so that he was the one holding me open as Cole flicked at my entrance. By the third pass of his tongue, I was truly afraid this would be one part of lovemaking that I wouldn't be able to get into but then I started to feel a tingle in my belly as Cole kept up the gentle kisses. Mace never let up on my mouth so my senses went into overdrive as my body tried to adjust to the dual torture.

Minutes could have been hours for all I knew as they each teased me, and when Cole pulled his mouth away from my body, I actually reached behind me to try and stop his retreat. But then Mace was lowering us both to the bed, me on top of him, and I felt

Cole settle in behind me. He went right back to kissing, sucking and licking my hole as Mace made love to my mouth. I was so hot by the time Cole dribbled lube on my opening that it actually felt good against my heated skin. I tried not to tense when Cole's finger began to push inside of me but I couldn't help it.

It didn't hurt exactly, but it was uncomfortable. Mace kept up his kissing so I tried to focus on that and I really enjoyed the feel of Cole's tongue running up and down my spine as he continued to finger me. I was panting by the time he got all the way inside of me. The burn was sharp and the tugging sensation as he began to withdraw his finger felt strange, but when he massaged my prostate, I groaned against Mace's mouth.

Mace chuckled and said, "Did Cole find your sweet spot?"

I only managed a nod because Cole kept rubbing circles over my gland and I was sure my head was going to blow off as the ecstasy inside of me began to build.

"Do you want Cole to make you come before we get inside you?"

I managed a nod and let out a muffled moan against Mace's chest as Cole increased the pressure. My dick was pressed up against Mace's balls so Cole had easy access to it and began giving it long, hard tugs. Mace's hands went to my hips so that he could push me back and forth onto Cole's finger and the added friction in between strikes on my prostate had me begging them to let me come. When Mace finally whispered in my ear to let go, I did just that and cried out in relief as my orgasm overtook me. My body clamped down on Cole's finger as the climax continued to roll through me and each subsequent tug as he continued to push into me had me seeing stars as my release went on and on. When Cole finally pulled his finger free of my body, all I could do was lay there. And when he pushed two fingers into me, I was too worn out to feel the added burn.

I was still lying on top of Mace as Cole continued to prepare me and I reveled in the feel of his rough hands dragging over my sensitized skin. He touched me everywhere he could reach and continued to pepper me with sweet, drugging kisses that soothed me at first but then started to build up my need again. I heard the cap on the bottle of lube being opened behind me and I fought back the tension that threatened to overwhelm me.

Mace sat up, taking me with him. He leaned me back against Cole who was kneeling between Mace's spread legs and I stilled when I saw him take the bottle of lube from Cole and slather a generous amount on his dick.

I could feel Cole's slickened cock bumping up against my ass and his arms wrapped around my chest as he skimmed kisses along my neck. Once Mace tossed the bottle of lube aside, he pulled me against his chest and lifted my hips. But it was Cole's hand who maneuvered Mace's cock into position and I realized they were going to let me control the pace of taking Mace inside of me.

Mace leaned back and used one arm to brace himself and left the other on my hip as Cole guided me down. I felt Mace's tip press against me, but I knew I'd need a lot more pressure to get it inside of me. The burn was intense as I forced Mace's crown past the resistant outer muscles, but something about the idea of knowing he'd be filling me soon had me pushing past the discomfort. I gasped when Mace's first few inches slipped inside of me. We'd been going without condoms for a while so I knew the heat of being inside someone bare was intense but I hadn't expected the pleasure of feeling the unique texture of Mace's cock to feel so good against my inner walls. I raised myself up a little bit before dropping back down, and I moaned at the burn that shot through me and then changed over to something else. I did it again over and over until I couldn't get any more of Mace inside of me.

I hadn't realized I'd closed my eyes at some point but when I opened them, I saw that Mace had his head flung back, his eyes closed and sweat was dotting his brow. Even though he was fucking me, I felt like I had all the power. I kept my eyes open as I lifted myself up again and I saw Mace's jaw harden. When I lowered myself slowly, adding a little bit of a twist to my hips as I reached his pelvis, I saw Mace blow out a breath. Cole's hands were stroking up and down my spine and over my ass as I rode Mace.

"So fucking tight," Mace muttered as I picked up the pace. But before I could get too far into it, Mace sat up and gently lifted me up until his dick slipped free of my body. I wanted to protest the loss but then he was shifting my ass backwards and I felt Cole's dick nudging against me. Cole slid into me in one easy move and he began thrusting into me in earnest. I was sitting astride Cole's thighs with his arms wrapped around my chest and weight to support me as he glided in and out of me and I reached back to wrap my arm around his neck to draw him to my mouth for a kiss. It was a raw, dirty kiss that had me groaning for more and then Mace was giving it to me. Within seconds I was back on Mace's dick and as he pumped into me, I felt Cole's hand tug on my turgid cock which was pressed up tight against my abdomen.

I didn't know how long they passed me back and forth for but just as I was nearing the edge, they both stopped and Cole, who was inside of me, pulled free. I wanted to beg them to keep going but then they shifted our positions so that Mace was lying flat on his back and I was lying on my back on top of him. His legs were raised just enough to spread me open and allow Cole to fit in between them. I was confused by the positon but didn't care as soon as I felt a dick slide back inside of me. I knew it was Mace's when he began thrusting his hips up against mine. I managed to look down to see Cole putting some lube on his finger but it wasn't until his hand disappeared down by the bedding and Mace groaned that I realized what was happening. Cole was going to fuck Mace while Mace fucked me.

Mace's thrusts slowed as Cole got him ready and within a minute he was sliding into Mace. My head was lying against Mace's shoulder and I pulled his mouth to mine as Cole began shuttling in and out of him. Mace's own glides into me had slowed but as Cole began to pick up the pace, Mace slung his arm around my waist and used it to slide me up and down on his dick. It took only a couple of plunges to get me back to where I'd been before Cole entered Mace and within minutes we were all desperately writhing and bucking against each other in search of relief. Cole's hand searched out my dick and began fisting it to match the rhythm he was using to fuck Mace.

None of us spoke but our grunts and moans filled the silence of the apartment. I knew I was close when my balls drew up tight against my body and my spine started to tingle, but I couldn't find the breath I needed to form the words. Mace beat me to it because his arm became like a steel band against my abdomen as his cock rippled and pulsed inside me. Hot, wet liquid spurted inside of me as Mace cried out in relief. My own orgasm started the second Mace's come coated my inner walls and I dug my fingers into his arm as my release shot all over my abdomen and Mace's arm. Cole gave Mace a few more hard thrusts before he shouted his pleasure. Mace groaned in my ear as Cole filled him and then Cole was leaning over us both, his mouth searching out ours. I couldn't move or speak except to whimper when I felt Mace's cock slip out of me. Someone washed me off but I had no idea who and then I ended up in my favorite position – between the two of them.

I was resting my head on Mace's shoulder while Cole's head was on my chest. "I love you," I said. I didn't bother with their names because they knew I was talking to both of them.

"Love you," Cole murmured against my chest. I could tell from his slurred words that he would be out in seconds.

Mace leaned down to brush a kiss over my lips. "Love you," he said simply and then he shifted to his side so he could drape his arm over Cole while the arm underneath me drew me as close to his body as I could be.

As I drifted off to sleep, I realized that I hadn't gotten to play with Mace's new piercing.

"Next time," I managed to murmur a second before I was out.

Epilogue

JONAS

TWO MONTHS LATER

I COULD BARELY HOLD STILL AS I WATCHED THE JET ROLL TO A STOP several hundred yards from us. I gave the banner that Cole, Mace and I were holding between us a quick once over to make sure we didn't have it turned upside down by mistake but it looked perfect.

"Damn dog," Mace muttered as he used all his strength to hold the Mastiff back. We'd driven up to the Hamptons to pick up the dog who'd been in the care of Devlin's housekeeping staff for the nearly four months that Devlin and Casey had been out of the country. I'd done my best to go up to the house to spend time with Sampson, Jack and the other rescue animals but it had been hard to get out there on a regular basis.

Devlin was the first one off the plane but he had Isabel in his arms and as soon as his feet hit the tarmac, he put her down and she came running right to me. I dropped the banner and Cole pulled it out of the way before she reached me and I managed to catch her when she launched herself at me.

Mace let Sampson go at the same time Izzy reached us and the dog made a beeline for Devlin, who managed to brace himself against its impact.

"Hi, baby girl," I said as I squeezed Izzy.

"You've gotta call me little girl now 'cause I'm not the baby anymore," Izzy announced. I smiled at that and then greeted Ryan as he gave me a hug.

"Hey buddy, welcome home," I said as I ruffled his hair.

"Thanks."

"He's sad 'cause he had to leave his new girlfriend," Izzy said.

"Am not!" Ryan returned.

The kids went back and forth with each other but my eyes were on Devlin as he held his hand out for Casey who was at the top of the stairs. My gaze fell to the baby in her arms and I felt tears sting my eyes.

"I've got her," Cole said to me as he lifted Izzy from my arms. I managed a quick "thank you" before I started walking forward and as I passed Devlin, I brushed his arm with my hand. He gave me a smile and then headed towards the car.

Neither Casey nor I spoke as I wrapped my arms around her, careful not to jostle the baby. This time around I was the one to wipe at Casey's tears and then I turned my attention to the baby.

"Oh God," I whispered. "She's perfect."

"I know," Casey said, her voice thick with emotion. "Here," she said as she passed the baby to me.

It took me a second to adjust to the feel of the wriggly baby in my arms but a rush of rightness overcame me. Someday I would have this. It wasn't something Mace and Cole and I had discussed yet but I knew in my bones that it was in our future.

"Did you decide on a name yet?" I asked.

Casey nodded. "Amanda Carrie Prescott."

I smiled. Amanda had been Casey's sister. And I knew my friend had chosen Carrie as a way to keep the girl who'd been one of us with us forever. Cole was going to be thrilled.

I shifted the baby so that I was holding her with one arm against my chest and put my other arm around Casey's shoulders as we began walking towards our family.

"Welcome home, Casey," I said even though I knew, as my eyes locked on Mace and Cole, that I was the one who'd finally come home.

The End

Scroll to the next page for a Sneak Peek of Ronan & Seth's story

About the Author

Dear Reader,

I hope you enjoyed Jonas, Mace and Cole's story. They will be back in Ronan's story.

As an independent author, I am always grateful for feedback so if you have the time and desire, please leave a review, good or bad, so I can continue to find out what my readers like and don't like. You can also send me feedback via email at sloane@sloanekennedy.com

Join my Facebook Fan Group: Sloane's Secret Sinners

Join my Facebook Fan Group: Sloane's Secret Sinners
Connect with me:
www.sloanekennedy.com
sloane@sloanekennedy.com

Also by Sloane Kennedy

(Note: Not all titles will be available on all retail sites)

The Escort Series
Gabriel's Rule (M/F)

Shane's Fall (M/F)

Logan's Need (M/M)

Barretti Security Series
Loving Vin (M/F)

Redeeming Rafe (M/M)

Saving Ren (M/M/M)

Freeing Zane (M/M)

Finding Series
Finding Home (M/M/M)

Finding Trust (M/M)

Finding Peace (M/M)

Finding Forgiveness (M/M)

Finding Hope (M/M/M)

Love in Eden
Always Mine (M/M)

Pelican Bay Series
Locked in Silence (M/M)

Sanctuary Found (M/M)

The Truth Within (M/M)

Crossover Books with Lucy Lennox

Made Mine: A Protectors/Made Marian Crossover (M/M)

The following titles are available in audiobook format with more on the way:

Locked in Silence

Sanctuary Found

The Truth Within

Absolution

Salvation

Retribution

Logan's Need

Redeeming Rafe

Saving Ren

Freeing Zane

Forsaken

Vengeance

Finding Home

Finding Trust

Finding Peace

Four Ever

Lost and Found

Safe and Sound

Body and Soul

Made Mine

Made in the USA
Las Vegas, NV
12 April 2023